A Girl Named Candy

A Novel

First Edition

By L. Walker Arnold

ARNOLD
PUBLICATIONS
Nicholasville, KY 40356

A Girl Named Candy

© 1995 By L. Walker Arnold
Published by Arnold Publications

First Edition, September, 1995

Cover Art by Dan W. McMillan

Library of Congress Card Number: 95-094669
ISBN: 0-9629688-5-4

Printed in the United States of America

Arnold Publications
2440 Bethel Road
Nicholasville, KY 40356

Phone (606) 858-3538

In memory of Miss Renda Pettus, who encouraged me in high school, led me closer to the Lord, and inspired me in my early ministry.

Chapter 1

*I*t is not unusual for rain to fall in the Ohio River Valley in January, but in January of 1937 the rainfall was unusually heavy. Rains were frequent and hard along the valley, and they flooded the streams that fed the Ohio River. The rains fell for three solid weeks from where the river was formed by the confluence of the Allegheny and the Monongahela, near Pittsburgh, to its egress into the Mississippi at Cairo, 980 miles downstream.

By mid-January the river had flooded lowlands and was rising four tenths of a foot an hour. Radio stations and newspapers were predicting a crest of 59 or 60 feet, but people were not greatly alarmed, for the river was not expected to rise as high as it had the preceding March.

Candy Mays lived with her stepmother in a small house near the river, but so far the constant rain and the high water had been little more than a nuisance to them.

One morning, the third week of January, Candy awoke with a start and bounded out of bed, aware that she had overslept. She stumbled sleepily, stripped off her nightgown, and started dressing, knowing that her stepmother, Lillian, would scream at any minute for her to hurry or she would be late for school.

Last night she had fallen asleep to the sound of

rain on the tin roof above her, and this morning the same sound had lulled her into oversleeping. She glanced out the window at the pouring rain as she buttoned her blouse. She picked up a comb from the dresser and pulled it through her tangled hair as she walked to the window for a look at the river. It was muddy and laden with debris, and the water was swirling and roaring as it raced down the valley. Some houses near the river had already been flooded, she had been told, and some had washed away with the people in them.

Only a few days ago the river had overflowed its banks and started inching toward their house. She knitted her brow, wondering how many raindrops it had taken to make the big river rise so high, and she wondered if the rain would ever stop falling.

For one frantic moment she hoped there would not be another flood like Noah's flood--but that could not be. God had put a rainbow in the sky and promised that He would never again destroy the earth with a flood.

"Can-dee, are you up?" her stepmother called at that moment in a strident, half-angry voice.

Candy jumped, in spite of herself. She should be used to her stepmother's voice by now, but she was not. Her own mother had been gentle and kind, and her voice had never sounded like that.

"I'll be there in a minute, Mom," she responded, though it was distasteful to her to call Lillian Mom, as she demanded.

Candy was still thinking of her mother as she went back to her dresser to give her hair a hasty brushing. She had only been eight when her baby brother died at birth, and her mother died a few hours later. That had seemed like the end of her world to her. After they buried her mother, her father had done his best for her, but she had never been as close to him as she had been to her mother.

She had never forgotten things her mother taught her. She could still almost hear her say, "You must be a good girl, Candy. You must be honest and truthful and decent, and you must have integrity. There's not much to a person who doesn't have integrity."

Candy did not understand what the word meant, but it was important to her because it had been important to her mother. Integrity had been one of her mother's favorite words.

"And, Candy, you should never hold a grudge or have bitterness in your heart," her mother had told her. "You can't be happy if you do."

Her mother had taken her to church from the time she could remember, and she had taught her to believe in Jesus and to love and serve Him.

Four years had passed since her mother's death, and now, at twelve, she thought she was almost grownup. A year after her mother had died, she had gained a stepmother. Only six months later her father had been killed in an accident. That had left her to live with her stepmother in the small house her father had built. Lillian had accepted the responsibility of rearing her stepdaughter none too graciously, doing only what she felt obliged to do for her. She had never shown Candy any affection.

"I don't care," Candy said with a shrug.

The rain started pouring harder, and she cast another glance at the river, wondering if it would get high enough to reach their house. Lillian must be wondering about that also.

Last night Jason Conn, who lived in a shack a quarter mile away, had come by the house and told her that the road between Ashland and Russell was blocked by rising water.

"Surely the river won't get much higher," he had commented. "If it stops where it is, people can get around on the back roads until it goes down."

"It will go down in a few days. It always has," Lillian had said hopefully.

Candy looked at her light brown hair, so like her mother's hair, and gave it a final stroke with the brush. She smiled sadly as she remembered how pretty her mother had been, then made a face at herself in the mirror and giggled.

"I'd be pretty too if my mouth wasn't so big," she shrugged. *She had to have a mouth so she could eat and talk, didn't she?* Mama had said she would look like her when she grew up. She hoped she would.

"Are you coming, Can-dee?" Lillian called more angrily than before.

"Yes, Mom. I'm on my way." She got the Bible her mother had given her from under her pillow. With her other hand, she got her doll from the doll bed where she had placed it last night before she went to bed. She put both of them in her lower dresser drawer under her clothes.

"Now, Nellie, you stay there, and you be good," she told the doll as she pushed the drawer closed. Then she hurried to the kitchen where Lillian was fussing with the cook stove.

"What took you so long?" Lillian shouted above the radio that was blaring from a shelf in the kitchen. Lillian lifted her eyes from her task and glared at her.

"I'm sorry, Mom," she managed evenly.

"You ought to be. Now you go feed and milk the cow, and hurry, you hear? You'll be late for school."

"Yes, Mom." She got her raincoat and gum boots from the closet and put them on. Trying to ignore her stepmother grumbling at the stove, she got the milk bucket from the side table and left for the barn. As she followed the ascending path to the barn, she heard Lillian's angry voice following her, but when she went inside, the rain on the tin roof drowned it out.

Candy fed the cow and chickens, did the milking, and hurried back to the house. She removed her coat and boots on the porch, went in and put the milk on the kitchen table, and went to their tiny bathroom and washed her hands. When she returned to the kitchen, she strained the milk in a crock and covered it with a tin lid.

"Breakfast is on the table," Lillian said when she saw that Candy had finished with the milk.

Candy sat down at her place at the table, bowed her head, and, because Lillian objected to her praying, she silently offered thanks.

Lillian sat down and started eating. Candy ate in silence, because Lillian never talked when she was eating, and she didn't want her to talk either. When Candy finished eating, she arose from the table.

"You'd better hurry or you'll be late for school," Lillian reminded her. "I'll have to hurry too, so I'll be ready when my ride gets here."

"All right, Mom," she answered, realizing that it was almost time for Katherine Blake to come and give her stepmother a ride to Friendly's Restaurant in Ashland, where they both worked. Lillian would ride home with Katherine this afternoon at the end of their shift, arriving shortly before she got home from school.

Candy ran to her room and dressed for school. On her way to the back porch to get her coat and boots, she picked up her books. "I'll see you tonight, Mom," she called as she was going out.

"Don't you be late gettin' home."

"I won't, Mom." She closed the door, put on her coat and boots, and left. She was glad to be away from the sound of her stepmother's voice, even if it did mean walking to school in the rain.

That afternoon when school let out, water had risen around three sides of the schoolhouse, so the children had to climb the back fence to get out of the school yard, and walk a mile through the fields to get to the road that ran along the foot of the hill.

There was none of the usual running and playing that afternoon, and there was little talking as the children walked across the soggy fields. When they reached the road, the walking was easier, but they still had to pick their way between ankle-deep puddles of water.

"It's still raining," Candy announced from the back door when she reached home and paused to remove her raincoat and boots.

"Where've you been since school let out?" her stepmother asked sharply.

Candy put her books away before she answered.

"You didn't answer me. Where have you been all this time," Lillian demanded.

"The road up the river was covered with water, so I had to walk through the fields to the other road, and it took longer."

"Hump! It wouldn't have hurt you to wade through a little water."

"It was too deep to wade. I saw a car stalled in the road, and water was halfway up on the door."

"Well, at least you're home, but you look like a drowned rat. Go change to your work clothes."

Without answering, Candy went to her room and changed. She hurried back, lest she make her stepmother even more angry.

"I hear the cow at the gap bawling her head off. Go let her in the barn and feed and milk her before you help me cook supper," Lillian ordered.

"Yes, Mom." She put her raincoat and boots on and went to the barn and fed and milked the cow.

"I sure hope the river starts going down by tomorrow," she said when she returned to the house.

"I hope it don't keep risin'. If it rises much higher, we'll be flooded out."

"I'm worried about Mary Worth and her family. The water was up on their front steps when she got home from school."

"If the water was that close to our house, I'd be movin' out. I won't wait to be washed away like some people have."

"Mary hollered from her front door that her pa and uncle were moving their furniture upstairs."

"Since we don't have an upstairs, we'll have to get Jake to help carry our things to the barn, if we see that the water's goin' to get in the house."

Jake would be glad to help, Candy thought. *For the past year he had been hanging around Lillian a lot. Lillian was struck on him, and he seemed to think a lot of her.*

"I don't care," she told herself in a fierce whisper. "Even it she marries Jake, things can't be any worse than they are now."

Early the next morning, Lillian's screaming voice awoke Candy. "Get up this minute, Can-dee," she was screaming. "We've got to get out, and we ain't got much time. Water is all around the house except in the back, and it's risin' fast."

Candy bounded from bed, threw off her nightgown, scrambled into her clothes, and ran to Lillian without taking time to tie her shoes.

Lillian had the front door open and was looking out at the rising water. She had a vexed, half-frightened expression on her face. "Run get Jake as fast as you can, Can-dee," she ordered. "We've got to get out in a hurry."

Candy jerked on her boots, threw on her coat, and started to leave.

"Tell Jake I'll be gettin' out what I can, and please hurry, Candy."

That was the first time Lillian had ever said please to her, Candy realized, and she had actually called her

Candy instead of Can-dee.

Candy started running toward Jake's shack in the blinding rain, splashing through puddles, and slipping in the mud.

When she came in sight of Jake's shack, he was standing on the front porch, looking out at the rain. Her eyes swept his tall, lank frame and his bearded face, but she avoided his bloodshot eyes. His eyes always made her feel uneasy.

"Jake, the river is about to get in our house, and Mom wants you to help get our things out," she shouted.

"I've been afraid of that." He ran in, grabbed his coat and hat, and put them on as he started running toward Lillian's house. Candy ran after him, but she was so tired she could not keep up. When she came in sight of the house, he was already helping Lillian carry out a small table.

"Where have you been, Can-dee?" Lillian screamed. "Don't you know we need your help?"

"I reckon I outrun her. My legs are longer than hers," Jake said mildly.

"Anyway, you start carryin' out the things you can lift while me and Jake carry the big things out. We have to hurry."

"We've got more time than you think, Lillian," Jake said. "A big river like that don't rise all that fast."

"It come up all around the house last night," she countered.

"Yeah, but that was eight or ten hours. We can carry your things out in an hour or two."

Lillian looked at him uncertainly. "Will we need Candy?" she asked. "I had thought of keeping her out of school to help."

Jake glanced at Candy, then at Lillian. "We won't need her." He smiled and winked at Lillian. "We can move all but the heavy pieces, and I'll get a couple of fellers I know to help get them out."

"Then you hurry and get dressed and go on to school, Can-dee," Lillian ordered.

Candy noticed that Lillian was smiling at Jake.

"I'm hungry," she complained.

"There's no time for breakfast this morning. You hurry and go on to school."

"Yes, Mom," she managed in spite of the lump in her throat. *Her own mother would never have sent her to school without breakfast,* she was thinking.

She went to her room to dress, wondering if the high water had blocked the way to the schoolhouse.

When Candy was ready to go, Jake and Lillian were not in sight. They must be at the barn, she decided, so she went by the kitchen and picked up some cold biscuits that had been left in the pan on the oven door the might before. She stuffed them in the satchel with her books, then went out and started walking to school in the rain.

As she walked she watched raindrops splattering in the puddles that had collected in the road. Each drop made a tiny yellow splash. She looked at the river, and it was so wide that she thought it must look like the ocean, though she had never seen the ocean.

A boat was going down the river with a load of furniture piled on it. She wondered if the rain would ruin the furniture before they got to where they were going. Two other boats were going down the river, and another one was moving toward the distant shore.

When she came in sight of the schoolhouse, she saw that the water was higher than it had been the day before. She had not seen any boys or girls on the road, and there were only a few huddled beside the schoolhouse, shivering in the cold rain.

Candy climbed the fence and joined them. For a while they waited for the teacher to come, then one of the big boys climbed in a window and opened the door from the inside, and they all went inside. Someone turned up the thermostat so the furnace would warm the building, and they all gathered by the windows and watched for the teacher to come. While they were waiting, Candy ate the cold biscuits she had brought, but they did little to satisfy her hunger.

Finally, one of the older girls announced that she would teach until the teacher arrived, and they all went to their seats. She started teaching, trying to mimic the teacher's style. That made some of the students smile, but there was no misbehavior. The constant rain and the rising water had dampened their spirits, and they were quite subdued. Slowly the morning passed and still the teacher did not come.

When they went out at noon, water was almost up to the schoolhouse door. "We had better go home while we can," the girl who had been teaching told them.

The others agreed, and they climbed the fence and crossed a field to the road that ran on high ground. No one was going Candy's way, so she sadly started walking home alone.

The walk home was more precarious than it been in the morning, but Candy carefully found her way between the puddles of water. Finally she topped the last hill and came in sight of the house.

"Oh," she cried, and drew in a sudden breath. The water was halfway up the walls of the house. The doors were open and water was flowing through them. When Candy reached the path that led to the barn, half of it was under water. From there she looked through the back door of the house and saw that water was almost up to the windows on the inside.

Her stepmother and Jake were nowhere to be seen, so she went to the barn. "Mom, Jake, where are you?" she called.

There was no answer, so she started looking around. Furniture and clothing were piled in the stalls and in the loft of the barn, but Jake and Lillian were not there.

"Oh, Nellie," she cried, thinking of her doll for the first time since she had put her in the bed beside her last night. In her haste this morning she had not put her away. She climbed the ladder to the attic, found her bed and bedclothes, but she did not find Nellie. She pulled open her dresser drawers and searched them one by one, hoping against hope that Lillian had put her doll away. But Nellie was not to be found. Her Bible was also missing.

"Oh, what did they do with them?" she wailed.

Lillian had often told her she was too big to be playing with dolls, and several times she had threatened to burn her Bible. That made her feel sure that Lillian had found her doll and her Bible and done something with them. "I bet she threw them in the river," she said bitterly, and turned away, choking with sobs.

As she descended the ladder, she saw the cow standing at the gate, lowing. Her sack was strutted as if she had not been milked today. Candy felt sorry for the cow, so she let her in the barn and put her in a stall that didn't have any furniture in it. She fed the cow, then milked her in the can they used for measuring her feed.

Candy was so hungry she drank the warm milk until she could drink no more. Then she poured the rest of it in a trough for the chickens. For a long time she stood in the doorway of the barn, lonely, frightened, and cold. She watched the river and wondered what she should do. Finally she decided that Lillian and Jake must have gone to his shack. It was on high ground so it would not be flooded. The shack would be warm, and surely they would have something to eat.

She left the barn and ran up the path toward Jake's shack as fast as she could, but when she came in sight of it her heart sank. No smoke was coming from the chimney. That meant they were not there. She slowed to a walk and continued to the shack and tried the door. As she expected, it was locked. She went to the window and looked in. It was dark inside, and she knew that it was almost as cold inside as it was outside.

Weeping silently, she retraced her steps to the barn and stood in the doorway, looking at the rising water that was now almost up to the eves of the house. Hard as it was to live with Lillian, she wished that she would return. She stood there, shivering and weeping until it was almost dark. Then she went in the cold, damp, darkening barn and climbed to the hayloft.

The milk had not satisfied her hunger. *Surely Lillian and Jake had brought what was in the pantry and stored it in the barn,* she thought, so she started looking for something she could eat. Finally she found a box of things from the pantry. There was some shortening, a box of matches, soda, baking powder, a can of corn, and a can of peas. That was all. She could eat the peas just as they came from the can, she decided, so she started looking for a can opener.

She found the can opener in a box with the knives and forks and spoons and opened the peas, got a spoon, and started eating. They were cold and tasted raw, but she ate them anyway. She was still hungry, and she thought of opening the can of corn and eating it, but she decided to save it for her breakfast.

She went to a small window at the end of the loft and looked out at the house. Only the roof was now above the water. Beyond the house was nothing but water as far as she could see. For a long time she stood there, weeping silently. Only when the coming night statrted darkening the attic did she decide to look for a place to sleep.

She found some blankets Lillian and Jake had carried to the loft, made herself a bed in the hay, removed her wet coat and boots, laid down, and pulled the blankets over her. But she was so cold and lonely she could not go to sleep. So she lay there watching the last faint light disappear from the rafters.

After it was dark, she finally fell asleep. Some hours later, the sound of breaking timbers, followed by a heavy scraping noise, awakened her. She leaped from her bed in the hay, felt her way to the window at the end of the loft, and looked out into the darkness. Faintly she saw the roof of the house above the water. Then, greatly distressed, she realized that the house was moving. It had washed off its foundation and was floating down the river!

Great sobs shook her body. Her father had built that house, and she had lived there happily until her mother and little brother had died. After that she had lived there with her father, and with her father and Lillian after they they had married. She had not been happy after her father married Lillian, and it had been worse after he was killed in the accident. But that house was the only home she had ever had. Big tears rolled down her cheeks, but there was no one to see them or to care.

"Dear, Lord, I wonder if you care," she sobbed. Then she dried her eyes and went back to her place in the hay and pulled the blanket over her. Gradually she grew warm, and she finally sobbed herself back to sleep.

Chapter 2

*T*he next morning Candy awoke to another cold, rainy day. Her stomach was aching from hunger, so she decided she would milk the cow and drink some milk and eat the can of corn she had found last night. That would not be much of a breakfast, but it would keep her from starving.

She crawled from her bed in the hay, and brushed the hay from her clothes. She searched around and found a comb and combed the tangles from her hair. There was no water for a bath, so she decided that later she would find a washcloth, wet it with rain water, and wash her face. The water would be cold, but it would have to do.

Her coat was still damp, and her boots were wet and stiff, but she put them on anyway. She found her scarf, tied it over her head, then climbed down the ladder. Somehow the cow's stall had come open in the night, and the cow was gone. She went out to see if she was at the gap. She wasn't there, so Candy turned away disappointed. Maybe she would go bring her up later, she decided.

She left the barn and went down to the water's edge and tried to see where the house had been, but the foundation was hidden under the muddy water. For several minutes she stood there, cold, hungry, lonely, and frightened. She wondered where her stepmother and Jake had gone. Didn't they care what happened to her?

In a moment she stamped her foot and brushed her tears away. "You're too big to cry," she told herself sternly, trying to mimic her stepmother's voice. Then she giggled, but the tears did not stop falling.

"Lillian and Jake should at least come to see about me," she muttered with sarcasm that was unusual for one so young.

She looked at the river and saw that it was full of floating logs, pieces of furniture, and broken pieces of lumber. A small building was floating past, and, a short distance up the river, she saw a house floating near the shore. A moment later she heard a voice calling, "Help! Help! Somebody get me get off this house."

The house came nearer, and she saw a boy, somewhat older than she was, clinging to the roof. He had on a coat and hat, but he still looked cold, and he looked like he was terrified.

The house passed her, and she started running after it, wishing there was something she could do to save the boy.

"Can't you swim?" she called.

"Yeah, but I might drown in that swift water," he called back.

"Maybe I can find somebody with a boat," she called.

"I hope you can. Run and keep up with me," he called back.

"I will." She continued to run after the house, but she slipped and fell in the mud. She muddied her dress and skinned her knees, but she scrambled up and ran on, determined to keep the boy in sight until she found help.

Soon she was panting for breath, and she had to slow her pace. "Dear Lord, help me," she prayed as she struggled on.

The house was getting ahead of her, and she knew she was soon going to lose sight of it. Then she saw a boat floating near the shore. It was tied to a post with a rope. She untied the rope and pulled the bow of the boat up to the shore and got into it. Thankful that her father had taught her how to row a boat, she picked up an oar and rowed out into the current.

The boat had water in it, but there was not time to bail it out, for the house was already way ahead of her. She started rowing after the house with all her strength, hoping she could keep it in sight until someone saw them and came to help. The current of the river increased her speed, and she started gaining on the house.

"Keep rowing and you'll catch up with me," the boy called from the housetop.

"I'm rowing as hard as I can," she called back.

"You're gaining on me."

She kept pulling on the oars, and the boy climbed off the roof and down onto a windowsill, just above the water.

"Be—be care—careful," she called between puffing breaths.

"I will. An' you be careful that you don't bump into the house." He was quiet for a moment as he watched her bring the boat closer.

"The boat won't support us both with all that water in it," he lamented when she had almost caught up with him.

"There's a bucket in the boat, but I haven't had time to bail the water out."

"You can stop rowing while you bail it out. The boat will keep up with the house."

"All right, but it'll take awhile." She laid down her oar and started bailing. She was weak from hunger and tired from exertion. Her arms were aching, but she kept bailing.

The house drifted closer to the shore, struck something, and swung around, and the boy lost his footing and fell into the water and went under.

"Oh!" Candy screamed, thinking that he would surely drown.

In a moment he surfaced and swam to the back of the boat and caught hold of it.

"Hurry and row to the shore. I'm freezing," he called through chattering teeth.

"Aren't you going to get in?"

"I'll upset the boat if I try. Keep rowing, hard as you can."

She started rowing toward the shore with all her remaining strength, and the boy started kicking with his feet to help move the boat. Slowly the boat moved across the heavy current, and finally it reached shallow water. She got the rope, climbed over the side of the boat and waded toward the shore, pulling it after her.

The boy soon reached solid ground also and waded to the shore.

"Let's pull the boat to shore and tie it. Somebody else may need it," she said.

"Sure," he said through chattering teeth.

Together they pulled the boat up on the shore as far as they could, and the boy tied it to a fallen tree. They were both exhausted, wet, and freezing, but Candy tried to smile.

"We did it!" she cried.

"What's your name?" the boy asked.

"Candy Mays."

"I'm Ralph Roberts."

"Ralph, I'm glad I found you, because I don't have anybody to take care of me."

"Me neither."

"We'll have to take care of each other."

"Candy, we'd better find a place to get inside before we freeze."

"I know, Ralph, but where? There's not a building in sight."

"Let's run until we find some place."

"All right."

They climbed the bank to a road that ran around the base of the hill.

"Which way should we run?" he asked.

"This way." She pointed down the river, deciding to get farther from home. Lillian had not come back to take care of her, so she would not go back and try to find her.

A cold wind was sweeping off the river, and it chilled them to the bone. Ralph's clothes became stiff with ice, and he started shivering beyond control. Candy's wet feet and legs throbbed with pain, and the rest of her body ached from the cold.

"We—we've got—to keep run—ning," Ralph puffed.

"I—I know." The water sloshed in her boots as she ran.

"I—hear a—a car," Ralph managed, glancing over his shoulder.

"Maybe they'll give us a ride."

They moved to the side of the road and turned toward the approaching car. Ralph was still shivering, but he managed to hold out his hand and motion for a ride. Candy was jumping up and down, and swinging her arms.

The car slowed and stopped beside them, and a man opened the door. "Get in," he invited. "You look like you're freezing."

"We—we are," Candy shivered as she climbed into the car.

"I—I feel like—like an icicle," Ralph managed between shivers as he got in beside her and closed the door.

The man looked Ralph and Candy over, then turned

up the heater. "What are you kids doin' wet?" he asked.

"My house washed away with me on top of it," Ralph answered.

"And I got wet rescuing him," Candy added.

"Where are your parents?" the man asked, looking at Ralph.

"Don't have any. My mother died when I was a baby, and they buried Pa yesterday."

"Are you his sister?" the man asked.

"No sir. I just saw him floating by on his house and went after him in a boat."

The man looked at her with an air of skepticism. It was obvious that she and the boy had both been in the river, but it was hard to believe that this small girl had really rescued the boy from a floating house.

"Where do you live?" he asked.

"I don't live anywhere. My house washed away too. The barn's still there, though."

"And where's your family?"

"My mother and father are dead. I've been living with my stepmother, but she left, and I don't know where she went."

"What are your names?" he asked.

"My name is Candy Mays, and his name is Ralph Roberts," Candy answered.

"Weren't you scared, Ralph?" the man asked, turning his attention to the boy.

"Sure I was—that is till I seen Candy a-runnin' after me. Soon as I seen her, I knowd she'd get me off the house somehow."

The man whistled softly and turned his attention to the road.

Candy was quiet for a minute, listening to the buzz of the heater and feeling warm air blow on her legs. At last she turned to the man. "What's your name, mister?" she asked.

"I'm Joe Sanders. I guess you had both better go

home with me where it's warm and get your clothes dried. I'll bet you're hungry too."

"I am," Candy said eagerly. "I've only had some milk and some canned peas since yesterday."

"I ain't had nothin' to eat since yesterday either," Ralph said.

"My wife will get you both something to eat when we get to my house."

Mr. Sanders fell silent then, and the hum of the motor, the buzz of the heater fan, and the slapping of the windshield wipers were the only sounds. The windshield wipers cut momentary clear places on the windshield, giving a view of the brown, swirling water that filled the wide valley. In places the water was clawing at the shoulder of the road. The sky was gray. Rain was pouring again, and the rutty road was filled with puddles of water.

Candy stole another glance at Mr. Sanders. He was about the age her father had been when he died, but he was larger than her father and not as handsome. He did have pleasant, blue eyes though, and they crinkled in the corners when he smiled.

Soon Mr. Sanders turned onto a graveled driveway that circled to a house on the side of a hill.

"This is where I live," he said as he stopped the car by front gate. "Let's go in and get you something dry to wear, and, while you're thawing out, my wife will fix you something to eat."

As Mr. Sanders was getting out of the car, Ralph jumped out and Candy followed. The cold wind chilled them again. Candy wanted to run ahead of Mr. Sanders to get out of the cold, but she walked to the house beside him. Ralph hugged himself against the cold and walked beside her.

"Let's go in," Joe Sanders said when he reached the door and opened it.

"Look what I found on the road," he called to his

wife as she turned to see who was coming in.

"Well, what have we here?" she asked, looking Ralph and Candy over.

Candy looked Mrs. Sanders over also. She looked like a schoolteacher, she thought.

Mrs. Sanders continued looking at her and Ralph as if she could not believe what she was seeing. "What are you two doing so wet?" she asked. "You look like two drowned kittens."

"The boy got washed away in his house, and the girl went after him in a boat," Mr. Sanders answered for them.

"Really? What are your names?" she asked, still looking at them in her schoolteacher manner.

"I'm Candy, and he's Ralph," Candy answered, edging toward the fireplace where a fire was smoldering sulkily.

"I thought we could get them something dry to put on, and give them something to eat," Mr. Sanders said.

"I'll see what I can find. Joe, you build up the fire. I know they're freezing," she told him as she started to another room.

He put another log on the fire, picked up the poker and punched at it, making the sparks fly. Soon a blaze was leaping up the chimney.

Ralph and Candy moved their chairs close to the fire and sat down.

"My wife's name is Sarah," Joe said when she returned.

"I'll call her Mrs. Sanders?" Candy said decidedly.

"Why, you polite little girl," Sarah exclaimed.

"Ma'am, you look so neat and proper. . . . you look like I should call you Mrs. Sanders. Besides my mother told me to always be respectful to people older than I am."

"Then I'll call her Mrs. Sanders too," Ralph said.

"Well I'll declare, he's polite too," Sarah exclaimed, holding out the clothes she had brought.

"Joe, I got some of your clothes for the boy. You take him to the spare bedroom and let him put them on, though goodness knows he'll be lost in them. I'll take Candy with me and help her get into something dry."

In a few minutes Mr. Sanders brought Ralph back and set him down by the fire. He looked awkward in Joe's big pants and shirt, with the pant legs rolled up to his ankles and the shirt sleeves rolled up to his wrist.

When Mrs. Sanders brought Candy back, she burst into laughter at the sight of Ralph.

He looked at Candy, dressed in one of Mrs. Sanders' blouses and a long sweater that covered her down to her knees, and he started laughing too.

"Laugh if you want to, Ralph," she giggled. "At least I'm dry."

"I'm glad you children have a sense of humor," Mrs. Sanders commented. "I'll wash your clothes and dry them in front of the fire, but first I'm going to fix you something to eat."

"I have to go to work," Mr. Sanders said as she started to the kitchen. "Mrs. Sanders will take care of you kids, and I'll see you when I get home tonight."

"I'll have supper ready when you get home," Mrs. Sanders called from the kitchen.

"I don't think I'll ever get warm," Candy murmured, moving her chair still closer to the fire.

"Me neither, but I'm sure glad Mr. Sanders is lettin' me wear his clothes. I'd be freezin' sure 'nough if he hadn't," Ralph exclaimed.

"They sure are good to us," Candy commented as she ran her fingers along the sleeve of the sweater Mrs. Sanders had loaned her to wear.

"I wish we could live with them forever," Ralph whispered.

"Me too, only . . ." she shrugged.

"Only what?"

"Only, Mrs. Sanders. I . . ."

"You children come and eat. I have your breakfast on the table in the kitchen," Mrs. Sanders' precise voice cut in at that moment.

"Thank you. I sure am hungry," Candy responded as she led the way into the kitchen.

"I'm hungry too," Ralph echoed.

Mrs. Sanders had put two large bowls of hot oatmeal on the table, and there were some biscuits and butter and a dish of blackberry jam.

"This looks good," Candy said as she sat in the nearest chair.

Ralph went to the chair on the other side of the table.

"Is it all right if I pray before I eat?" Candy asked Mrs. Sanders.

Startled, Mrs. Sanders looked at her. "Why, of course, if you want to."

"My mother told me to always thank God for the food before I eat."

"I wasn't taught to do that when I was a child. Your mother must have been some kind of a religious fanatic," Mrs. Sanders added under her breath.

"Oh no, ma'am. My mother was just a good Christian."

Candy prayed, but Ralph did not bow his head. Apparently he was not used to praying before eating either.

They soon emptied their bowls, and Mrs. Sanders brought them each a second bowl of oatmeal. After they finished that, they ate the biscuits and jam.

"Mrs. Sanders, do you want me to do the dishes?" Candy asked when she and Ralph finished eating.

"No, you thoughtful little girl!" Mrs. Sanders responded, looking at her over her glasses. "You go back to the fire and finish thawing out."

She treats me like I'm a child, Candy thought as she followed Ralph back to their chairs by the fire.

That night after supper, Mrs. Sanders hustled Ralph to a bedroom off the kitchen and sent Candy to a bedroom across the hall from where she and Mr. Sanders slept.

Candy did not soon fall asleep in the strange bed, so she was still awake when the Sanders went to bed a great while later. Soon she heard them talking in hushed tones.

"I wouldn't mind keeping the girl, she's such a pretty little thing, but of course we can't keep the boy," Mrs. Sanders said.

"He's the one that don't have any family. The girl has a stepmother, though she doesn't know where she is. We'll have to find her and take the girl back to her."

"Too bad! I'd like to keep her, but I don't want the boy. We'll have to get him placed in an orphanage."

"That shouldn't be too hard," Mr. Sanders said as he closed the bedroom door.

Candy sat up in bed, thoroughly alarmed. She had only met Ralph today, but she liked him, and she did not want be separated from him. She certainly did not want to go back to live with her stepmother.

Ralph is the only family I've got, and I'm the only family he's got, she thought. "I won't let them separate us. I won't!" she vowed in an inaudible whisper.

She sat on the side of her bed, determined to stay awake until she was sure that Mr. and Mrs. Sanders were asleep. Then she would go to Ralph's room and awaken him, and they would slip out of the house and leave.

Some while later she heard both of the Sanders quietly snoring behind their bedroom door, and she slipped from her bedroom and tiptoed to the fireplace in the living room. Mr. Sanders had replenished the fire before he went to bed, and the flames were still curling around the logs and sending shadows dancing along the walls.

She felt of their clothes that Mrs. Sanders had hung before the fire, and found that they were dry. Noiselessly she slipped into her clothes, but she did not put on her boots. She listened for any sound from the Sanders' bedroom and heard only their snoring. So she got Ralph's clothes, and, carrying them and her boots, moved soundlessly down the hall on her bare feet. Ralph's door was open, so she tiptoed inside.

Ralph was wide awake, for he had not been able to sleep either. He had heard Candy creeping along the hall and was sitting up in bed, looking into the darkness when she entered his room.

"It's me, Ralph. Don't make a sound," she whispered from the doorway. "I brought your clothes. Hurry and put them on, because we've got to leave while the Sanders are asleep."

"What for?" he demanded in a whisper.

"Be quiet! I'll tell you later. Here's your clothes." She laid them on the bed. "Put them on, but don't put your shoes on until we get outside. Don't make a sound," she cautioned. "I'll be waiting for you by the back door."

She placed her boots by the back door, then went to the fireplace, and, by the light of the fire, found a pencil and a piece of paper. Holding the paper to the light of the fire she wrote:

Thank you, Mr. and Mrs. Sanders for all you have done for me and Ralph. We don't want to be any more trouble, so we're leaving.

Candy

She placed her note on the table where Mrs. Sanders would find it the next morning, then she went to the back door and waited breathlessly for Ralph to come.

"What's this all about?" he asked in a soft whisper when he came a few minutes later.

"I'll tell you later." She put on her coat and motioned for him to put his on. "Don't forget your shoes," she told him as she picked up her boots.

She turned the doorknob and the door opened with a loud click. They waited anxiously for a long minute. There was no sound in the house, but Candy could hear her heart pounding in her ears.

At last they stepped outside and gently closed the door. Soundlessly they felt their way across the porch in the darkness. They found the steps and Candy sat down and pulled Ralph down beside her.

"Put your shoes on," she whispered as she started tugging her boots on.

"Why are we leaving when we had good warm beds to sleep in?" Ralph asked in a whisper.

"Wait till we get away from the house," she whispered.

Ralph pulled his shoes on and tied the laces. Then they arose and walked slowly down the steps. The rain had stopped, but the night was very dark.

"Hold my hand so we don't get separated," Candy whispered.

Ralph took her hand, and they walked slowly across the yard until they came to the fence.

"We've missed the gate," she gasped.

"We've been walking on the grass instead of the driveway," Ralph told her.

"Wonder which way the gate is."

"It's over this way," he said, guiding Candy to the left.

They felt their way along the fence, until they came to the gate. Ralph opened it and led her through.

By the feel of gravel under their feet, they followed the driveway until they reached the road. There Ralph pulled her to a stop. "Now why did we have to leave a warm house and come out in the dark and cold for?" he demanded.

"Because the Sanders want to separate us, that's why," she blurted. "They want to put you in an orphan's home, and they want to take me back to my stepmother."

"Where'd you get that idea?"

"I heard them talking after they went to bed, that's where. I don't want us to be separated. Do you?"

"No I don't. There ain't neither one of us that's got anybody else. So I reckon we'll have to look out for each other. Which way do you think we ought to go?"

"Let's go up the river toward where I used to live. Maybe someday, if I'm sure my stepmother's not around, I can get some of my clothes out of the barn where she put them."

"Will she ever come back since your house is gone?"

"She might come after her things."

"We'd better get goin'. We have to get far enough away while it's dark so the Sanders won't find us."

"Let's hold hands again so we won't lose each other in the dark," she said.

He took her hand, and they started walking on the hard surface of the road. Each time they got out of the road, the soft, muddy ground warned them to turn back.

"What are we goin' to do if the Sanders miss us and come huntin' us?" he asked.

"They won't know which way we've gone, so maybe they'll go the wrong way."

"What if they don't?"

"We'll see their lights before they see us, and we'll hide in the bushes."

A chilling wind was blowing off the river, and the sound of rushing water filled the night. Candy and

Ralph continued to follow the road. Hours passed, and they grew weary. They lost all track of time, but plodded on. Candy became so cold that her mind was numbed, and she came to wonder where she was and why she was walking in this cold, dark night. She stopped frequently, and Ralph had to pull her along to keep her moving.

Ralph grew tired also, and, when it seemed he could not possibly walk another step, he saw the first light of dawn in the east.

"It's almost day, Candy," he said, trying to encourage her, but she stumbled on without answering.

"I see the shape of the hills," he said a bit later, still trying to encourage her.

"I'd give anything to get out of the cold," she answered numbly.

"We can walk faster when it gets light so we can see. That will help us get warm." He tugged at her hand, but she held back, too numb to move faster or to care. Dismayed and frightened by her condition, he kept pulling her along, and she followed as in a dream.

Chapter 3

Soon it was light enough to see details, and Ralph saw a small cabin on a high bluff in the woods.

"Candy, there's a cabin up there. Maybe whoever lives there will let us in out of the cold," he exclaimed.

"I hope they will. I'm freezing," she mumbled.

They found the dim outline of a path that led to the cabin and followed it. Fallen, water-soaked leaves made the path slippery, so he took Candy's hand for fear she would slip and fall. She stumbled along beside him on feet that were numb with cold. The path led though a patch of dense trees, then up a steep bank to the cabin. The effort of climbing the muddy bank, with Ralph half pulling her, partially revived her.

"There's no smoke coming from the chimney, and there's no light in the window," she mumbled as they reached the top of the bank.

"Maybe they ain't up yet," Ralph suggested. "Let's find out."

He climbed the half fallen steps and crossed the small, slanted porch to the door and knocked. She followed him, and they waited for a response.

"They must not be home," she murmured sadly.

Ralph tried the knob. It turned and he pushed the door open enough to put his head in and looked around. "There ain't nobody here," he said.

"Should we go in?" Candy asked. "The people who

live here wouldn't care if they knew how cold we are."

"Come on," Ralph said as he pushed the door open.

They went in and closed the door and looked around.

The cabin smelled of burnt wood and dampness and mildew. There were ashes in the fireplace from a fire that had gone out long ago. There was wood in a box by the fireplace and kindling by the hearth.

"Looks like somebody camped here and left some of their stuff when they went home," Candy said, looking around the cabin.

"I hope they left some matches so I can start a fire."

"Me too. I don't think I'll ever be warm again."

Ralph roamed around the room, looking for matches. He soon found a half of a box of matches on the mantle above the fireplace.

"Here they are," he cried excitedly. He found an old newspaper to use to ignite the kindling, and he quickly kindled a fire. As it started blazing, they huddled before it, watching the flames eat through the kindling and finally catch in the larger pieces of wood.

"Are you getting warm?" Ralph asked, rubbing his hands together before the fire as the flames started leaping upward.

"I'm beginning to, but now I'm hungry. I wish we had something to eat." She brought up a chair with a broken back and sat before the fire.

"Maybe they left something we can cook," he suggested.

"But it wouldn't be right to take somebody's food."

"We can leave a note that we'll pay for it."

"Well . . . I guess that would be all right—if we sign our names."

"I'll see what I can find."

She huddled before the fire while Ralph looked on shelves and in drawers. Finally he found a small piece of salt bacon.

"There ain't nothin' here 'cept some ol' chunk of salty bacon," he said, turning away with disgust.

"That'll beat starving, Ralph. Mama taught me how to cook salt bacon. I'll need some water though, so I can parboil it."

"Whoever stayed here had to have water, so there must be a spring somewhere. Let's go find it," Ralph suggested.

"I'm awfully tired, and I'm still freezing, but I'll go with you," she mumbled.

"Sure. Come on. That'll be better'n stayin' here in the cabin shiverin'."

"Here's a bucket with a dipper in it," Candy said as she lifted a rusty bucket from a peg in the wall.

"Ain't it awfully rusty?"

"Sure it is, but it'll have to do. I'll wash it good."

She found a piece of lye soap on a table by the stove. "I'll use this," she said.

They went out and scouted around the back of the cabin, and in a valley beside a small cliff, they found a bubbling spring of clear water. Candy washed the bucket and dipper in the cold water with her hands and rinsed them. Then she handed them to Ralph.

He filled the bucket and they started back to the cabin. She ran ahead of him and was shivering before the fire when he got there.

There was a rusty teakettle on the small cook stove, and Candy found an equally rusty skillet in the oven. A dishpan was hanging on the wall.

"We need a fire in the stove so I can heat water to clean these," she said holding up the skillet and teakettle with disgust.

"I'll build a fire in the stove, but I sure wish we had something to eat now," he complained. "Maybe we should have stayed with the Sanders."

"And let them separate us?" she cried, looking at him with blazing eyes.

"You know I don't want that." He turned his attention to the stove and soon had a fire blazing in it.

When the stove got hot, Candy heated water in the teakettle, washed it, and refilled it. While it was heating again, she found an old butcher knife and a cutting board. When the water was hot, she got the dishpan off the wall and rinsed it. Then she put hot water in it and washed the cutting board and the knife and skillet. Then she handed the knife to Ralph. "You have to slice the bacon in thin slices," she told him.

Ralph looked at her in wonder. She was younger than he was, and she was smaller than he was, but she was telling him what to do, and she was managing housework in this terrible cabin as if she were a grown woman.

"Where'd you learn to keep house?" he demanded.

"I learned it from my mama, that's where. She taught me lots of things. I used to help her do housework when I was a little girl," she said as if she were really quite grown-up.

Ralph sliced six slices of the bacon and handed them to her.

She set the skillet on the stove and poured water in it and put the bacon slices in to parboil. After she had boiled the excess salt from the bacon, she emptied the water from the skillet and put the bacon in to fry. Soon the aroma of frying bacon filled the cabin.

"See if you can find some flour," Candy said when the bacon was almost done.

"You're not goin' to make biscuits with nothin' but flour are you?" he asked.

"Of course not, I'm going to make some bacon gravy if you find some flour."

"Oh!" He started opening cabinet doors and drawers. "Here's some," he cried after he pulled aside a curtain that was hanging on the front of a small corner cabinet. "And here's some salt if you need it."

"I won't need the salt. The bacon grease will make the gravy salty." While she was talking she poured most of the grease in a small jar. "Milk makes better gravy than water, but we'll have to do with water gravy," she said as she stirred a small quantity of flour in the grease that was left in the skillet. When it started thickening, she poured in some water and continued to stir until it thickened again. Then she set it on the back of the stove.

"I hope there are some plates here," she said.

"I saw some when I was looking for the flour." He went to the cabinet and brought out two cracked plates.

"Those will do fine. See if you can find some forks while I wash them. And see if there are some glasses. We'll drink water with our breakfast."

"There's part of a bag of coffee, and there's a coffeepot."

"I'll make coffee for you if you want it. I don't drink coffee."

"I'd like coffee. Tell me how and I'll make it."

"Bring me the pot and I'll wash it."

Candy washed the battered old coffeepot, then poured hot water in it, added coffee, and set it on the stove to boil.

"I'll wash the rest of the dishes while it's boiling," she said.

When she finished with the dishes, she set the plates on the table and took up the slices of bacon and put half of them on each plate. She also put some gravy on each plate.

"We can start eating, Ralph. Your coffee will be ready in a few minutes," she said. "You sit over there, and I'll sit here by the stove so I can get your coffee when it's ready." Ralph sat down and picked up a piece of bacon with his fingers.

"Wait. Before you eat, we have to offer thanks," Candy told him.

"Ain't this an awful little to be thankful for?"

"My mama always said we ought to thank God for whatever He provided for us, be it much or little. I reckon this is little, but maybe God will give us more after awhile."

"Prayin' before you eat seems silly to me."

"Didn't your parents pray before they ate?"

"I don't remember nothin' about my mama, but my old man never prayed about nothin'. Besides, what makes you think God had anything to do with us finding this old salty bacon?"

"He made somebody leave it, didn't He? And He helped us find the cabin. Now you bow your head while I pray."

Reluctantly, Ralph bowed his head.

"Dear Father, we thank You for this food, and we trust You to send more when we need it. Amen. Now we can eat."

"What do you mean praying for more food when we need it?" he demanded. "We need it right now."

"I wish we had some bread," she said as she bit into the crisp bacon and dipped gravy with her fork.

"I found some sorghum molasses on a shelf. Maybe we could eat it with the bacon," Ralph said. He went to the corner cabinet and got a tin pail of sorghum and brought it to the table and opened it.

"I feel like offering thanks again," Candy said as she poured some of the thick, brown syrup on her plate and dipped her bacon in it.

Ralph followed her example, and tasted it gingerly. "It tastes pretty good," he commented.

They were so hungry that they ate the rest of what she had cooked in silence.

"I wonder when God will send us something else," Ralph said skeptically as he got up from the table.

"What's that?" Candy asked, turning her head to listen.

"It's some kind of a bell or somethin'."

"It sounds like a cowbell, but what's a cow doing where nobody lives? Let's go see." She jumped up from the table and ran to the door.

"Oh, Ralph," she cried, "it's a brown and white goat."

"Sure it's a goat. I've seen goats before," he said as he joined her at the door.

"Oh! You beautiful creature," Candy cried, walking slowly toward the goat with her hand extended.

"I don't see why you're so excited about a goat," Ralph complained.

"Don't you see, Ralph. We asked for more food, and God has sent it."

"I don't see how you get that. We can't eat a goat."

"Ralph, look at her sack. She needs milking, and we need milk to drink. Goat milk is good for you."

"I don't know how to get milk out of her. When I lived with my old man, we got our milk out of bottles."

"Well I know how to get her milk."

"You really know how to milk a goat?" he asked incredulously.

"Of course. Mama used to have goats, and she taught me how to milk them."

"Come, goat," she said turning to the animal. "I'm going to call her Sandy Bell. Don't you think that's a pretty name for her?" she asked.

"It's as good a name as any, I reckon. How are you going to make her stand still while you milk her?"

"We'll have to put her in the cabin. I saw a shed out back, but it's probably full of stuff."

"Open the door and I'll drive her in."

"Wait. Maybe I can toll her in. Come, Sandy Bell," she called again, as she opened the door and held out her hand to the goat.

The goat looked at her with large, intelligent, brown eyes. Then she made a tentative step toward her.

"Get out of the way, Ralph. She may not like you."

He stepped aside and the goat slowly followed Candy into the cabin.

"Ralph, watch and see that she doesn't eat our coats while I find something to milk her in." She found a small bucket hanging on a wall, washed it, and started milking the goat.

"Do you like hot milk?" she asked Ralph when she finished.

"Never tried it, but I'm hungry enough to try anything."

She found two cups and washed them. Then she poured each of them full of milk and handed one to Ralph. He tasted it, made a slight face, then drank it down. "Can't say that I like it, but I'm not hungry anymore," he said.

"Next time I make gravy, I'll make it with milk instead of water. That will make it taste better."

"There's enough bacon for another meal or two."

"We have to find something to feed the goat," she said.

"Can't she find her own food?"

"Sure she can, but we need to give her a treat. We need a way to cut some cedar branches. She would like them."

"I've got a pocketknife. I can cut some little branches with it."

"Then go cut some for her, and if you can find some small bushes, she'll eat the bark off of them."

Ralph went out, and in a few minutes he returned with some cedar branches and two small bushes.

Candy let the goat out of the cabin, and she ate the cedar branches hungrily, but she ignored the bushes.

"I guess that's not what Sandy Bell likes," Candy observed.

"Whoever owns her will feed her when she goes home," Ralph suggested.

A shadow crossed Sandy's face. "I hadn't thought about her belonging to somebody. I thought she'd got lost because of the flood. I hope her family don't need the milk I took from her."

"Maybe she'll have more milk when she gets home."

"Not if she goes home this morning. I'm sorry I milked her, but I thought God had sent her."

"I reckon we needed her milk more than whoever owned her does."

"I wish we could keep her, but we have to let her go."

"She hasn't tried to go anywhere since we put her out."

"She will. A goat won't stay anywhere long unless it's shut up or tied."

"If we had some rope, we could tie her and milk her again tonight," Ralph suggested. "There may be some rope in the shed."

"Ralph, it wouldn't be right to keep somebody's goat." She went to the goat and patted her neck. "Thank you for the milk, Sandy Bell, but you better go home now," she said.

The goat turned and rubbed the side of her head against Candy.

"Maybe she's still hungry," Ralph suggested. "There's a grassy place back of the shed. Let's take her around there and see if she likes grass."

Candy tolled the goat past the shed to the grassy place, and she started grazing at once.

"We'll leave you now, Sandy Bell, and when you get through eating, you go on home," she told the goat firmly.

"What will her family feed her when she gets home?" Ralph asked.

"Some corn, and maybe some hay. I'd give her some hay if I had some from our barn," Candy said.

"How far do you reckon it is to your barn?"

"A long way, I think."

"We could walk up that way and see one day."

"Somebody might see us and want to separate us."

"I reckon you're right."

"You know, Ralph, people wouldn't want to separate us if we were brother and sister," Candy said, brightening as a sudden idea came into her mind.

"But we're not."

"You could adopt me."

"How could I do that?"

"Easy. I've seen couples get married, and all they had to do was say some vows."

"Could we say vows like that?"

"Of course. It's easy."

"But wouldn't we need a preacher or somethin'?"

"I'll be the preacher and ask the questions. You can answer for yourself. Then I'll be me, and I answer for myself."

"Why don't you adopt me?"

"That wouldn't do. You have to adopt me so I can take your name. A wife always takes the husband's name, so I'll take your name after I'm your sister."

"Well, if you say so," he said doubtfully.

"All right, we have to stand up beside the wall."

"Why do we have to do that?"

"When couples get married, they always stand by a wall or a stairway. We don't have a stairway, so we'll stand by the wall."

Looking puzzled and a bit embarrassed, Ralph allowed her to push him back against the wall in the only free space in the cabin.

"You stay there," she said. Then she stepped out in front of him, cleared her throat, and asked in the coarsest voice she could muster, "Do you, Ralph Roberts, take the girl whose hand you hold to be your lawful, wedded sister?"

"I'm not holding your hand."

"You will be in a minute. Now stop interrupting." She stepped back beside him and took his hand. "Now say, 'I do,'" she prompted.

"I do," he repeated, grinning shyly.

Solemnly she stepped back in the role of preacher. "And do you, Candy Mays, take the boy whose hand you hold to be your lawful, wedded brother?" She stepped back to her place beside Ralph and took his hand again.

"Of course I do," she said firmly. Then stepping back in the role of the preacher, she said, "I now pronounce you brother and sister."

"Now I'm supposed to kiss you," Ralph said.

"No you're not, Ralph Roberts."

"Why not? The man always kisses the woman after they get married."

"Don't be silly. I'm only your sister, and brothers and sisters don't kiss. They fight, though, sometimes," she added.

"I'm glad to have you for a sister," he said, "and I'm going to kiss you the way a brother is supposed to kiss his sister.

"You can kiss me there," she said, pointing to her cheek.

He solemnly kissed her on the spot she had indicated.

"I'm glad to have a brother," she exclaimed with delight. "I've wanted a brother ever since my baby brother died."

"I'm glad to have you for a sister, Candy. I never had a brother or a sister. After my mama died, I didn't have nobody but my old man, and he didn't stay at home much. After he died, I didn't have nobody till you got me off the house."

"How come you were in your house when it washed away?" she asked as the thought occurred to her.

"After they buried my old man, some people I don't like was going to make me go live with them. I told them I had to pack my things, and they said they'd come get me the next day. I intended to leave before they come, but the next morning, while I was upstairs gettin' my things together, I heard a big noise and the house felt like it fell in a hole. Water started coming up in my bedroom, and I felt the house moving, so I crawled out the window and climbed on top of the roof."

"That's where I first saw you," Candy said.

"And I seen you running down the riverbank after me."

"I'm glad I rescued you."

"Me too. If you hadn't, I wouldn't have a sister."

"And I wouldn't have a brother."

Now that I'm your brother, it's my place to make a livin' for you," Ralph said, moving away from her and shrugging off his embarrassment.

"Then you better find a way to do it. We can't live on the salt bacon you found very long."

"I'll go look for a job today, while it's not rainin'."

"Aren't you too tired to work after walking all night?"

"I'll be all right," he shrugged.

"What if somebody starts asking questions?" she asked. "We don't want anybody to know we're living in this cabin."

"If anybody asks where I live, I'll tell them that I've moved since the flood, and I don't know my new address."

"While you're gone I'll clean up this cabin. I declare it's a sight," she said, repeating the phrase she had heard her mother use so often.

"If I make any money, what do you want me to buy for us to eat?"

"Maybe you can get some potatoes and some bread

. . . and some beans. Mama used to buy things like that when we didn't have much money."

"I'll get what I can. Don't you leave while I'm gone."

"Why do you think I'd leave my brother?"

He looked away, slightly embarrassed. "Reckon I'll be goin'," he said turning back to her.

"Good-bye. I hope you make some money."

He went out and she followed him to the door and watched him go down the path to the road. He turned up the river, and she watched him until he was out of sight. Then she giggled and went back into the cabin.

Chapter 4

After Ralph was gone, Candy went out and looked behind the shed for Sandy Bell. She was delighted to find that she was still there, lying down, contentedly chewing her cud.

"Sandy Bell, I'm glad you're still here," she told the goat. "And I hope you're going to stay. . . . that is if you don't have a family."

Before returning to the house she looked in the shed to see what was there. There wasn't much—a few old tools, a piece of well-used tarpaulin, some rope, rolled up and hanging on a peg, and some steel traps, hanging from a nail in the wall. There was a washtub in the middle of the floor.

"Just what I need," she said aloud, and she got the tub, took it to the cabin, and set it on the floor near the fireplace. Then she got the water bucket and made several trips to the spring to get water. She filled the tub half full, then filled every container she could find. She replenished the fire in the stove and put a kettle and a bucket, both filled with water, on the stove to heat.

While the water was heating, she went out to the shed and got the piece of tarpaulin, brought it in, and carefully covered the window with it so no one could see in. She searched the cabin unsuccessfully for a towel, but she did find a small cake of toilet soap in a dish on a shelf. On impulse she pulled back several covers that were on the cot and was relieved to find that the mattress was covered with a clean sheet and that the pillowcase was clean.

When the water was hot, she emptied the teakettle and the bucket into the tub and added enough cold water to make it comfortable to her touch. Then she stripped, took a bath, and dried herself before the fire. She took the sheet off the cot and wrapped herself in it while she heated more water and washed her clothes. When she finished washing them, she wrapped a blanket over the sheet and went out to hang the clothes up to dry.

There was no clothesline, so she hung her clothes on low bushes. She had barely finished when the clouds returned and a slow drizzle started to fall. She made a face at the clouds and quickly gathered up her wet clothes and carried them back in the cabin.

She took off the blanket, but she continued to wear the sheet. For a moment she looked around hopelessly, then started removing things from nails and pegs and hanging her wet clothes where they had been. The last of them she hung before the fire on the only chair in the cabin that had a back. Then she swept the cabin, made the bed, and washed the dishes.

Long before noon she grew hungry, so she cut two slices of bacon, fried them, and ate them with molasses. She was still hungry, but she saved the rest of the bacon for supper in case Ralph did not make any money to buy food.

She would milk Sandy Bell before Ralph came home, if she was still around. If Ralph did not bring home any groceries, she would fry more bacon, and they would eat it with molasses and gravy as they had this morning.

"Only this time I'll make milk gravy," she told herself aloud.

During the day, Candy wondered how she and Ralph would sleep that night. There was only one cot, and there was no way she was going to sleep on that cot with him, even if he was her adopted brother. Her mother had taught her better than that.

Several times during the day she went out to see if Sandy Bell was still back of the shed. Once the goat had gone to nibble on some tree branches on the hillside, but she came running when she saw Candy. "I do believe you're going to stay, Sandy Bell," she said.

At last the long day passed, and, though the sky had cleared, it was darkening with the coming night. Candy stood in the doorway, wearing her clothes that had finally dried, and watching the lengthening shadows of the leafless trees creep along the ground. A large flock of crows was flying against the reddening sky in the west. They were far away, but she could faintly hear them cawing.

"I better milk Sandy Bell before Ralph comes home," she told herself, and, feeling quite grown-up, she went in and got the milk bucket and went out and tied Sandy Bell to a tree and milked her.

It was getting dark in the cabin when she returned with the milk. She remembered the oil lamp she had seen on a shelf earlier that day, so she got it, cleaned the chimney, and lighted it. By the light of its yellow flame, she kindled a fire in the stove so it would be ready to cook on when Ralph got home. It was almost dark, and she was growing worried when she finally saw him coming up the path, carrying a sack of groceries.

"You found work!" she cried, delighted, when he was in hearing distance.

"It wasn't hard," he called back.

"I'm glad."

"Some people were movin', and they needed help," he continued when he was almost to the cabin.

"I'm glad you brought something for us to eat."

"They paid me when we got through, so I went to the store down the road and bought what I could." He held the sack open for her to see.

"If you weren't my brother, I'd kiss you."

"I hope you like what I bought."

"Oh I will, no matter what is is. I milked the goat so we'd have milk."

"I bet you're hungrier than I am. I ate dinner with the people I worked for."

"I ate some bacon and molasses."

"While I was eatin', I wished you was there so I could divide with you."

"Where'd you work?"

"For some people up the river. They'd stored their furniture in a barn, and I helped them move it to a house." He set the sack of groceries on the table.

"Food!" she exclaimed as she took potatoes and bread and a can of beans from the bag. There were also some eggs and some onions.

"The eggs will be good for breakfast, but what are the onions for?"

"I like onions. Maybe you could cook them with the potatoes."

"My mama used to do that." She reached in the bag again and brought out a tablet and a pencil. "What are these for?" she asked.

"I like to draw pictures, and sometimes I write things."

"Oh! Will you draw something for me?"

"While you're cookin' supper, I will. You may not like my drawin' though."

"I'll like anything you draw."

She moved quickly, as she always did, and soon had supper cooking on the little stove. She fried some bacon first, then fried the potatoes and onions in the grease from it.

"Open the beans, and I'll put them on to get hot," she told Ralph.

He found an aged can opener and opened the can and handed it to her. She dumped the beans in a pan and put it on the stove to cook.

"It smells good cookin', and it's makin' me hungry," Ralph said.

"It'll be ready in a few minutes."

Ralph got his pencil and tablet and sat down by the table, so he could see by the light from the lamp. He sharpened the pencil with his pocket knife, then started drawing on the tablet with his left hand.

Candy glanced at him.

I don't care if he is a southpaw, long as he's my brother, she thought. She knew he was drawing a picture by the movement of his hand.

After she had put the food on the table, he brought the picture for her to see. She looked at it and gasped in surprise. He had drawn a picture of her in the boat as she had rowed out to rescue him.

"Ralph, it looks just like me," she exclaimed. "I want that picture, and I'll keep it forever."

"I'll give it to you later. I'm not through with it yet, but let's eat first. I'm hungry."

"I haven't made the gravy yet," she said, "but it will be ready in a few minutes."

After supper, while Candy was clearing the table, she continued to wonder how they could sleep. Apparently Ralph had not even thought about it, for he was working on his picture as if that was all that was on his mind. To her great relief, before she finished washing the dishes, he laid aside his picture and made himself a bed in front of the fire with a cover from the cot, then laid down and promptly fell asleep.

Carefully she spread a cover over him, put a log on the fire, and went to bed in the cot, thankful that the sleeping arrangements had been so easily taken care of.

Candy went to sleep wondering what had become of her stepmother. "I don't miss her nagging, but I hope she's all right," she whispered in the covers as she was drifting off to sleep. She awoke once in the night when Ralph was putting more wood on the fire, but she promptly went back to sleep.

The next morning it was not raining, but it was cloudy and cold, and it looked like snow could start falling any minute. After breakfast Ralph left to go look for work, and Candy stood in the door and watched him out of sight. Then she put on her coat and went to look for Sandy Bell. She found the goat on the hill back of the cabin, eating leaves from some bushes. Snow was beginning to fall.

"Come here, Sandy Bell," she called, and the goat came running. She tied the goat and milked her. Then she went in and washed the dishes and made the bed.

There was little for her to do after that, so she became restless and decided to go for a walk up the riverbank. That would pass some time, and perhaps she would find something useful that had washed ashore. Maybe she would even find something she could wear after she washed the mud out of it.

She dressed warmly in the clothes she had and left the cabin. When she reached the river, she found that the bank was dank and muddy. A cold breeze was blowing off the river, driving falling snow before it. She decided to go on anyway.

All kinds of things—pieces of broken furniture, water-soaked magazines and books, stained and muddy articles of clothing, and pots and pans were strewn along the riverbank. Everything, except maybe the pots and pans, was ruined by mud and water.

At last she grew discouraged and decided to go back to the cabin. She had walked quite a distance along the riverbank, so she decided to go to the road that ran around the side of the hill and return to cabin that way. The road would not be as muddy as the riverbank, and she would be away from the foul odor of the river.

Snow was falling fast when she reached the road, but little of it was sticking to the soggy ground. The snow dimmed the visibility, but she soon saw a woman coming up the road. When they met, the woman stopped and looked her up and down. "I'll bet you lost your clothes in the flood," she said bluntly.

"The rest of my clothes are stored, but they're a long way from here. I've been trying to find something on the riverbank that I could wash and wear, but I didn't find anything that was any good."

"You won't, but I know where you can get clothes. The Red Cross is in Ashland giving away clothes and food. They are even giving away some furniture. It's a long way to walk, but I'm on my way there. Why don't you go with me?"

"Thank you, ma'am, but I can't go today. Maybe I'll go tomorrow."

"I know your mother will be glad to hear what the Red Cross is doing."

Candy was on the point of saying that she didn't have a mother, but thought better of it. "Thank you for telling me," she said instead.

Candy returned to the cabin and passed the rest of the day wishing that Ralph would come home so she could tell him about the Red Cross.

Late that afternoon she milked Sandy Bell. Then she rekindled the fire in the stove and prepared more potatoes and onions and beans for supper. After she finished, it was too cold for her to stand in the doorway and wait for Ralph, so she sat down before the fire to wait. Soon she heard his footsteps on the path outside, and sprang up and ran to the door to meet him.

"Oh, Ralph, I'm glad you're home," she cried.

"I didn't make much today," he greeted. "I helped a man cut some wood and put it in his shed, but he only gave me a dollar. I bought some bologna with it." He tossed the bologna on the table. "I was goin' to kill a rabbit for us to eat with a rock on the way home, but I didn't find one."

"You couldn't kill a rabbit with a rock," she said without looking up from her task.

"I could too. My old man used to be a ball player, and he taught me how to throw hard and straight. He taught me to throw curveballs too."

"What's curveballs got to do with killing a rabbit?"

"Nothin', I reckon. I just thought of it."

"I'll fry some of the bologna. It will be good with what I've already cooked."

"I'm glad you're not disappointed."

"Ralph, I'm not, and just wait until you hear the news I've got."

"You left the cabin," he accused.

"I only went walking up the river. Ralph, I can't stay in this place every minute. On my way back, I met a woman, and she told me something wonderful."

"What was that?"

"The Red Cross is giving away food and clothes in Ashland."

"Will they give us something to eat?"

"Sure they will. The woman said they are giving food and clothes to everyone who has lost things in the flood. They are even giving away furniture."

"We ain't got room for no furniture."

"I was just telling you what she said."

"It'll be a long walk, but I'll go to Ashland tomorrow and see what I can get."

"I'm going with you. I need clothes as much as you do. Besides, you'll need me to help carry back

56

what they give us."

"Ain't you afraid somebody will want to separate us?"

"If they do, I'll tell them that you are my brother."

"I reckon you're right. We'll both go."

The next morning, after a hurried breakfast, they dressed for the outside and started to Ashland. Three or four inches of snow had accumulated on the ground during the night, but now it had almost stopped falling.

"Will we pass your barn on the way?" Ralph asked when they were on the road.

"No we won't. It's on the road by the river. That road is covered with water, so we have to go to Ashland on this road."

They walked about a mile, then caught a ride on the back of a pickup truck. It still took them almost an hour to get to Ashland and find the place where the Red Cross was operating in the shelter of a big warehouse.

Candy reported to the lady in charge that her house had washed away and they were in need. To her relief, she did not question Ralph.

"Have you found a place to live?" the lady asked.

"We're living in a cabin down the river. It was all we could find," Candy answered truthfully.

"Do you have a way to get the food home?" the lady asked.

"We'll carry it," Ralph told her.

"Won't it be too heavy to carry that far?" she asked, looking them over.

"No, ma'am. We'll get it home."

"This lady will see that you get what you are able to carry," she said. "Why didn't your parents come with you?"

Someone asked for her assistance at that moment,

and, while she was distracted, they went with the lady she had said would help them.

They selected enough food to fill two large boxes, and the lady packed it for them.

Candy thanked her, and she and Ralph picked up the boxes and started home. They had walked only a short distance when a man stopped in a car and offered them a ride. They gladly accepted, but a short distance before they reached the path that led to the cabin, Ralph asked him to let them out.

"We have to walk from the road to our house," Ralph told the man as they were getting out of the car.

"I wondered how we were going to keep him from finding out where we live," Candy said.

"We have to be careful."

After the car was out of sight, they carried their groceries to the cabin and put them on the shelves and on the table.

"I'm hungry," Ralph said when they finished.

"I'm cold and hungry, but we'd better hurry back to Ashland and get some clothes before they close."

"They gave us some soft drinks. We could at least drink two of them on the way."

"And we can make some sandwiches and eat them. They gave us some bread and cheese and more bologna."

Hurriedly Candy made sandwiches, and they started back, eating as they walked.

It was mid-afternoon when they got back to the Red Cross station. Candy went directly to the lady who was in charge of distributing clothes and told her they needed clothes. The lady was deeply moved by the appearances of the two wet, ill-clothed children, and she gladly assisted them in selecting clothes that would fit them. After that Candy found a window shade and a pair of curtains for the window of the cabin.

"It looks like you children have quite a load there,"

a man who had been watching them observed. "You going far?"

"A few miles past Russell," Ralph replied.

"I'm goin' that way, so I'll give you a lift."

"We'd be much obliged," Ralph said as the man took one of the boxes Candy was carrying and led them to his car.

Ralph asked the man to let them out on the roadside as he had the man who had given them a ride earlier in the day.

"Are you sure you kids can carry all that stuff?" he asked.

"Sure we can," Ralph said. "Thank you for the ride." The man shook his head in unbelief as they got their boxes out of the car.

Ralph and Candy watched the man drive out of sight, then started across the field without a backward glance.

The next day, they returned to Ashland and found a folding cot and some sheets and covers so Ralph would have a bed. A man with a pickup truck offered to haul what they had home for them.

In the days that followed, Ralph went out each day to look for work. Most days he found something to do. He brought what he earned to Candy each day, and she put what they did not spend for groceries in a jar and hid it so they would have money when they needed it.

So they settled into to a reasonably comfortable life, considering that they were children fending for themselves. Candy was especially pleased that she had a brother, and she was proud that she was keeping house for him. He was proud that he was earning money for them to live on.

Candy tried not to think of her stepmother, but she could not keep from worrying about her. She wondered where she had gone and how she was living.

She must have settled in Ashland so she could keep her job at Friendly's Restaurant—if it had not been forced out of business by the flood. If she did not have a job, surely Jake would take care of her. If she had left the area, most likely he had gone with her.

It never occurred to her that her stepmother was a grown woman and far more able to look out for herself than she was to care for herself. I'd try to find her if I wasn't afraid she'd separate me and Ralph, she finally concluded. After that she tried to put Lillian out of her mind and spent her energy keeping house and in making the cabin more livable.

Chapter 5

*A*fter several days the river started slowly receding, and the day came when Ralph and Candy heard children passing on the road on their way to school. On the third day, Candy decided that they should go back to school.

"You can go if you want to, but I'm goin' to keep on working. We can't expect the Red Cross to feed us forever," Ralph countered.

"All right, if you say so, but you have to keep up with your lessons. I'll teach you at night."

"I don't see how you can do that. I'm older than you, and I'm in the ninth grade. You're probably just in the seventh."

"Well, so what. I'm not too far behind you."

"But you haven't studied my lessons."

"Then I'll study them before you do."

"I don't see how you can do that and keep up with your lessons too."

"I'll study twice as fast as I usually do."

"We don't have any books," he objected.

"I'll borrow books, silly. Somebody will let me have them, if I promise to bring them back the next day."

"You'll borrow books for both of us and carry them home every night? You'll break your back."

"I won't either. Maybe I can buy some used books

with part of the money we've saved. I'll bring yours home and leave them."

"Oh, all right," he conceded. "I reckon I can study some at night."

The next day Candy started to school and was pleased to find some used books she could buy for both of them. They were not too expensive, and happily she counted out the money and paid for them. At noon she became acquainted with Sally Fields, one of the ninth grade girls, and asked her to write down her assignments for the next day and give them to her at the close of school.

"What are you going to do with them?" she asked, trying to look superior, Candy thought.

"I'm getting them for my brother. He can't come to school right now."

"Then I'll get them for you, and maybe I can meet your brother when he starts coming to school."

"I'm not sure when he can start."

Sally looked disappointed, then brightened. "Tell him to come to school with you some day so I can meet him. No, don't tell him that. After I see him, I may not want to meet him. Anyway, I'll give you the assignments."

After school that afternoon, Candy started home carrying a heavy load of books with Ralph's assignments tucked inside of one of them. The minute she got home, she started looking over Ralph's lessons. They were more difficult than she had imagined, so she decided to use every spare minute studying them before he came home. They would work together on them after supper, and surely, between them, they could learn his lessons.

On the second Saturday afternoon after Candy started to school, her English teacher, Miss Conrad, came to the cabin to visit. Candy was mortified, and she could not imagine how Miss Conrad had found the cabin.

Miss Conrad could not believe that Candy was from such a primitive home. "Where are the other members of your family today, Candy?" she asked as she entered.

"My brother's working," Candy answered. "Here is a chair for you." Candy placed the only chair with a back by her.

"And where are your father and mother?" Miss Conrad asked as she sat down.

"They are both dead," she answered truthfully. Her mother's teachings were too strong in her memory for her to attempt deceit.

"Oh, I'm sorry. Then your brother must be older than you," the teacher persisted.

"Yes, ma'am."

"Has your brother finished school?"

"No, ma'am, but I'm teaching him at night."

"He's older than you, and you're teaching him?" her teacher asked in astonishment.

"Yes, ma'am. We're kinda learning his lessons together."

"How much older is he than you?"

"Two years."

"And you're learning your lessons and his too?"

"Yes, ma'am." Candy was greatly upset that Miss Conrad kept asking questions, but she continued to answer them truthfully.

"And who keeps this place. I notice that it's clean and that everything is in place."

"I keep it. My brother has enough to do, making a living for us."

"Your brother makes a living for you?"

"Yes, ma'am."

"That's too much responsibility for you and your brother," the teacher observed gently. "I'm going to try to get something done about this."

"Oh no, Miss Conrad! Please don't tell anybody that my brother and I are living here. I'm afraid they'll separate us and send us off to orphan's homes. I don't want to lose my brother, and I don't want to leave the only home I have. Besides, I don't want to leave Sandy Bell."

"And who is Sandy Bell, pray tell?"

"She's my goat."

"You have a goat?" the teacher asked, shaking her head in dismay.

"Yes, ma'am."

"Candy, what do you do with a goat?"

"I milk her. She keeps me and Ralph in milk."

"This is too much," Miss Conrad said again as she arose and started buttoning her coat. "My heart goes out to you, Candy, but something has to be done. Two children can't go on living like this." Her eyes roamed around the cabin as she spoke.

"I don't see why not!" Candy cried in alarm. "We'd be just fine if people would let us alone."

"You are a brave little girl, Candy, and I'll do all I can to see that you and your brother are not separated."

"I'm not sure you can, Miss Conrad," Candy said evenly. She opened the door and waited for the teacher to leave.

"I have your best interests at heart, Candy. I hope you understand."

"Yes, ma'am."

The teacher smiled and left. Candy watched her go out to the road and out of sight, then she started packing.

She had most of their things packed when Ralph came home late that afternoon.

"What are you doin', Candy?" he demanded looking around the room.

"I'm packing, that's what. I already have most of our things packed."

"What are you packin' for, Candy? Where do you think we're goin'?"

"I don't know where we're going, but we have to leave here, and we have to do it tonight."

"What are you talking about? I thought you liked livin' here."

"I do, but my teacher, Miss Conrad, came this afternoon and asked all kinds of questions. Then she said that something had to be done about us. So we've got to leave before she sends people to make trouble for us. I don't want to be separated from the only brother I have," she wailed.

"I don't want us to be separated either, but where can we go?" he asked with rising temper.

"We'll have to find a place, same as we found this one."

"I'll never stand for us bein' separated," he stormed, looking like a small version of a man.

"We could go to my barn," she suggested.

"What if your stepmother comes back? Can we live with her?"

"I don't never want to live with her again. Besides the barn would be too cold for us to live in."

"I know where there's a cave. One time when my old man and me was huntin', it come up a hard rain, and we spent the night in it."

"What's a cave got to do with us?"

"We could live in it," Ralph suggested.

"I've read that people used to live in caves," she murmured, thinking.

"You finish packing while I go wall up the front of the cave with some rocks. That will help keep the cold out."

"You hurry. We have to move before dark."

When Ralph returned a short time before dark, she met him at the door.

"I've got everything packed," she said.

Ralph looked tired, and his hands were bleeding. "I'm sorry," she said, gently touching his hands.

"It's all right. I've got the cave almost ready."

"I tried to put everything in the cabin back like it was, except we'll have to leave your bed."

"Maybe we can come back and get it later," he suggested, surveying the boxes she had stacked near the door.

"Ralph, you'll have to put the money I've saved in your pocket. It's in the jar over there on the shelf."

"Sure, we'll need it." He got the money and put it in his pocket.

"I don't know how we'll carry all I've packed," she said soberly.

"Besides all this we'll have to take some dry kindling to start a fire. I'll put it in a sack so I can carry it. What are we going to do about Sandy Bell?"

"Take her with us, of course. I have her tied out by the shed."

"Then we'll let her carry some of this stuff. I've heard that goats are real strong."

Sandy Bell didn't object as they tied some of the bundles on her back, but Candy had to scold her to keep her from eating the cardboard boxes she could reach.

After they had tied all they could on Sandy Bell, they picked up the rest and started through the fields in the early darkness. Soon a strong wind began to blow, and it started raining. The wind buffeted them, making their progress more difficult, and the rain pelted them, stinging their faces and wetting their clothes. Sandy Bell didn't like the rain, and Candy had to keep talking to her and occasionally giving a tug on the rope to keep her moving.

It was soon dark, and they had difficulty finding their way. From time to time, the headlights from a car, passing on the road, illuminated the hill ahead of them. When the lights were gone, they felt their way slowly in the darkness until the next light flashed ahead of them.

"If we just keep goin' toward that hill, we'll come to the cave," Ralph said to reassure Candy.

When they reached the foot of the hill, Ralph felt his way along its base, talking softly so Candy could follow by the sound of his voice. At last they came to the opening of the cave, and he led the way in. Candy followed, still leading Sandy Bell.

"I don't think I'll ever be warm again," she managed between chattering teeth.

"I'll build a fire," he said as he searched his pocket for the matches.

"I'm glad you brought the dry kindling."

"Me too. The wood I brought in this afternoon is wet, so it'll take a while to get the fire going."

He struck a match, dumped the kindling he had brought in the floor, found a small sliver of pine, and set it ablaze.

"Hold this so I can see," he told her as he held the blazing splinter out to her.

She took it and held it up.

By its flickering light, he quickly placed some of the kindling in wigwam fashion near the door.

"I learned to do this from my old man the night we stayed in the cave," he said. "And he taught me to build the fire near the opening of the cave so the smoke would go out. Now, let me have the fire." He took the burning splinter and held the blaze under the kindling. Soon it caught, and the fire started creeping up the small sticks to the top of the wigwam. Carefully he added small pieces of wood to the fire, and soon its warmth began to radiate back into the cave.

"That feels delicious," Candy said, holding her hands toward the fire.

Sandy Bell looked at the fire with her big, brown

eyes and moved to the back of the cave.

"How am I going to cook," she asked, looking puzzled.

"I'll put some rocks on each side of the fire when it burns down, and you can set the skillet on them. Me and my old man used to cook that way when we went camping."

"If you'll move the loose rocks out of the way, I'll get the covers and make the beds while we're waiting for the fire to burn down," she said.

"There won't be enough quilts to make two beds," he said, looking at the roll of bedclothes they had brought. "The floor of the cave is goin' to be awfully hard and cold. We'll have to put two quilts under us, so we'll just have enough for one bed."

"Then only one of us will sleep at a time," she said firmly. "My mama taught . . ."

"I know. Your mama taught you better than that. We could sleep in one bed with a big rock between us."

"No," she said sharply.

Ralph shrugged, turned away, and started clearing a place for the bed.

"I'll make the bed. Then I'll fix supper," she said in a controlled voice.

Ralph knew she was upset, so without reply, he started placing some large rocks on each side of the fire.

After she finished spreading the quilts on the place Ralph had cleared, she searched through the groceries and found a can of soup. "Open this," she said, holding the can out to him.

Ralph cut the can open with his knife and silently handed it back to her.

She dumped it in a pan and set it over the fire to heat. When the soup was hot, she found some crackers. Then she looked helplessly around.

"Where are we going to eat?" she asked, forgetting that she was angry and breaking into laughter.

"I thought of that while I was walling up the front of the cave, so I brought in a big flat rock and propped it up on some thick rocks. We'll have to sit on the floor, though." He pointed to the flat rock in the back of the cave.

"You'll have to move Sandy Bell or there won't be room for us to sit down. Maybe you can tie her some way so she can't reach our clothes and eat them."

"There's room for her against the side of the cave." He moved the goat and tied her to a big rock. "I'll go cut a cedar branch for her to eat. Maybe that will keep her busy while we eat," he said.

"You'll get wetter than you are already," she objected.

"It won't take me long."

He went out and soon came back dragging a cedar branch and put it near the goat. Immediately she started eating the twigs from it.

Candy giggled as they sat down to eat. "This would be like a picnic if we were outdoors and the sun was shining," she said.

After they finished their soup, Ralph found a long slab of stone in the back of the cave and put it in the middle of the bed. Then he went to bed on the far side and turned his face to the wall of the cave.

She looked helplessly around for several minutes, then she took off her shoes and crept under the cold, damp covers on her side of the bed and turned her face toward the fire. She lay there a long time, looking at the fire and wishing it would dry her damp clothes and drive the chill from her bones. Finally she fell into a troubled asleep.

Several times during the night, she awoke and turned, trying to be comfortable on the hard bed. She awoke also when Ralph was up, adding wood to the fire.

The next morning Candy awoke with a chill shaking her body, but she got up anyway and cooked their breakfast.

"I'll milk Sandy Bell," Ralph offered.

She was feeling so miserable she did not object.

It was the first time Ralph had milked. It took him a long time, but he finally finished and brought the warm milk to the rock table. Then he took Sandy Bell out and tied her to a cedar tree so she could eat from its branches.

Candy did not eat, but she drank some of the milk. Then she fell back into bed.

"I'm not goin' to try to find work today, Candy. I'm goin' to stay here and keep a fire going for you," Ralph told her.

"I'm glad, Ralph. I don't want to be alone."

He sat by her side all day, leaving her only to bring in wood to replenish the fire. At noon he heated more soup and a can of beans. She tried to eat, but could not. Ralph was distressed when she fell back into bed.

Late in the afternoon, Ralph brought Sandy Bell in, tied her, and milked her. He offered some of the warm milk to Candy, but she barely tasted it

"I'm going out to cut wood, Candy, so we'll have enough to last all night. And I'm going to set up and keep the fire goin'."

"All right, Ralph, but hurry."

"Sandy Bell will be with you," he said, trying to pacify her.

"I know." She looked at the goat and smiled weakly. "But I still want you here."

"I'll hurry," he said and went out. He found a fallen tree and cut some limbs from it. They were water-soaked, but so was all the wood that was outside. He chopped the limbs into lengths he could use and made several trips carrying them into the cave. At first Candy smiled each time he came in, but she fell asleep before he brought in all the wood.

He added wood to the fire and sat down and leaned his back against the wall of the cave, determined that he would stay awake and keep a fire going. In the early hours of the night he dozed, then awoke and replenished the fire. After that he slept.

"Ralph I'm freezing," Candy called as the gray light of another rainy dawn was creeping into the cave. "And I think I have a fever."

Instantly he was at her side. He placed his hand on her forehead and found it hot to his touch.

"I'll build up the fire. Then I'm goin' for a doctor," he said.

"No, Ralph. If people find out we're living in this cave, they'll separate us for sure. I'll soon get better."

"You need a doctor, Candy."

"No," she said, and started tossing from side to side on her hard bed.

All morning he stayed by her side, only getting up to replenish the fire. By noon she was delirious, and his anxiety mounted. *What if she should die here in the cave? How could he explain why they had been living here?* He knew he should get a doctor, but she cried out each time he arose to go.

"I have to go out and get some feed for Sandy Bell," he finally told her in one of her lucid moments.

She turned her burning eyes on the goat. "I'll bet she is hungry, but hurry. I don't want to be alone."

"I'll hurry, but promise me that you'll stay in bed till I get back."

"I promise."

He knelt beside her and kissed her burning brow, then he went out and started running in the rain. He had to get a doctor in a hurry, he knew, but he didn't know where to find one. Russell was not far up the river, and there should be a doctor there, he reasoned, so he ran to the road and turned that way. If there was not a doctor at Russell, there would certainly be doctors in Ashland, but he hoped he would not have to go that far.

He ran until he was out of breath, slowed briefly, then ran again, with fear gnawing at his heart. Candy could become delirious again and wander out in the rain while he was gone. If she did, that would make her worse. She could get lost, and she could die before they found her. She might die anyway if he did not soon get a doctor for her.

Chapter 6

*R*alph continued to run with his heart beating fast and hard, both from exertion and from fear. He wondered how much farther it was to Russell and how long it would take him to find the doctor if there was one there.

At length a car passed him, slowed, pulled to the roadside, and stopped. The driver, a teenaged boy, opened his door and looked back. "Want a ride?" he called.

"I'd—be—much o—bliged," Ralph panted.

A lady opened the door on the passenger side and moved over to make room for him. "You must be in a hurry," she said as Ralph got in beside her.

"Yes, ma'am. My sister's real sick, and I'm goin' after a doctor."

The driver put the car in gear and revved the motor. The car lunged to a start and sped along the rain-soaked, rutted road.

"Who is your doctor?" the lady asked.

"Don't have one, ma'am. I thought maybe there'd be one in Russell."

"Dr. Short had an office in Russell before the flood, but I heard he had to move," the driver replied.

"His house is on high ground. Somebody told me that he moved his office there," the lady said. "Will he be all right? . . . what did you say your name is?" the lady asked.

"I ain't said, ma'am, but my name's Ralph Roberts. Any doctor will do, long as I can get him in a hurry."

"Ralph, I'm Mary Neal and this is my son, Robert. What's wrong with your sister?"

"She caught a cold, and it got worse. I think she's runnin' a fever, and she's talkin' out of her head."

"You really do need a doctor," Mrs. Neal said.

"I'm sorry about your sister," Robert told him, and he started driving faster, dodging the potholes and sending muddy water flying from puddles that had collected on the road.

"I hope we can find a doctor quick," Ralph worried.

"Dr. Short may have moved back to his office. We'll find him if we can. If we can't, we'll find you another doctor," Mrs. Neal assured him. "Are your parents with your sister?"

"She's by herself," Ralph answered, hoping he could avoid telling Mrs. Neal that they were living alone.

"With all the rain, it's a wonder everybody isn't sick," Mrs. Neal said.

"Yes, ma'am," Ralph said, breathing a sigh of relief.

They talked little after that until they reached the outskirts of Russell.

"Do you know where Dr. Short's house is?" Robert asked his mother then.

"It's on the first street to the right."

Minutes later, Mrs. Neal pointed out the street, and Robert turned. A short distance up the street she pointed to the doctor's house, and Robert stopped by the front walk.

"Thank you," Ralph said as he bounded from the car.

"We'll wait and see if the doctor is here," Mrs. Neal called after him.

Ralph ran up the walk, bounded up the steps, and rapped on the door.

A nurse in a white uniform opened the door.

"Is the doctor here?" Ralph asked so earnestly that she sensed his anxiety.

"He's with a patient. Is this an emergency?"

"Yes, ma'am. My sister is awfully sick. She's runnin' a fever, and she's out of her head."

"I'll speak to Dr. Short," the nurse said, and she disappeared behind a door.

A moment later Dr. Short came out. "What's wrong with your sister, young man?" he asked.

"She's got a cold, and I think she's got a fever 'cause she's hot when I touch her, and she don't make sense when she talks."

"Where is she?"

"She's at home.... 'bout five miles down the road."

"I'll be with you in a few minutes," the doctor said as he went back to his office.

Ralph went out and told Mrs. Neal and Robert that the doctor was going to go with him in a few minutes.

"Thank you for the ride," he told them.

"You're welcome, Ralph," Mrs. Neal responded.

"I hope your sister gets all right," Robert said.

Ralph watched them drive away, then went back in to wait for the doctor.

Dr. Short soon came from his office. "Let's go see what's wrong with your sister," he said.

"Yes, sir." Ralph went out with the doctor and got in his car beside him.

Dr. Short started the car and drove along the street at a reckless pace and turned on the road down the river. "You tell me if we have to turn," he told Ralph.

"We don't turn off. Just keep goin' till I tell you to stop."

The doctor did not seem inclined to talk on the way, and Ralph was too worried to talk. He was greatly relieved when they came in sight of the cave and he did not see her outside.

"You can stop here," he told the doctor when they reached the place where the path to the cave turned off. "We live kinda in the woods," he told Dr. Short.

"You do live out in the woods," Dr. Short observed as he got out of the car with his bag.

"Our house washed away, and we had to move," Ralph explained.

"That happened to a lot of people, but I didn't know there was a house out here."

"It ain't a regular house, but it was all we could find in a hurry," Ralph said.

At the mouth of the cave Ralph paused and turned to the doctor. "This is where we live," he said, trying to hide his embarrassment.

"You live in a cave?" Dr. Short snorted.

"It was the only place we could find," he repeated.

"No wonder your sister is sick. It's a wonder the whole family's not down with pneumonia!"

"There ain't no family but me and Candy. I hope you won't tell nobody where we're livin'," Ralph said pathetically.

"Let's go in," Dr. Short said gruffly.

Ralph pulled the curtain aside from the opening of the cave and led the way into the smoky enclosure.

"Candy, you're up!" he exclaimed in amazement when he saw her attempting to cook over the fire.

"I wanted to have something ready for you to eat when you got back." She looked at him with glazed eyes, and he saw that she was staggering.

"You ought to be in bed," he sobbed. "I've brought the doctor to see you."

"Oh, no, Ralph! Now everybody will know where we live," she cried in alarm.

"Calm down, young lady, and let me see what I can do for you," Dr. Short said. He looked around for a chair and saw that there was none. "Sit down on that pallet over there, and I'll kneel beside you," he said to Candy. "I want to take your temperature and check your pulse."

Mechanically, as if she hardly knew what she was doing, Candy went to the pallet and sat down.

Dr. Short set his bag on the floor of the cave and opened it. He took out a thermometer and put it in Candy's mouth. Then he took her blood pressure and counted her pulse. He took out his stethoscope and listened to her lungs and her heart. Abruptly he took the ear pieces from his ears and put the instrument away. He took the thermometer from her mouth and read it and shook his head.

"Just as I expected—she's got pneumonia," he observed as if he were talking to the walls of the cave. "We'll have to take her to the hospital at once," he added, turning to Ralph.

"Oh, no. I can't go to the hospital," Candy sobbed, catching his meaning in spite of her clouded brain.

"Young lady, you won't live unless you do."

"You have to go, Candy," Ralph told her brokenly.

"I can't," she sobbed, and the tears rolled down her cheeks.

"You must," the doctor said firmly. "Get her warmest clothes and help her get into them. There's no time to lose," he added turning to Ralph.

Despite Candy's protest, Ralph helped her put on her coat and boots. Then they left the cave, and started to the doctor's car, with Ralph and Dr. Short supporting Candy as she stumbled along the pathway.

When they reached the car, they helped her get in, and Ralph got in beside her.

"We'll take her to King's Daughter Hospital in Ashland," Dr. Short announced as he got in and started the motor. He turned the car around and started driving toward Ashland with all possible speed.

Candy closed her eyes, rested her head on Ralph's shoulder, and went to sleep. She did not awaken on the way, but when the doctor wheeled in the drive to the emergency room entrance of the hospital, she sat up.

"Wait in the car," Dr. Short ordered as he jumped out and ran into the hospital. In a moment two orderlies came out with a gurney. They helped Candy from the car, lifted her to the gurney, and rolled her into the emergency room where Dr. Short was already issuing orders.

"Ralph, you sit in the waiting room, while I get her admitted to the hospital and get some medication started. After we get her in a room, you can stay with her," Dr. Short said, in what was for him an unusual show of compassion.

Unhappily, Ralph went to the waiting room and sat down to wait and to worry. A great while later, a nurse came to tell him that Candy had been taken to a room on the second floor. She was sleeping, but he was welcome to sit in the room with her.

Relieved, he went to the second floor and found her room. He thought his heart would break when he saw her in a clean, white hospital bed with a needle in her arm and a tube running from it to a bottle above her bed. She was so still and so pale, he thought she had died. Then he saw her chest gently rising and falling and realized that she had not.

With a sigh of relief, he sat down beside her. He did not leave her until late in the afternoon, when a nurse suggested that he go and get something to eat.

"I don't believe you ate any lunch," she observed.

"No ma'am. I was afraid she would wake up while I was gone and get out of bed and leave the hospital."

"She'll not wake up soon. The doctor has given

her something to make her sleep. Besides, I'll keep an eye on her while you're gone."

He went then, though reluctantly, found a restaurant, and ate a sandwich. Then he returned to Candy's bedside.

Long after dark, Dr. Short came in to see Candy. He took a critical look at her chart and shook his head. "She's a very sick girl," he told Ralph bluntly.

"Is she goin' to get well?" Ralph asked in a hoarse whisper.

"We'll do all we can for her," the doctor shrugged.

After Dr. Short was gone, Ralph continued his vigil, more worried than before. Through most of the night he did not sleep. From time to time he arose and stood by Candy's bed, looking down at her. She was so still, so pale, and so beautiful, he thought his heart was going to break. Just before daylight, in utter weariness, he closed his burning eyes and went to sleep. He did not awaken until meals were being served to patients down the hall. Then he stretched, sat up, and looked at Candy. Her eyelids were moving ever so slightly.

"Candy, are you awake?" he asked softly.

She opened her eyes and looked up at him. Then her eyes roamed around the room. "Where am I?" she asked softly.

"In the hospital. Dr. Short and I brought you in yesterday."

"Now I remember. Are they going to separate us?"

"I won't let them. You just get well, and I'll find a better place for us to live."

"Who's taking care of Sandy Bell?"

"I'll go feed and milk her soon as the doctor comes. I want to know you're goin' to get well before I leave."

"Of course I'm going to get well. I have to, so I can take care of you and Sandy Bell." Her eyes closed as if she were too weary to keep them open.

Soon a nurse came to the room. "I thought I heard you and her talking. Is she awake?" she asked.

"She was a minute ago."

"I'm awake," Candy said, opening her eyes again.

"The doctor says you can have some hot soup if you feel like eating."

"That sounds good," she said softly.

"I don't feel like eating, but I thought you could eat it," she whispered, turning her sunken blue eyes on Ralph after the nurse was gone.

"Will they care if I eat it?"

"They shouldn't care if I don't eat it."

"I wish you would eat it."

"Maybe I'll eat something later."

Minutes later an aide brought the soup and set it on the table by Candy's bed.

"You better wake her so she can eat while it's hot," she told Ralph.

"Candy, they brought your soup. Wake up and see if you can eat it," he said, shaking her gently.

"I'm not hungry, Ralph," she said weakly as she opened her eyes.

"Try to eat it, Candy."

"I want you to eat it,"

Uncertainly Ralph reached for the soup and tasted it. "It's good," he said. "Candy, please try to eat it."

"I'll watch you eat," she responded.

Ralph thought he was going to choke on the soup, but he ate it to please her.

"Now go and take care of Sandy Bell," she said when he finished eating.

"The doctor hasn't come yet."

"I'll be all right. Just go and hurry back."

"If I have to go, I will, and I'll hurry."

"Ralph, I've been thinking." She stopped for breath. "If—if my stepmother hasn't come back, our barn would be a good place for Sandy Bell. There's stalls in the barn, and there's hay in the loft for her to eat."

"I don't know where your barn is."

"It's above the river, not far from where I first saw you on your house. On your way, you'll come to a real big rock beside the road, and you can see the barn from there."

"I'll look for it on the way."

"If my stepmother isn't there, lead Sandy Bell to the barn and feed her."

"It's a long walk to the cave. I may not have time to move Sandy Bell if I don't catch a ride, and I'll be late gettin' back."

"I'll be here when you get back," she smiled faintly.

He smiled back in spite of his concern, kissed her gently on the forehead, and turned to go. He paused at the door and looked back for several minutes before he turned away and left.

"I'd turn Sandy Bell loose if it wasn't for Candy, but I believe she'd die if anything happened to that goat," he said aloud when he reached the street. But he knew he would never turn Sandy Bell loose. He would take care of her, just as Candy would, and when Candy got well, he would find a place for them to live, and they would take Sandy Bell with them.

Chapter 7

*R*alph did not try to catch a ride to the cave, but walked all the way for fear he would not find Candy's barn. Finally, beside the road, he saw the big rock that she had told him about, and, looking toward the river, he saw the barn a quarter of a mile away. There was an almost invisible pathway that led toward the barn. He left the road and followed the path to the barn door. There he listened for a moment, and, when he did not hear anyone inside, he slid the wooden latch aside, opened the door, and looked in.

There was no one in the barn, so he went in and looked around. Two of the stalls were empty. There was hay in the loft with furniture and clothes piled on top of it. There were a few pigeons on the rafters near the roof, and a few bedraggled sparrows fluttered to a start and flew from the barn. A rooster was standing on one foot near the door, and a few hens were foraging for food in the barn lot.

Ralph left the barn, relieved that Candy's stepmother was not there, and started on to the cave. Nobody offered him a ride, so he walked the rest of the way.

It was mid-afternoon when he reached the cave, and he was hungry. He wanted to find himself something to eat, but Sandy Bell was bleating and tugging at her rope.

"You must be hungry and thirsty, you old goat," he said to Sandy Bell as he untied her. He led her out of the cave and let her go. "You hurry and eat, 'cause I have to tie you up again before I leave. But tomorrow I'll come early, and move you to a nice barn where there's hay for you to eat."

He went back in the cave and looked through the groceries they had left. He found a can of mixed fruit, opened it with his knife, ate the fruit, and drank the juice. Then he went out and cut some cedar branches for Sandy Bell and put them in the cave where she could reach them after he tied her up.

He waited until the goat finished eating and put her back in the cave and tied her. He milked her in a syrup bucket Candy had brought from the cabin. On his way back to the hospital, he carried the milk to the barn and gave it to the chickens.

It was almost dark when he got back to Ashland. He was tired and hungry, but he was so worried about Candy he did not stop, even to get a sandwich. Instead he hurried on to the hospital and up to her room. She was sleeping, and he was relieved to see a half empty bowl of Jell-O and a half piece of toast on her bedside table. *She must be better,* he surmised as he sat quietly down in the chair by her bed.

Some while later an aide came, bringing Candy's supper.

"Do you want me to wake her up?" Ralph asked.

"Maybe you'd better not. The doctor probably still has her sedated. I'll leave her tray in case she wakes up."

The aide left, and with a troubled heart, Ralph continued to sit by Candy's bedside. Time dragged slowly, and he grew weary, but he kept up his vigil.

Finally Dr. Short came to Candy's room. "Well I see that you're still here," he grunted at Ralph.

"I ain't leavin', Dr. Short, long as she's here."

"I'm glad somebody cares for her," Dr. Short growled.

"She's all I've got, an' I'm all she's got."

Dr. Short started taking Candy's pulse, and she opened her eyes and looked up at him. Then she looked to see if Ralph was there and smiled when she saw him.

"How are you, young lady?" Dr. Short asked.

"My head's not hurting like it did, but I feel awfully tired."

"Has she had anything to eat?" Dr. Short asked Ralph.

"I think she ate a little at noon, but she didn't wake up when they brought her supper."

"The food on that tray's cold. I'll tell them to bring her something fresh."

He turned back to Candy. "Young lady, you're getting better, but you're not out of the woods yet. I want you to take your medicine and rest, and eat everything they bring you."

"What are you eating, Ralph?" he asked, turning to him.

"I opened a can of fruit and ate it this afternoon when I went to the cave to see about Candy's goat," he replied.

"Is that all you've had today?"

"Candy wouldn't eat her soup this morning, so I ate it," Ralph admitted.

"You can't live on that," Dr. Short snorted. "I'll send word to the kitchen for them to bring your meals too while you're here."

"Thank you, Dr. Short," Ralph said, trying to swallow the lump in his throat.

"Where did you sleep last night, Ralph?" Dr. Short asked.

"I slept some in the chair by Candy's bed."

"I'll have them bring in a cot for you to sleep on."

He turned back to Candy.

"Young lady, I don't want to hear of you giving Ralph any more of your food. You need it yourself," he scolded.

"Yes, doctor. I'll feel more like eating when Ralph has something to eat too."

"Ralph, you come with me," Dr. Short said when he was ready to go. "He'll be back in a minute, Candy."

Dr. Short led Ralph to a remote corner of the hall and stopped.

"Ralph, how long have you and Candy been living in that cave?" he asked.

"Not long. It was the only place we could find," he defended.

"Where's your family?"

"Candy is all the family I've got."

"What about your parents? Don't you have a father or mother?"

"They're both dead."

"For heaven's sake! Two children, here in the United States, living in a cave!" Dr. Short exploded. "It's a wonder you both didn't die of pneumonia."

"Is Candy goin' to get well?" Ralph asked soberly.

"I'm sure she will, but you can't take her back to that cave to live."

"I'll find a better place," Ralph promised.

"You both belong in a home," the doctor growled.

"Please, Dr. Short. It would break Candy's heart if anyone put us in a orphan's home, and it would kill her if they separated us."

"Don't mention it to her. The last thing she needs is something to worry about. We'll see what is to be done when she gets well." He dismissed Ralph with a shrug and started down the hall.

Ralph went back to Candy's room greatly troubled, but determined not to let her know. He would talk Dr. Short into waiting until she left the hospital before he made any move to get them in a home, he decided. Then they would run away again.

Soon an aide came, bringing the food Dr. Short had ordered.

"This is for Candy," she said as she set a cup of broth and some toast on the table. "And this is for Ralph." She smiled at Ralph as she set a well-loaded plate of food on a side table.

"That smells good," Candy said as the aide cranked up the head of the bed and propped her up on a pillow.

"Can you feed yourself, Candy?" she asked.

"Sure I can. I ate by myself at noon."

Ralph got up and stood by Candy, ready to help her after the aide was gone.

"You sit down and eat, Ralph. I can eat by myself."

"I'm glad you're better, Candy." He moved his plate to her table and pulled his chair up beside it.

"I'm glad Dr. Short told them to bring your supper."

"Me too. I'm starved."

"I'll pray before we eat."

He bowed his head, glad that she was well enough to start praying again.

When they finished eating, Ralph removed the pillows from behind her head and cranked her bed down.

"What did Dr. Short want?" she asked, turning her blue eyes on him.

"He said we can't live in the cave anymore," he replied before he thought.

"Where does he think we're going to live?" she demanded.

"I'll find us a place before you get out of the hospital."

"We'll have to convince people we're old enough to take care of ourselves," she mused.

"I'm plenty old enough to take care of you."

"I'm glad I have a big brother. It keeps me from feeling so alone."

"And I'm glad to have a sister."

She smiled, closed her eyes and fell asleep.

It was quiet in the room, and Ralph felt drowsy after being out in the cold. His head soon slumped to the side and he fell asleep in his chair.

The next morning Candy was well enough to be fretful. She complained about having to stay in bed, and she worried because they were slow bringing her breakfast.

"Did you move Sandy Bell?" she asked while they were waiting.

"It was too late to move her when I got to the cave. I did cut her plenty to eat though. I'm goin' to move her today."

"Did you milk her?"

"Yeah, I milked her, but I can't do it good like you can."

"What did you do with the milk?"

"I poured it in the trough for your chickens."

"I'm glad. I reckon nobody has fed them since the day I found you."

After breakfast Ralph left to go to the cave. As he started along the street, a car drew up at the curb, and a man leaned across the seat and opened the door on the passenger's side.

"Want a ride?" he called.

"Thank you," Ralph responded as he got in.

"Where are you going?" the driver asked.

"Down the river."

"Glad I came along, because I'm going that way. My name's Joe Stark. What's yours?"

"Ralph Roberts. I appreciate the ride, Mr. Stark."

Ralph had no way of knowing that Joe Stark was

a reporter for the local newspaper. Nor did he know that word had leaked from hospital staff that he and Candy were alone in the world and that their home had been lost in the flood.

That had given the reporter an idea for a human interest story, and he had been watching for Ralph to come from the hospital, hoping he could gather more information from him for his story.

"Do you live down the river?" Joe Stark asked as he guided his car out into traffic.

"I've been living different places since my house washed away," Ralph said evasively, put on guard by Joe Stark's questions.

"You live with your family?"

Ralph hesitated, and his hesitation was not lost on Joe Stark.

"I will as soon as we get moved," Ralph finally answered, thinking that he was not being untruthful. Candy was his family, and he would be living with her when she got out of the hospital. She would be glad he had not told a lie.

"Where are you going to move?"

"Don't know yet. Stop the car, and I'll get out and walk," Ralph concluded hotly.

"I'm sorry. I didn't mean to pry," Joe said.

"That's all right. Just let me out."

"You might as well ride. I'm going your way."

"I'll walk. If you don't stop the car, I'm goin' to jump out."

"Sure, if that's the way you want it," Joe said, and he stopped the car at the curb. Ralph got out without thanking Joe, and stood on the roadside and watched him drive away. When Joe's car was out of sight, he started walking toward the cave.

When Joe was well ahead of Ralph, he backed his car down a side road and parked behind some overhanging tree limbs. The car was well concealed, but he could still see the road.

He watched Ralph pass and gave him time to get well ahead, then he drove the car out on the road and started following him. Joe drove slowly and stopped frequently, staying close enough to keep Ralph in sight. At last he saw him turn from the road and go up a small hill and out of sight. He turned his car and drove a short distance back up the road and parked behind a barn. Then he concealed himself in the barn and watched, hoping that Ralph would come back up the road.

Some while later he saw Ralph coming up the road, leading a goat. Puzzled, Joe waited until he passed the barn and walked out of sight. Then he followed him in his car, always staying far enough behind so he would not know he was being followed.

After a few miles, Joe saw Ralph turn from the road and lead the goat into a barn. Again he parked out of sight and waited. After awhile, he saw Ralph come back to the road without the goat and turn toward Ashland.

When Ralph was out of sight, Joe went to the barn and looked around. The goat was in a stall eating hay, and a few chickens were drinking milk from a trough. He saw the furniture in the hayloft and climbed the rickety ladder to look it over. What he saw told him only that someone had stored their furniture, some clothes, and some personal items in the loft. *But where had Ralph been keeping the goat? And why had he brought her here?*

He went to his car and drove back to where Ralph had left the road when he went after the goat. He got out of his car and followed Ralph's tracks to the cave.

"Somebody's been camping here," he commented aloud when he saw the smoke-blackened opening of the cave. He pulled aside the curtain and an acrid smell assailed him. He went in and looked around, and what he saw amazed him. A skillet filled with some kind of food that had burned to a crisp was sitting on some rocks. There were some girl's dresses on hangers, hanging from crevasses in the wall of the cave. On other hangers were some boy's clothes that he thought would fit Ralph. Other garments, bedclothes, and cans of food were scattered over the floor of the cave, as if someone had made a hasty departure. Joe left the cave more intrigued than before.

On the way back to his car, Joe saw three sets of tracks, close together, that led to the road. The tracks told him that a man and a boy had walked close to a girl, as if they were supporting her. Her tracks looked as if she had faltered from time to time. *Could Ralph and a girl possibly have been living in the cave?* he wondered. *Could she have been ill? Was that why Ralph and a man had helped her walk to the road?* He walked back to his car thinking that he was onto an unbelievable story.

That same day Miss Conrad decided to visit Candy again. To her dismay, she found the cabin empty. Sudden panic filled her heart. Perhaps the children had been kidnapped. She returned home, phoned the police, and told them that two children who had been living alone in a cabin had disappeared.

The police went to the cabin to investigate. They easily tracked Ralph and Candy and the goat to the cave. There their trail ended, but they saw many tracks around the cave. They went inside and found evidence that a boy and girl had lived there, but were now gone. Scouting around, they found tracks leading from the road to the cave and more tracks leading back to the road. It was evident that the boy and girl had left the cave or been taken from it. Miss Conrad had told them that the girl's name was Candy Roberts, but she did not know the boy's first name. They returned to the police station in Russell and put out a missing persons bulletin on the missing children.

In some way Joe Stark learned that the Russell police were looking for a boy and a girl who had been living in a cave, and he knew at once that Ralph and the girl in the hospital were the ones they were looking for.

He went at once to the hospital to see the girl, but he found a "No Visitors" sign on her door. He started to go in anyway, but a nurse who looked and talked like a drill sargent, stopped him. In the brief instant that the door was open, he saw Ralph seated by the bedside of a girl who did not look like a patient who was too ill to have company.

"Can't you read?" the nurse demanded, coming from Candy's room and closing the door behind her. "You're not family, are you?"

"No, just a friend."

"You're not an undercover policeman?"

"No. Why did you ask?"

"None of your business. All you need to know is that Dr. Short has ordered that this patient is not to be disturbed."

"Thank you, ma'am," Joe Stark said and turned away. He walked the halls of the hospital until he saw Dr. Short come from a patient's room.

"I'd like to talk with you a minute, Dr. Short," he said, falling in step with the doctor.

"What about?" Dr. Short asked suspiciously.

"About the girl on the second floor with the "No Visitors" sign on her door. Who is she?"

"None of your business," the doctor snapped, bristling.

"Thank you," Joe answered. He turned on his heel and left the hospital. Next he went to the police station in Russell. There he learned that Candy's teacher had given the police the tip that had led to their search for Candy and Ralph Roberts. Joe went to the school and questioned Miss Conrad. She told him only that Ralph and Candy had no parents, and that she had lost track of them, but that was enough for him to piece together his story.

Joe wrote a long article about Ralph and Candy living alone in a cave a few miles below Russell until she became ill, most likely from exposure. She was now in the hospital being treated for pneumonia. His article also stated that Ralph and Candy had no parents and no home.

Following the publication of his article, there was a public outcry for something to be done for the children.Some irate citizens even wrote letters to the editor, demanding that the children be put in a home.

Ralph saw Joe Stark's article in a paper somebody had laid aside and sat down and read every word of it.

"I'd like to kill that Joe Stark," he gritted between his teeth. For several minutes he sat clenching and unclenching his fist and wishing that he was big enough to knock Joe Stark's teeth down his throat.

The next day he read some of the letters to the editor. They made him so angry that he threw caution to the winds and told Candy about the article and the letters.

She listened with her face white and her eyes blazing.

"We'll leave here tonight," she said evenly when he finished. "We'll slip out after dark and leave."

"I'll go get the things we need from the cave and put them where we can get them after we leave the hospital," he said firmly.

"You hurry. Then come straight back," she told him.

"I will, and don't you worry."

Ralph left the hospital and started to the cave, walking rapidly. When he reached the road to the cave, he started trying to catch a ride. Soon a lady with a car full of children stopped and offered him a ride. The children all piled in the back seat, and he got in beside the lady. He was glad the children kept up a chatter all the way, because that kept the lady from asking him questions.

When he reached the cave, he quickly put some food and some clothes for himself and Candy in a box. Then he hurried back to the road and caught a ride back to Ashland.

When he reached the hospital, he hid the box behind some shrubs, then went up to Candy's room. To his great disappointment, he found Candy tossing in her bed, with a nurse standing beside her.

"What's wrong?" he asked the nurse.

"Your sister has suffered a backset, and her doctor wants a nurse with her. I am to call him if she gets any worse."

Candy roused momentarily and looked up. "Don't worry Ralph. I'll be better before long," she said.

Greatly worried, Ralph sat down beside Candy. He did not talk for fear he would make her worse. The nurse did not talk either. Soon Candy went to sleep.

Ralph squirmed in his chair, listened to footsteps in the hall, heard the bell buzzing as some patient rang for a nurse, counted the panes of glass in the window, and thought. Candy would have to get better before she could leave the hospital, and that could be days from now. He certainly could not leave their things where he had hidden them. Someone would find them for sure, so he would have to get them tonight and put them in the wardrobe in Candy's room. He would take them out and hide them again when she was able to run away from the hospital. He would just have to wait for her to get better, but he was afraid she wouldn't. He wished he knew how to pray.

Chapter 8

*T*he next morning, in the big old house on top of the hill at Oakcrest Farm, near Maysville, Marsha White was conferring with Dora, her housekeeper, about preparations for lunch when she looked out the front window and saw the mail carrier come into view on the road.

"I see the mailman coming," she said to Dora.

"I'm glad the river has gone down so he can run our route again," Dora commented.

Marsha watched the mailman's car until he stopped at their box.

"He left mail in the box for us, Dora. Please go and get it. You had better put on your coat; it's cold outside this morning."

"Yes, ma'am," Dora replied. She stopped what she was doing, put on her coat, and started to the mailbox.

Marsha watched her go down the drive to the mailbox beside the county road.

Dora got the mail and started back up the drive, but Marsha's eyes did not follow her. Instead, she looked at the river, across the valley from the road. She saw that it was within its banks, but it was still muddy, and she sighed, wondering how long it would take for life in the valley to return to normal.

Maysville, their county seat, only a few miles away had been especially hard hit during the flood. Goodness knows, it had been hard on her husband, Judge Austin White, and all the other officials in the county. Their home at Oakcrest had escaped only because it was on high ground.

"You got the Ashland paper," Dora said as she entered the house. She handed the paper and the other mail to her mistress.

"Thank you, Dora. It's always good to get my hometown paper." She laid aside some business letters, then glanced at the paper, and a headline caught her attention.

Boy and Girl Living In Cave, she read aloud as she sank to a chair to read the article.

Her heart was greatly touched as she read about Candy and Ralph living in a cave, and her eyes filled with tears when she read that Candy was in the hospital.

It seemed an injustice to her that she and her husband had been denied the children they wanted, and these children were without parents and had actually been living in a cave. She decided to show the article to her husband when he came home that evening, and to suggest that they consider adopting the children.

"Dora, I want you to read this article about some children living in a cave," she said, holding up the paper.

"In a cave? My goodness, I can't believe it!" Dora exclaimed. "I'm busy right now, but I'll read it when I get a free minute."

That evening when Marsha showed the article to Judge White, he was touched, as she had been, but he thought they should see the children before they considered adopting them.

"Let's go see them tonight," Marsha urged. "I have not been able to think of anything but those children all day."

"Good idea, but we'll have to hurry if we are to get to the hospital before visiting hours are over."

"Then hurry and dress while Dora is putting dinner on the table. I've already dressed, because I was hoping I could talk you into going to see them."

Judge White did not answer, but he went upstairs to dress.

"Dora, please hurry dinner. Judge White and I are going to Ashland to see those children I read about in the paper," Marsha called to her housekeeper.

"Yes, ma'am. I hope you and the judge can do something for them, maybe get them in a home or something."

"Something has to be done, Dora. We'll see."

Judge White came downstairs, dressed to go, just as Dora was putting dinner on the table. They sat down and ate hurriedly, then drove to the hospital in Ashland.

When they reached Candy's room, they were disconcerted to find a sign saying that she could not have visitors."Oh, I hope she's not worse," Marsha whispered worriedly.

"Let's go to the desk and find out," Judge White suggested.

They went to the nearest nurses' station and waited until a nurse looked up from her task.

"We want to ask about Candy Roberts. Is she worse?" Marsha asked anxiously.

"She's had a bit of a backset, and her doctor decided she should not have company," the nurse answered.

"Is she serious?" Judge White persisted.

"We think she's going to get well, but her doctor doesn't want anything to worry her."

"I'm glad she's going to be all right," Marsha said, relieved.

"Are you related to her?" the nurse asked, looking

from Marsha to Judge White and back again.

"No, but we are interested in her and her brother. We'd like to talk with her doctor," Judge White responded.

"Dr. Short is her doctor, and he's somewhere in the hospital. I'll page him and ask him to come to the waiting room. You can wait for him there." She pointed to the waiting room down the hall.

They went to the almost empty waiting room and sat down to wait.

In a few minutes a short, balding doctor appeared at the door. "I'm Dr. Short. Are you people looking for me?" he asked, when Judge White and Marsha arose to meet him.

"Yes, we are. I'm Judge Austin White, and this is my wife, Marsha. We want to talk with you about Candy and Ralph Roberts."

"What about them?" the doctor asked, bristling slightly.

"We read about them in the paper, and we may want to offer them a home when the girl is able to leave the hospital. But of course we want to see them and talk with them before we make the decision."

"They need a home all right, but I guess it would be up to Candy whether they would live with you or not. She has some pretty strong ideas about what they will or will not do, and Ralph goes along with her," Dr. Short said, still sizing them up.

"We've wanted children for years," Mrs. White said.

"We can give them a good home," Judge White added.

"I've become right attached to these youngsters since they've been here, and I want them to be happy wherever they go," Dr. Short said firmly. He was thinking that Candy and Ralph might not fit in with the polished judge and his refined wife.

"My husband is the county judge of Mason County. We're in a position to offer the children every advantage, and we would love them as if they were our own," Marsha continued.

"We have to see them before we make a decision, Marsha," the judge reminded her.

"Candy will have to see you before she makes a decision," the doctor remarked tartly.

"One would think they'd be glad to have a home," Marsha countered.

"You haven't met Candy. She's an independent little somebody."

"I can't wait to see her," the judge smiled.

"One thing is certain, Candy and Ralph refuse to be separated. If you want one of them, you'll have to take them both," Dr. Short told them.

"We wouldn't think of separating them," Marsha assured him. "When can we see them?"

"You can see them now, but approach the subject of offering them a home gently. And, Judge White, don't mention that you're a judge. Candy will think you've come to put them in a home, and that could make her worse."

"I understand, Dr. Short. We'll be tactful."

Dr. Short led them to Candy's door. "I'll go in first and tell them that they are going to have company," he told them.

He went in and closed the door after him, and the Whites waited in the hall somewhat impatiently.

"How is she, Ralph?" Dr. Short asked as he approached Candy's bed.

"She's restless. I think she's worried."

Candy turned and looked up at the doctor. "Dr. Short, I've been thinking about what will happen to me and Ralph when I leave the hospital," Candy said in a half sob.

"What if we could find both of you a home with

some nice people?" Dr. Short asked.

"There's not any nice grown-up people, Dr. Short, except you and maybe one of the nurses," Candy replied.

"I feel the same way," Ralph said bitterly.

"Well now, since you think that I and one of the nurses are all right, don't you think there just might be a few more good people?"

"I've not seen any," Candy declared.

"There are lots of good people, Candy, and I have two of them waiting outside your door. They want to see you and Ralph."

"No," Candy wailed. "Don't let them in, Dr. Short. They'll just want to separate us."

"They don't want to do that at all, Candy, but they may want to offer both of you a home," Dr. Short said.

"You won't let them take us if we don't like them, will you, Dr. Short?" Candy asked, near panic.

"Of course not, Candy. That's a promise," he told her as he opened the door.

Judge White and Marsha entered immediately.

"Candy and Ralph, I want you to meet Mr. Austin White and his wife, Marsha," Dr. Short said.

Candy cast a quick glance at the Whites, then turned her back and pulled the sheet over her head.

The Whites looked at each other with disappoinment. Then the judge nodded encouragement to his wife.

"Hello, Ralph," she greeted, turning to the boy. "And hello, Candy, if that's you under that sheet."

Ralph muttered a greeting, but Candy did not respond.

"Candy, my husband and I have come to see you and Ralph, because we want to help you," Marsha said gently toward the covered head.

"The only way grown-ups want to help is to split me and Ralph up," Candy cried from beneath the sheet.

"We will never do that, Candy," Judge White said in a gentle voice that he never used in a courtroom.

"I wish people would let us be," Ralph broke in bitterly.

"Ralph, why don't you and Candy listen to what Mr. and Mrs. White have to say?" Dr. Short suggested.

"We'll listen, but me and Candy ain't goin' to let nobody separate us," Ralph answered belligerently.

"That's one thing we won't do," Candy cried, suddenly pulling the sheet off her head.

Judge White looked at the tousle-headed, blue-eyed, big-mouthed girl, and his heart melted. He wondered what had happened in her young life to make her so untrusting and so defiant. He realized how much she needed the love he and his wife could give, and he decided at once that he wanted to adopt her and the boy. He turned to Ralph, who was still bristling with distrust, and his heart went out to him also.

Austin White was a good judge of people, and he decided that Ralph would be a fine boy, once he got the chip off his shoulder. And Candy would be a sweet, responsive girl after she got over her fear and her defiance. He turned to his wife and nodded approval.

She smiled her gratitude and turned to Ralph. "Ralph, after we get better acquainted, we hope you and Candy will like us. If you do, when she is ready to leave the hospital, we want you to come and live with us," Mrs. White said.

"I reckon that would be up to Candy," Ralph said cautiously.

"Ralph, look at me," Marsha said. "My husband and I have driven all the way here from Maysville to offer you and Candy a home. You will think about it, won't you?"

"Do you have a house me and Ralph can live in?" Candy interrupted, looking from one to the other with her big blue eyes.

"We want you to live in our house as part of our family, Candy. Wouldn't that be better than for you and Ralph to live alone?" Judge White responded.

"What do we have to do for all that?" Candy asked.

"Have to do?" Marsha gasped. "We don't expect you to do anything but be part of our family. We will love you and Ralph, and we hope you and Ralph will come to love us."

"Do you have work I can do to earn money for clothes and such for me and Candy?" Ralph asked.

"You won't have to earn money for clothes, Ralph. You and Candy will live with us, and we'll furnish your clothes. And you'll go to school like other boys and girls your age."

"I love to go to school," Candy cried with sudden interest.

"What if we don't like livin' with you?" Ralph asked.

"We hope you will like living with us, Ralph, but if you don't we'll help you find another place to live," Judge White assured him.

"Sounds fair enough to me. What do you think, Candy?" Ralph asked, turning to her.

Candy puckered her brow in thought for a long minute. "Do you have a place where I can keep Sandy Bell?" she finally asked.

"Is Sandy Bell your dog?" Mrs. White asked.

"No, ma'am. She's a goat!" Ralph said, somewhat embarrassed.

"A goat? I don't know. Will she eat my flowers and shrubs?"

"She'll eat everything in sight," Ralph admitted.

"She only eats what we give her when we keep her up," Candy defended.

"Surely we can do something with Candy's goat," Marsha said, looking at her husband.

"I'm sure there's a stall in our barn for Sandy Bell,

and she can share the pasture with the cows and work mules."

"Will they be good to Sandy Bell?" Candy asked.

"Of course they will, Candy. The cows and the mules will make Sandy Bell welcome, once they get used to her," Judge White told her.

"Do you have any ponies?" Candy asked.

"We don't have any ponies now, but some day we just might get a couple of ponies that would love to have you and Ralph ride them," Austin White said, watching Candy's expression.

"We'll go, won't we, Ralph?" Candy exclaimed, smiling for the first time.

"If you say so, Candy."

"I'm going to hug you, Ralph," Marsha said as she put her arms around the boy.

Ralph stood stiffly, but he allowed her to hug him. "And I'm going to kiss you, Candy." She leaned over the bed and kissed Candy on her cheek.

"Nobody's kissed me since my mama died, except Ralph, and he only kisses me on the forehead," Candy said in a half sob.

"You'll get plenty of hugging and kissing at our house, Candy. Marsha has lots of love to give," Austin White said. He patted Candy on the shoulder and turned to Ralph and tousled his hair.

"Candy, my husband can't come with me to see you in the daytime. He has a lot of extra work since the flood, but I'll come to see you and Ralph every day until Dr. Short releases you from the hospital," Marsha said.

"I want you to come back," Candy said, smiling up at her.

"Me too," Ralph said.

Marsha was near tears when she and Austin turned to go.

"Good-bye, Mr. and Mrs. White," Candy said when

they paused in the doorway.

"Good-bye, Candy and Ralph. I'll see you tomor-row," Marsha smiled.

"I'll see you one night soon," Austin told them.

"I'll see you kids in the morning," Dr. Short said. He went out with the Whites, and the door closed behind them.

"I like them," Candy exclaimed.

"Me too, but they're awfully uppity lookin'. They make me feel fidgety."

"I reckon they can't help how they look, Ralph. Some people are just made that way. My mama looked a lot like Mrs. White when she dressed up to go to church, and we might look as fine as them someday, if we get dressed up," she added thoughtfully.

"Maybe," he frowned, "but I can't say that I want to. I like us bein' the way we are now."

"Well, I want to be like them. When I grow up, I want to look as fine as Mrs. White, and I want to be as kind and good as Mr. White is."

"I reckon I would like to be a little like Mr. White," Ralph conceded.

Candy and Ralph talked quietly about the Whites long after the nurse had turned their light out. They were excited about their new home, and Candy decided that she would have to hurry and get well enough to leave the hospital.

Chapter 9

What do you want us to call you?" Candy asked Mrs. White the next day while she was visiting her at the hospital.

"I've been thinking about that, Candy. What did you call your mother?"

"I called her Mom. My stepmother made me call her that too, but I didn't like it."

"Oh! I didn't know you had a stepmother. What has become of her and your father?" Marsha asked anxiously.

"Papa died a long time ago. . . . about three years, I think. After he died, I lived with Lillian—that's my stepmother—until the flood washed our house away."

"Where is your stepmother now?" Mrs. White insisted.

"I don't know. She left before the house washed away, and I haven't seen her since."

"Had your stepmother adopted you?" Marsha asked, uneasily.

"No, she never adopted me. She didn't want me, but kind of put up with me after Papa died," Candy said, trying to keep the anger out of her voice.

"What about you, Ralph?" Mrs. White asked. "Did your stepmother want you?"

Ralph shrugged, not knowing how to answer.

"My stepmother never wanted anybody, except

maybe old Jake, and I think she left with him," Candy said, trying hard to change the subject.

"That's too bad," Marsha said. "Now, what were we talking about?"

"You were going to tell us what to call you," Candy prompted.

"Oh yes. Suppose you and Ralph call me Mama Marsha. I would like that, and it won't be the same as what you called your mother."

"Yes, ma'am," Ralph responded noncommittally.

"I'll like calling you that," Candy said, smiling happily. "What does Mr. White want us to call him?"

"Austin and I talked about that, and he suggested that you call him Daddy White."

"I'll like calling him that," Ralph said. He was on the point of telling her that he had called his own father the old man, but he caught himself in time.

"I'm kind of afraid of Mr. White . . . I mean Daddy White," Candy ventured. "Maybe it's because I've only seen him once."

"He was sorry he couldn't come with me today, but he has been real busy at the courthouse, especially since the flood."

"The courthouse!" Candy gasped. "What does he do there?"

"Austin is the county judge of our county, Candy."

"The county judge!" she echoed, greatly surprised.

Ralph started, looked quickly at Marsha, then turned away.

"He'll come with me tomorrow night."

"I'll call him Daddy White, but it'll take me a while to get used to having a judge for a daddy," Candy said thoughtfully.

"I think I'll be afraid of him," Ralph said as much to himself as to Marsha.

"You need not be, Ralph. He'll love you just as your own daddy did."

I'm not sure my old man ever loved me or anybody else, Ralph thought to himself.

The next day Marsha came to the hospital in the afternoon. "Guess what, Candy," she greeted. "Late this afternoon, Daddy White is coming in a pickup truck with a cattle rack on it to get Sandy Bell and take her to our farm."

"Oh, I'm glad, glad, glad. I've been wondering how I would get her moved."

"And Ralph, Daddy White wants you to go with him and show him where you keep Sandy Bell."

"I'll like doin' that," Ralph exclaimed.

Within a week Candy was able to leave the hospital, and Mrs. White came to check her out and take her and Ralph home to Oakcrest.

Candy was sitting on the side of her bed when Marsha arrived, and Ralph was sitting beside her, holding a bundle containing Candy's clothes. A bundle of his own clothes was on the floor at his feet.

"Oh, Mama Marsha, I'm glad you've come. I can't wait to get out of here," Candy cried, rising to accept Marsha's kiss on her cheek.

"I'm fed up with this place," Ralph complained, arising also.

Marsha gave him a quick hug.

"I have to check you out, Candy. I see that you and Ralph are already packed," Marsha said.

"Ralph packed our things last night."

"As soon as I check you out, we'll start home."

"How am I going to pay my hospital and doctor bills, Mama Marsha?" Candy asked. "I asked Dr. Short about them, but he wouldn't tell me a thing. Will they wait till I can get a job and make money to pay them?"

"You precious girl!" Marsha exclaimed. "Don't you worry about your bills."

"I'm already worried about them. My mama taught

me to be honest, and to pay my bills, and to have integrity."

"You must have had a wonderful mother," Marsha mused.

"Oh, I did, and I think you're a wonderful mother too," Candy said.

"I'll do my best to be a mother to you, Candy. You too, Ralph," she ended, turning to him.

For a moment Candy was without words. "Thank you," she finally said, "but you haven't told me how I can pay the hospital and doctor."

"Daddy White and I are going to adopt you and Ralph into our family, Candy, and we'll be responsible for your bills."

Candy considered that for a long minute. "We weren't in your family when I came to the hospital, so it's not right for you to pay what I owe," she concluded.

"Oh, yes it is, Candy. Daddy White and I will pay any bills you have now and any you make in the future."

"I'm glad you and Daddy White are going to adopt us, and I appreciate you not wanting to separate me and Ralph."

"Me too," Ralph agreed.

"We would never think of separating you two. Now, Candy, you wait here while I go check you out. It shouldn't take long," Marsha said.

"Can I go with you?" Ralph asked.

"You'd better stay with Candy. I have an idea she'd follow us if you went with me," she told him.

"Yes ma'am," Ralph agreed reluctantly.

"I don't think I could walk that far," Candy said. "The nurse said they're going to take me out in a wheelchair."

"I'll hurry," Marsha promised as she was leaving.

Ralph was standing in the doorway, but Candy was

still sitting on her bed when Marsha returned with an aide pushing a wheelchair.

Candy arose and got shakily into the wheelchair.

"I'm ready," she smiled up at Marsha. "Get our things, Ralph."

He picked up the two bundles and followed as the aide pushed the wheelchair out of the room and along the hall.

"This is the gladdest day of my life," Candy lilted as the aide pushed her wheelchair into an elevator and Ralph and Marsha got in beside her.

At the first floor, the aide pushed the wheelchair out of the elevator, along the hall, and down a ramp to the street.

"It's still winter," Candy exclaimed in surprise as she looked up at the bare trees and the gray sky. "I thought it would be spring by now."

"You weren't in the hospital that long," Marsha explained.

"This is only the first week in March. It just seems like a long time."

"It's beautiful outside, even if it is still winter," Candy exulted. "I think I'm going to die of happiness,"

"Candy, you can't be any more happy than I am," Marsha rejoined.

"I'm glad to get away from this place," Ralph said as Marsha led the way toward a luxury automobile.

"Gee smithers! Is that your car?" he cried as Marsha put the key in the door lock.

"Yes, Ralph, this is our car. I hope you like it."

"It's the most beautiful car in the whole world!" he exclaimed.

"It sure is, Ralph," Candy joined in.

They put Candy in the backseat on a bank of pillows Marsha had brought. Ralph and Marsha got in the front, and he sat staring at the instrument panel, wondering what all the gauges were for.

Marsha put the key in the ignition and turned it. With great interest both children listened as the motor turned over, started, and purred smoothly. They both gasped with pleasure as Marsha drove the car out into traffic and started along the street.

Lying on her pillows, Candy looked out the window, drinking in all she saw. Ralph watched Marsha drive the big car.

Marsha drove slowly in the city traffic, but when they reached the open road, she increased her speed.

The road ran near the river, and in places it came into view. It was within its banks, but it was still high and muddy, and it was flowing rapidly.

"I wonder where the river is going in such a hurry," Candy remarked.

"It's on its way to join the Mississippi at Cairo, Illinois," Marsha told her.

"Gee smithers, I didn't know it was goin' all that far piece," Ralph exclaimed.

Marsha looked at him quizzically. It was strange, she thought, that a brother and sister should have such different speech patterns. She glanced at Candy in the rearview mirror, thinking to herself, she talks like a little English teacher, and he talks like a regular boy. Then it occurred to her that perhaps Candy had patterned her speech after her mother, and Ralph had learned to talk like his father.

"I hope some day you will stop saying, gee smithers, Ralph. There are better ways you can express yourself," Marsha said.

"If you don't like it, I'll stop sayin' it right now, Mama Marsha," Ralph said.

"I appreciate that, Ralph. I really do."

Candy rode in silence for some time, absorbed in all she saw. There were signs of the recent high water everywhere. The river had left muddy stains on the ground, on the trees, on fences, and on buildings. She sighed, relieved that the flood was over.

"Is Sandy Bell all right?" she finally asked.

"Oh yes. She's well fed and she's made friends with the cows and the mules and with us. I can understand why you are so attached to her."

"I'm glad you have a farm for her to live on," Candy said. She was growing weary, so she closed her eyes, but she did not go to sleep.

Ralph and Marsha were silent, so Candy listened to the hum of the motor and the other sounds of the car. She tried to imagine she was flying in a big airplane, but she soon opened her eyes again. "I could ride in the car all day if I wasn't so tired," she sighed.

"We'll be home before long and you can rest," Marsha told her.

"I wish we didn't have to stop," Ralph exclaimed.

"After Candy regains her strength, one day Daddy White and I will take you both on a long trip in the car, and you can ride to your heart's content," Marsha told him.

"I hope Candy soon gets well so you can," Ralph exclaimed.

In less than two hours they reached the outskirts of Maysville, passed through town, and turned on a county road. After another mile, Marsha turned from the road to a driveway and started up a hill. Candy sat up and looked out, and her eyes grew wide when she saw the large, white, colonial house with a front porch and a balcony. Large posts reached all the way to the high roof above the balcony. There were many large, old trees in the big yard.

"Is that where you live, Mama Marsha?" she asked in wonder.

"Indeed it is, and that's where you and Ralph are going to live."

"I love your house, but it's so big, and the yard is so big," Candy marveled. "And I love all the big trees in the yard."

"Most of those trees are oak trees, Candy. That is why we named our place Oakcrest."

"I never thought I'd live in a house like that," Ralph exclaimed.

"Well, you're going to, Ralph, and I hope you will like living there," Marsha remarked.

"The river won't ever reach us up here," Candy exclaimed as the car stopped at the yard gate.

Just then a collie dog came bounding across the grassy lawn and stopped at the gate, barking a welcome.

"Ralph and Candy, that's our dog, Roger," Marsha told them.

"He's beautiful, and I love him," Candy cried, "but does he bite?"

"No he doesn't bite. He's barking because he's glad to see us."

"I'm going to love playing with him when I feel better," Candy declared.

"Me too," Ralph agreed, but he did not trust Roger enough to get out of the car.

Candy looked around, wondering where Sandy Bell was. She looked past the garage at the end of the house, to a stock barn a hundred yards away. There was a big field behind the barn, but she didn't see Sandy Bell anywhere.

"Where is Sandy Bell?" she asked.

"She's probably in the back of the pasture with the cows and the mules."

"I'm glad she likes them, but I want to see her."

"She'll come up with the cows at feeding time, and Ralph can lead her to the yard so you can see her."

"Then I reckon I'll just have to wait." She moved toward the door to get out of the car.

"Candy, do you think you can walk to the house if Ralph and I help you?" Marsha asked.

"Sure I can, Mama Marsha. There's no way I'm going to be carried to the house like a baby."

"Are you sure Roger won't bite me?" Ralph asked.

"I'm sure, Ralph. You can get out of the car and open the door for Candy," Marsha told him.

With his eyes still on Roger, Ralph got out and opened the door for Candy.

"We'll help her to the house, Ralph. You can come back later and get your things," Marsha told him.

Ralph took Candy's hand and she got out of the car. Marsha took her arm and together they walked her to the gate. Marsha opened the gate, and Roger bounded out, barking and wagging his tail. He ran around the car, then went to Candy and licked her hands. Then he reared up on Ralph and barked as if asking him to play with him. Ralph shied away from the dog, but he did not let go of Candy.

"Roger, I know I'm going to love you," Candy said.

Just then a small coupe started up the drive. "It's Austin," Marsha exclaimed. "Candy, he said he was coming home to welcome you and Ralph, and he's here."

"I hate for him to see me being helped like a baby," Candy said.

"You shouldn't mind, Candy. He knows you've been sick."

"But I ought to be well by now."

"You will be soon. Let's go to the chair under the big oak tree, so you can sit down and wait for Daddy White," Marsha suggested.

They led Candy to the chair, and she sat down. Then she watched Daddy White's coupe come up the hill. Ralph stood beside her chair watching also.

Austin stopped his car behind the big car and bounded out. "Welcome home, Ralph and Candy," he called as he started jauntily toward them.

"Hi, Daddy White," Candy called, clapping her

hands.

Ralph was still awed in the presence of Judge White, so he only watched him and smiled.

"I'm glad we have them home at last," Marsha exclaimed, going to meet her husband.

He kissed her on the cheek, took her hand, and walked her to where Candy and Ralph were waiting.

"I'm glad you're here, Ralph," Austin said, tousling the boy's hair. He stooped beside Candy so his eyes were on a level with hers. "I'm glad you're here too, Blue Eyes," he told her.

"My daddy used to call me blue eyes a long time ago," she giggled.

"If you'd rather I didn't call you that, I won't," Austin offered.

"I'd like for you to call me that."

"All right, blue eyes. Now, if you feel up to it, I'll help you into the house. Do you want me to carry you?"

"I can walk, but I stagger a little," she grinned.

"Then I'll steady you." He took her hand and helped her to her feet. Then he put his arm around her shoulders and helped her walk to the house. Ralph and Marsha followed close behind them. At the steps, Daddy White picked Candy up and set her on the porch.

Dora had been watching from the door, and she held it open wide for them to enter. "I've got Miss Candy's bed all ready," she said.

"Candy and Ralph, this is Dora, our housekeeper, and Dora, these are our new children," Marsha said.

"Oh, Miss Candy and Master Ralph, I'm glad to meet you," Dora said.

The Whites were not at all surprised that Dora had used the courtesy title before the children's names. That was Dora's way. She had grown up neighbors to some children from somewhere overseas, and had picked up that manner of addressing people from them, and she still did it.

"I'm glad to meet you, Miss Dora," Candy said, using the same manner of address. She was surprised that the Whites had a housekeeper, and she wondered why Marsha did not keep her own house as her mother had kept hers.

Because of his timidity, Ralph did not respond to Dora at all.

Gently Austin led Candy into the house.

She looked around and marveled at the size and the beauty of the house as Daddy White led her to the back bedroom he and Marsha and Dora had carefully prepared for her.

As she entered she looked around the large, high-ceiling room. Her eyes rested for a moment on the long, curtained windows, then surveyed the heavy, walnut bedroom furniture. Last she looked at the beautiful patterned carpet that covered most of the hardwood floor. She was surprised and pleased and somewhat awed by her surroundings. Never had she dreamed of sleeping in such a room.

Austin led her to the bed, and she got in. She was weary, and she was thankful to get off her feet.

Marsha gently arranged the pillows under her head.

"I want to see Sandy Bell when she comes up to-night," Candy sighed.

"I told her we would have Ralph to lead Sandy Bell to the yard so she could see her," Marsha explained.

"Oh, I see. Then, since Sandy Bell is coming to see you, Candy, I'll help you go out to meet her."

"Thank you, Daddy White," Candy said. A few moments later, with a smile playing across her face, she closed her eyes and fell asleep.

"Can I sit by Candy like I did at the hospital?" Ralph whispered.

"Of course you may, Ralph," Marsha said softly.

"Thank you, Mama Marsha," he said as he sat down beside Candy's bed. The others quietly left the room.

"I'm not going to stay in bed today," Candy announced the next morning when Marsha gently awakened her.

"Why don't you let Dora bring your breakfast to you in bed?" Marsha suggested. "You can get up later if you feel like it."

"I'm going to get out of bed this minute," Candy announced firmly, and she threw back the covers and put her feet on the floor.

"But, Candy, you've been very ill."

"I'm better now, and I want to eat breakfast at the table with you and Daddy White and Ralph."

"It's a bit late for that, Candy. Daddy White and I ate breakfast early this morning. He came to your room to see you before he left for the courthouse, but you were asleep. You can eat with Ralph, though. He hasn't had breakfast."

"I wish I had been awake so I could see Daddy White," Candy said, swaying slightly as she stood to her feet.

"Are you all right, Candy?" Marsha asked.

"I'm fine."

"Then I'll get your clothes so you can dress."

"After I eat, I want to go outside," Candy said as she took the first tentative step toward her dresser.

"Can't you wait until you're stronger, Candy?"

"I'll be stronger after I eat breakfast."

Marsha grimaced, shrugged, and went to get Candy something to wear from the garments she had taken from her bundles and put in the wardrobe the night before, after Candy had fallen asleep.

"I'll take a bath and dress," Candy announced when Marsha returned. She took her clothes and went to the bathroom and closed the door.

"Call me when you finish dressing," Marsha called through the door. In a few minutes Candy came out, dressed and smiling.

"Getting dressed makes you look better, Candy," Marsha commented.

"I'm hungry," Candy announced.

"I'm sure Dora has something for you to eat."

"Where's Ralph?"

"Outside. I'll call him." She preceded Candy to the breakfast room and pulled out a chair for her. Then she went to call Ralph.

"My, my, look who's up," Dora greeted as she entered the breakfast room, bringing a bowl of cereal and some bananas. "I'll bring you some milk in a minute, Miss Candy."

"Thank you, Dora. Will you please bring something for Ralph to eat too? He'll be here in a minute."

"Sure I will, Miss Candy. You and Master Ralph can have anything you want, long as we've got it."

Ralph soon came in, pleased to see Candy up. "I waited to eat with you, but I was gettin' hungry," he said.

"What have you been doing?"

"Playin' with Roger. He's a lot of fun."

"I'm going outside after breakfast. Maybe I'll play with him too, if I feel like it."

"I found a man at the barn named Bill Hanks. He lives by himself in a tenant house, he called it, down by the creek. He takes care of the farm, and he's goin' to let me help him," Ralph said excitedly.

"Ralph, I'm glad Bill is going to have a helper," Marsha smiled.

"I'm going to help Mama Marsha and Dora when I feel better," Candy announced.

"I'm glad you're going to help Dora and me," Marsha said, smiling.

Chapter 10

Candy and Ralph soon adjusted to their new home
and to their new parents, though for several days they
were both somewhat in awe of Judge White.

They both liked Dora from the beginning, and
Ralph took up with Bill Hanks the first time he saw
him. The morning after they came to Oakcrest, Candy
saw Bill come through the back door, dragging his
left leg, and she liked him on sight.

"Hello, blue eyes," he greeted when saw her. He
smiled and his eyes crinkled at the corners.

"Hello, Mr. Bill," she greeted in return.

"Just call me Bill," he responded.

"All right, Bill," she giggled. "What's wrong with
your leg?"

"He hurt it a long time ago," Ralph answered for
him.

"His leg don't slow him down, though. He can still
do more work than any two men I've ever seen," Dora
said.

Bill smiled, winked at Candy, slapped Ralph on
the back, and went out.

"I'm goin' with Bill," Ralph said, and he followed
him out.

Candy was soon well enough to move to a bedroom upstairs that Marsha and Dora, with some help

from Ralph and Bill had arranged for her. The first night in her new room, she was so pleased and happy, she could scarcely sleep.

The next morning after breakfast, she went outside and wandered about the yard. Before the end of the week, she went to the barn and to the pasture behind the barn where Sandy Bell was grazing with the cows. The mules were standing in the corner of the field. She soon grew tired and returned to the house.

Ralph spent most of his time outside, watching the cows and the mules and helping Bill feed and care for them. He especially enjoyed feeding and milking Sandy Bell.

Each day, after the morning chores were finished, he roamed the fields and played beside the creek that ran through the farm, returning only at mealtime to eat and to see Candy.

On the second Saturday after Ralph and Candy came to live with them, Marsha left Candy in Dora's care and took Ralph to Maysville shopping. Marsha bought him a new suit, dress shoes, underwear, socks, shirts, and a necktie. For Candy she bought a beautiful white dress with rose trim, a pair of black patent leather pumps, some silk stockings, and some undergarments.

Ralph was filled with excitement when they returned home. He could hardly wait to see the look on Candy's face when she saw what Marsha had bought for her, and he wanted to show off what she had bought for him. He helped Marsha carry all the packages and bundles into the house, and they paused in the hall.

"Where are you, Candy?" Marsha called.

"I'm in here, listening to the radio," Candy called from the library, and came running out.

"Look at all the stuff Mama Marsha has bought for us," Ralph exclaimed.

"She bought all that for us?" Candy gasped.

"Just wait until you see what she bought." He took his bundles in the library and put them on the settee, and Marsha laid what she was carrying beside them.

"Look!" Ralph exulted, as he took his suit from the box and held it up for her to see. "Mama Marsha says I can wear it to church tomorrow. And look at these." He brought out his dress shoes and held them up.

"Oh, Ralph, I'm glad," Candy cried, almost as excited as he was.

"Ralph, I imagine Candy would like to see her things," Marsha laughed.

"I didn't expect you to buy things for me," Candy said.

"Of course I bought things for you, you goose. I want you to look nice too. The clothes you already have are all right," she hastened to add when she saw Candy's hurt look, "but I wanted you and Ralph to have something new to wear."

"My stepmother never bought me anything until I wore out what I had," Candy reminisced.

"Ralph, everything is piled up together. Get Candy's things out so she can see them," Marsha said.

Candy hurried across the room and turned the radio off, then watched Ralph separate the boxes.

"Open this first," he said handing her the box that contained her dress.

Candy clasped the box to her, and danced around the room. Then she opened it and took out the dress. She let the box fall to the floor as she held the dress up in front of her. She ran to the mirror in the hall and looked at her reflection, then clasped the dress to her and danced back into the room.

"It's beautiful! I love it!" she cried, looking at Marsha with shining eyes.

"I hope it fits you, Candy," Marsha said. "I hope the other things fit also."

"I know they will, but I have to try them on."

"I can't believe she bought all this for us," Ralph said.

"Ralph, let me see all she bought you before I go try my things on," Candy said.

Ralph proudly put on his suit coat and held the tie up to his neck. Then he showed her his shirts and socks and dresss shoes.

"Can I go to my room and try my things on?" he asked, turning to Marsha.

"You tried them on at the store, so you know they fit, but you may put them on so Candy can see how nice you look in them."

"All right!" he cried, and he ran up the stairs, taking them two at a time. He dressed quickly and came back down.

Mama Marsha was waiting in the hall.

A moment later Candy came from her bedroom, wearing her new dress and slippers, and walked down the stairs with her head held high and trying to imitate the way Mama Marsha walked.

"My new clothes are perfect, Mama Marsha, just perfect!" she said when she reached the hall. Then she saw Ralph in his new suit and looked him up and down. "Ralph, you're the handsomest boy in the whole wide world," she cried.

"I like your new dress," he said, trying to cover his embarrassment.

"Candy, now that we know everything fits, you should take your new clothes off and put them away so they will be fresh for you to wear to church tomorrow."

"I'm glad we're going to church. I haven't been for the longest time," Candy exclaimed with shining eyes.

"I'm going to take my new clothes off too, so they'll be fresh for tomorrow," Ralph said. He walked back upstairs, taking the steps one step at a time, with his shoulders back and his head high.

The next morning, on the way to church, Candy could scarcely contain herself. Her heart was near bursting with pride that she was riding in the big car with Judge White and Marsha. She was proud of Ralph too. He looked nothing like the rag-muffin boy she had rescued him from the river. He now looked as the son of Judge White should look. Dressed in her new clothes, she felt that she also looked like a daughter in the family.

She looked at Marsha, seated beside her husband, and straightened herself in the seat, and tried to sit the way she was sitting.

When they reached Maysville, Daddy White turned the car down a shaded avenue and parked in front of the biggest church building she had ever seen. She looked up at the high steeple and thought it must reach almost to the sky. People were walking along the street and turning toward large steps that led up to a pair of great swinging doors.

"Well here we are," Austin said as he got out of the car and walked around to Marsha's side and opened the door for her.

Ralph was already out of the car, and Candy was struggling to get her door open.

Ralph opened the door and looked in. "Am I supposed to help you out the way Daddy White helped Mama Marsha?" he asked in a whisper.

"Course not," she whispered as she got out. "That's for married people, and some of them don't do it." She hurried to catch up with Marsha and Judge White. Marsha took her hand, and Candy walked beside her, looking happily up into her face. Ralph quickened his step, caught up with Judge White, and walked beside him.

"Candy, we usually come to Sunday school, but we only came to church today. We thought both services might be tiring for you," Marsha said in an undertone.

"It wouldn't have made me tired. I'm almost well now," Candy assured her.

They went up the steps and through the big doors into vestibule. An usher met them, shook hands with Judge White and Marsha, smiled a greeting at Candy and Ralph, and led them to a pew halfway down the long aisle of the church. They all filed into the pew and sat down as strains of the great organ filled the sanctuary.

Candy sat in the pew between Marsha and Ralph, happier than she had been since she used to go to church with her mother.

Soon the members of the robed choir filed into the choir loft, and Candy looked at them in wonder. She had never seen a robed choir before, but she forgot the robes when they started singing. When the congregation started singing a familiar hymn, she joined in. Ralph did not sing, but he listened in wonder.

The pastor was a pleasant man who appeared to be sincere and in earnest. When the time came for him to preach, he talked about people being aliens from God and strangers in the world. He said that men who did not know God were like orphans and that they needed to be born into the family of God.

Candy glanced at Ralph and saw that he was listening, and he had an expression on his face she had never seen there before.

The preacher explained that everyone who received Jesus as Saviour would become the children of God. Then he asked everyone who did not have a Heavenly Father to come forward to be saved.

The choir and the congregation stood and started singing an invitation hymn, and Ralph immediately pressed his way past Candy and went to the front. Candy followed him down the aisle, thinking that she could not let him go to the front alone.

As Ralph took the extended hand of the pastor, she stopped beside him, and at that moment Judge White and Marsha joined them at the front. Judge White put his arm around Ralph, and Marsha put her arm around Candy.

Ralph was soon converted, but he did not understand about joining the church. He had a whispered conversation with Judge White, then agreed to be baptized and join the church.

Candy had her own whispered conversation with Marsha, and decided that she too would join the church.

The service soon ended, and they left the church and went to the car.

"I'm glad you got saved, Ralph," Judge White said as they started home.

"I'm glad too, Ralph, and I'm glad I joined the church," Candy trilled.

"I'm happy for both of you. Now we're all members of the same church, the way a family should be," Marsha exclaimed.

Chapter 11

*C*andy, would you and Ralph like to go to Lexington today?" Marsha asked as they were having breakfast one morning the next week.

"I'd love to go," Candy cried.

"I want you to go too, Ralph," Marsha said, when he did not answer.

"Do I have to go?" he asked dejectedly. "Bill promised to show me where I can catch some really big perch in the creek today, and he's already cut me a cane pole and promised to loan me some line and a hook and sinker."

"That's nice of Bill, but you can go fishing another day. I want you to go with me and Candy today. You'll enjoy seeing all the sights."

"OK," he agreed. "Reckon I can go fishin' some other time, but what are we goin' to Lexington for?"

"We're going to shop for school clothes for you and Candy. You both need new clothes before we start you in school."

"School!" Candy cried, fairly dancing with excitement. "I've been having such a good time living here, I'd forgotten about school—almost."

"I wish I didn't have to go to school. I'd druther get a job or somethin'," Ralph said.

"Ralph, there'll be plenty of time for you to get a job when you're older, but first you need to go to school. You'll need an education if you're going to get a decent job when you grow up. Besides, who knows, you might want to go into a profession."

"I reckon you're right," he said without enthusiasm.

Candy started to say that she had clothes stored in her stepmother's barn, but it occurred to her that Marsha might wonder why there were no clothes there for Ralph. "I don't want to be a lot of expense to you," she said instead.

"Don't worry about that, you little tightwad. I'm not about to send my children off to school inadequately dressed."

"Ralph, let's hurry and get dressed," Candy cried, and, without waiting for him to respond, she fairly flew up the stairs to her room.

A half hour later Candy and Ralph got in the car with Marsha, and they started to Lexington. On the way Candy filled the car with excited chatter, but Ralph had little to say. He entertained himself by watching Marsha drive the car, and by watching the traffic on the highway.

"I wish I could learn to drive," he said after watching the gauges on the instrument panel for a few minutes.

"Daddy White and I will see that you learn to drive when you are sixteen," Marsha smiled.

"Will you really?"

"Of course, and Candy can learn too when she is of age."

"I'm glad you and Daddy White found us," Candy exclaimed, smiling through tears of happiness.

"Me too," Ralph said, placing his hands between his knees and rubbing his palms together.

When they reached Lexington, Ralph looked around as if he were in a wonderland, but he still had little to say. Candy also fell silent as she drank in all the sights and sounds of the city. They were both especially excited when Marsha parked downtown and they got out and started walking along Main Street, past big stores with all kinds of beautiful things displayed in the windows.

Marsha soon led them into one of the stores, and Candy could hardly believe all the pretty clothes that were on display. Nor could she believe the pretty clothes Marsha had the saleslady show her. Marsha soon bought more clothes for her than she had ever expected to own in her life.

When Marsha started shopping for Ralph, he tried on the clothes she helped him select and proudly paraded in front of the long mirror that was on the wall near the dressing room.

"Thanks," he said as she made each purchase, but his eyes showed far more gratitude than his words expressed.

At noon Marsha took them to a restaurant on Main Street.

"Oh what a pretty restaurant," Candy cried. "It's the cleanest, shiniest restaurant I've ever seen.

"They will serve us more quickly if we sit on the stools at the counter," Marsha told them.

"I'm glad, 'cause I never set on a stool like that to eat before," Ralph said.

Late in the afternoon, with the car loaded with bundles, they started home. Candy and Ralph were tired from the day's activities, but they were so happy they laughed and talked all the way home. Marsha sometimes joined in their chatter, but most of the time she listened to them talk. Never before had she been so happy.

They got home late in the afternoon, and Marsha stopped the car at the front gate.

"Thank you for all the clothes you bought me, Mama Marsha," Candy said as she was getting bundles and boxes out of the car.

"I'm glad I didn't stay home to go fishin'," Ralph said as he started loading his arms with things Mama Marsha had bought.

The following Monday, Marsha took Ralph and Candy to school. "There's less than two more months of school this spring, but at least you'll get to know your teachers and your schoolmates. That will make it easier for you when school opens next fall," she told them on the way.

"I'm glad we're going to school now. I like to go to school," Candy responded.

"I reckon school is all right, but I don't like to go," Ralph commented.

"You'll both have to work hard to catch up on all the work you've missed," Marsha told them.

"I'll study night and day," Candy promised.

"When the river started goin' down, Candy went to school some, and I studied some at night," Ralph said.

"That should help," Marsha replied thoughtfully, "and I'll help both of you with your homework at night."

"I know we'll catch up," Candy said confidently.

"I'm sure you will, Candy," Marsha agreed.

"I have been thinking about something," Marsha said when they were almost to the school. "Your names will be White after Daddy White and I adopt you, so I'm going to enroll you in school as Whites. That way we won't have to change your names on the school record next year. Besides the other kids will never know you by any name but White," Marsha told them.

"I've been wondering about that," Candy said.

"I'll have to get used to being a White, 'cause I've

been a Roberts all my life," Ralph said.

"Well you are going to be a White from now on," Marsha said emphatically as she parked at the school.

They got out of the car and Marsha led the way into the school and to the principal's office.

"Good morning, Mrs. White," he greeted, smiling, as she ushered Ralph and Candy into the office.

"Good morning, Mr. Champion."

"And who is this pretty girl and this fine boy you have with you?" His eyes rested briefly on Candy, then on Ralph.

"I have brought my new son, Ralph, and my new daughter, Candy, to enroll them in school." Her hand rested briefly on the shoulder of each of them. "Candy and Ralph, this is Mr. Champion, the principal of Maysville High School."

"It's good to meet you, Candy and Ralph." Mr. Champion smiled down at them.

"I'm glad to meet you, Mr. Champion," Candy responded. "I like your school."

Ralph was too embarrassed to respond. He only stood on his tiptoes and twisted his right foot from side to side.

"Come with me and I'll show you to your homerooms," Mr. Champion offered, after he had asked their ages and the grades they were in. "Your homeroom teachers will enroll you." He led them to Candy's room first, and they paused outside until the teacher saw them and came to the door.

"This is Miss Robertson, the seventh grade English teacher, and, Miss Robertson, this is Mrs. White and her son, Ralph, and daughter, Candy. Candy is a new student for your room."

"I'm glad to meet you Mrs. White, and you Ralph and Candy. I'll be delighted to have Candy in my room. I believe you are a bit too old for my room," she smiled at Ralph.

"Yes, ma'am," he responded.

"Then, I'll take this young lady in and enroll her," Miss Robertson said, and she put her arm around Candy's shoulder and led her into the room.

"Thank you, Mr. Champion," Candy called over her shoulder, and she waved a discreet good-bye to Marsha and Ralph.

Ralph followed Mr. Champion stoically to his room and was taken in charge by a man teacher Mr. Champion introduced as Mr. Ford.

Ralph was silent as Mr. Ford took him into his room and directed him to a desk.

"I'll come for you and Candy after school," Marsha called after him.

"They can ride the bus home," Mr. Champion suggested.

"I'll let them ride the bus tomorrow, but today I'll come after them," Marsha rejoined.

Marsha was waiting in the car when Candy and Ralph came from the school building that afternoon. She expected them to come bounding out when classes were dismissed, but they came out slowly, and, without waving a greeting or smiling at her, they walked to the car with downcast eyes.

Marsha knew instantly that something was wrong.

"Hi, kids," she greeted when they reached the car.

"Hi," Candy said as she got in. Ralph got in and closed the door without responding.

"Hello, Ralph," Marsha said, glancing at him.

"Hello, Mama Marsha."

Marsha started home without questioning them, hoping that one of them would tell her what was wrong.

When they were well on the way, and neither of them had volunteered any information, she decided it was time to question them.

"You two are awfully quiet," she finally said.

"I ain't got nothin' to say," Ralph answered sullenly.

"What about you, Candy? Is there anything you want to tell me?"

"I reckon I don't have anything to say either," Candy said in a sad little voice.

"You could tell her what Norma Gray said," Ralph said hoarsely.

"It doesn't matter," Candy retorted, near tears.

"Matter nothin'. I don't want her nor none of the rest of them throwin' off on Daddy White."

Marsha's face went white. Her eyes narrowed to slits, and her knuckles whitened as she griped the steering wheel. "I see." She nodded slowly. "Ralph, there is something you and Candy need to know. It will help you understand why Norma is angry."

"I don't care if she is—she ain't got no cause to throw off on Daddy White."

"It's true that she shouldn't vent her anger publicly, but I know how she must feel. You see, a judge has to try people in court when they are accused of doing something wrong. If they are found guilty, he sometimes has to pronounce stiff sentences on them."

"What's that got to do with Norma?" Candy asked.

"A couple of years ago Norma's father was arrested on suspicion of killing young Dr. Brown, who had recently set up practice in Maysville. The jury found him guilty, and Daddy White had to sentence him to prison. You can imagine how much that hurt Norma, so you must try not to be upset by what she says."

"What she said about Daddy White ain't all she said," Ralph blurted, for once talking more than Candy.

"What else did she say, Ralph?" Marsha prompted.

"It don't matter, Ralph," Candy said unhappily.

"Ralph, tell me what else Norma said," Marsha insisted.

"She told some other girls that me and Candy didn't

have no regular mama and daddy. Then she whispered something I didn't understand, and the other girls all snickered."

"Being adopted is nothing to be ashamed of," Marsha said, measuring her words carefully. "Really it's something special. Some parents don't want their children when they're born; but Daddy White and I wanted both of you, and we love you as much as we would if you had been born into our family."

"I'm glad," Candy said, brightening.

"I'm glad too, 'cause you're the only mama and daddy we've got," Ralph said in a choking voice.

"Now, I want both of you to be your usual happy selves when Daddy White comes home," Marsha said as she turned the car into the drive to Oakcrest.

"I'll try," Candy promised. "I don't want to worry Daddy White."

"I'll try too," Ralph agreed.

"Thank you, Ralph and Candy. That takes a load off my mind." She shrugged, relaxed her tight grip on the steering wheel, and drove the car to the usual parking place by the yard gate.

Chapter 12

*T*he next few days in school were hard for Candy, but her smiling face and outgoing personality gradually made friends for her. Ralph did not make friends as easily as Candy, but one day something happened that made friends for him. The family of Bill Logan, the pitcher for the school baseball team, moved away, leaving the team without a pitcher. The coach had to find a replacement, and he looked long and hard at Ralph. He liked his lean, agile body and his long muscular arm.

"Boy, what's your name?" he asked.

"Ralph White."

"Ralph, can you throw a ball?"

"Never tried in a ball game, but I can throw hard and straight. I used to throw rocks and kill rabbits."

"Pitching ball is different, but let's give you a try."

"Coach, I bet he can't throw a-tall," one of the boys yelled.

"I bet I can throw straighter and harder than he can," Ned Potter shouted.

"All right, Ned. I'll give you both a try. You first, Ralph."

He led Ralph to the pitcher's mound and gave him a glove and a ball. "Now I want you to throw that ball straight across home plate and into the catcher's glove. Let's see if you can burn his hand through the glove."

Ralph wasn't about to tell how he used to practice throwing a ball, and how his daddy had trained him before he died. That catcher's glove wasn't too different from the half gallon syrup can he had nailed to the wall of the barn so he could practice throwing a ball into. It had been fun back then to pretend that he was a pitcher for the hometown team. Now he was going to get a tryout for a real team.

He put the glove on his right hand and took the ball in his left hand.

"He's a southpaw. That'll make him hard to hit," one of the boys yelled.

Ralph looked at the catcher, then wound up like a regular ball pitcher and threw the ball. It went straight over the plate and struck the catcher's mitt with a loud pop. The catcher dropped the ball, removed his glove, and shook his stinging hand.

"Let's see him throw a curveball," Ned Potter mocked.

"Let's see how he makes out pitching against a batter," the coach said. "Wadell Smith, come here and see if you can hit his fastball. Tom Jones, you be the umpire."

Wadell Smith was the best batter on the team, and his teammates thought there was not his equal in the county. They expected him to knock Ralph's fastball over the back fence on the first pitch.

Wadell picked up a bat, walked to the plate, spit on his hands, and touched the base twice with the tip of the bat. By that time every boy on the playground had gathered on the sidelines to watch Wadell hit the ball, and many of the girls had lined up behind them.

The first ball Ralph threw was a fastball on the inside. Wadell dodged as the ball crossed the edge of the plate, and the umpire called, "Strike one. . . . I think."

There followed a great sigh of unbelief from the

students, and some of them turned and looked at Mr. Ford, who was standing beside the umpire and had seen the pitch. "It was a strike," he affirmed.

Wadell scowled and dropped the tip of the bat to the plate. Then the took a stance like an angry prizefighter and waited for the next ball.

"You can hit him, Wadell. He ain't got nothin' but a fastball," someone called from the crowd.

Ralph took his time, wound up and threw the ball.

Wadell thought it was a fastball headed straight at the plate at knee level. He drew back his bat to make a swing that would knock the ball out of the school yard, but the ball curved downward just before it reached the plate. Taken completely by surprise, Wadell swung and missed.

"He threw a dropball," someone muttered in unbelief.

"Strike two," the umpire called.

Biting his lower lip in anger and frustration, Wadell came up to the plate again. This time the ball was a slowball, and Wadell swung a bit too soon. He tipped the ball and it went out of bounds behind him.

"You got one more strike, Wadell. You can still knock the ball over the fence," a teammate called.

The next ball was on the outside, and Wadell lowered his bat to watch it go by. But the ball curved and crossed the edge of the plate.

"Strike three," the umpire called in an awed voice.

"He can't do it again," Wadell growled.

"We're not having a contest to see whether he can or not. We only wanted to see if he has the makings of a pitcher, and I'm convinced that he does," Mr. Ford said.

"I know he can't strike me out again," Wadell muttered.

"I'm sure you could hit one of his balls sooner or later, Wadell," the coach consoled.

"Ned, are you ready for a tryout?" the coach asked, searching for Ned Potter in the crowd. "Oh, there you are. You ready to try."

"Naw. Let him be the pitcher," Ned said unhappily.

"I'd just as soon not," Ralph said. He thought he had already made an enemy of Wadell, and he didn't want to make one of Ned.

"With Ralph pitching for us, we'll beat every team in the county," Jeb Barns, the oldest and tallest boy in school, said.

"Yeah, Yeah," a half dozen students yelled. Several of the boys gathered around Ralph, now eager to make friends with him, and some of the girls looked at him with new interest.

The next day, Ralph started practicing with the team. Most of team members accepted him at once, and he gradually won his way with them all except Wadell. Wadell was not openly hostile, but he kept his distance, never speaking to Ralph unless he spoke first.

Candy made good grades, and with the teacher making assignments for her to study at home, she made steady progress on what she had missed while she was out of school.

Ralph managed to make passing grades, though he did not like to study. He preferred to draw pictures and write poems. Also he loved to be outside with the animals, or to be roaming the fields with Roger. So Marsha had to push him to study on his back lessons.

At the close of school, Ralph and Candy both passed to the next grade. Marsha met them that day when school let out at noon, and took them home in the car. When they came in sight of Oakcrest, Judge White's car was parked in front of the barn.

"How come Daddy White is home early today?" Candy asked.

"He arranged to get out of the office today so he

could be home when you and Ralph got home from school."

"I'm glad. I want to show him my report card," Candy said.

"I'm glad too, 'cause I want him to know I passed," Ralph said with more than his usual enthusiasm.

"I think Daddy White just might have a surprise for both of you," Marsha confided as she turned on the driveway.

"Oh, I wonder what it is," Candy cried.

Just as Marsha stopped the car in front of the house, Judge White, dressed in his farm clothes, came out of the barn.

"I'll bet Daddy White has bought another goat," Ralph exclaimed with little enthusiasm.

"I don't think so, Ralph. A goat would be just for me, and Mama Marsha says he has a surprise for both of us," Candy explained as they spilled from the car.

"We both passed," Candy shouted to Judge White.

"I passed too," Ralph shouted, as if Candy had not already said that he had. They ran to Austin, and he hugged them.

"I'm proud of both of you," he said. "Now run change to your play clothes and hurry back. I have something I want to show you."

"What is it, Daddy White? Can't you tell us before we change clothes?" Candy asked.

"I'll show you when you come back."

"Let's hurry, Ralph," Candy cried, tugging at him. "Yeah, let's do."

They ran to the house and up to their rooms and hurriedly changed their clothes.

Marsha and Austin were waiting in the living room, smiling knowingly at each other when Candy came down the stairs dressed in her play clothes. Ralph followed close behind her, still struggling with his belt buckle.

"Now let's go to the barn and see the surprise," Marsha said as she and Austin arose from the couch.

"Can we run ahead?" Ralph asked.

"I'd rather you didn't," Austin said, in his court-room voice.

Unable to restrain herself, Candy started prancing ahead of them.

"Wait Candy!" Austin called in a voice that stopped her.

She looked back at him and saw a tinkle in his eyes. Then she giggled.

"We'll let Daddy White go first," she said in the firmest voice she could muster, and she stood on her tiptoes, waiting for them to catch up.

Marsha and Austin both laughed at her. Marsha reached her first and took her hand. Austin took Ralph's hand, and together they continued toward the barn.

Daddy White walked slowly, restraining the ex-cited children, and prolonging their expectations. When he finally reached the barn door he stopped.

"Now watch while I open the door," he said, and ever so slowly he lifted the latch and pulled the door open.

"Please hurry, Daddy White, I'm going to die if you don't," Candy cried.

"I can't have you dying on me, Candy," he chuck-led, and he pulled the door open with more pleasure than he had ever experienced in releasing a prisoner.

Candy and Ralph leaned forward in their eager-ness to see inside the shadowy barn.

"Oh! Oh! Oh! Ponies! Ponies! They're beautiful," Candy cried, when she saw two spotted ponies stand-ing side by side, munching grain from a trough. Bill was standing beside them, smiling. "Oh, Ralph look. Both ponies have saddles and bridles on," Candy cried as she ran into the barn.

"Are the ponies really ours?" Ralph gasped, unbelieving. He walked, as if in a dream, to where Bill was standing.

"They really are yours, Ralph," Bill answered.

"Ralph, the one with the black spots is yours, and the one with the brown spots is Candy's," Austin told him.

"Are they boy ponies or girl ponies?" Candy asked.

"I understand that yours is a girl and Ralph's is a boy. That is right, isn't it, Austin?" Marsha asked.

"That's right," Austin said.

"I'm glad my pony is a girl," Candy exclaimed.

"I'd druther have the boy," Ralph said.

"I'm glad you're both pleased with the choices we made for you. We thought the mare would be easier for Candy to manage," Marsha explained.

"Is that what you call a girl pony?" Candy asked.

"That's right," Austin told her.

"Then what do they call a boy pony?"

Judge white, for all his wisdom, looked helplessly at Marsha, not sure how he should go about explaining that a male pony could be either a stud or a gelding.

"Ralph's pony is a gelding," Marsha said, hoping that would end the discussion for the time.

"I know why he's a gelding. A stud can be mean," Ralph supplied.

Marsha looked at Austin and slowly shook her head and smiled.

"Well, aren't you going to thank Daddy White for your pony, Ralph?" Marsha asked to change the subject.

"Oh sure. Thank you Daddy White, and thank you Mama Marsha. I'd druther have a pony than anything in the whole world."

"Thank you, thank you, thank you both for my pony. I'll love her more than I love Sandy Bell—

maybe." Candy exclaimed.

"You're both welcome. We bought the ponies because we love you," Austin said.

"May we ride them now?" Candy asked.

"Yes you may, Candy. That's why Austin and Bill put the saddles and bridles on them. Bill will lead them out of the barn for you," Marsha responded.

"I can lead mine," Ralph assured, and he took the reins of his pony from Bill. He led his pony out and stopped, and his eyes roved over it, taking in every detail.

Austin led Candy's pony out and stopped beside Ralph. Candy had walked beside him, and he handed her the reins.

Ralph put his foot in the stirrup and mounted the saddle.

Candy watched him, dancing with excitement, then turned to her pony and started running her hands over the saddle, feeling the smooth grain of the leather and the decorative pattern that had been pressed into it. She walked in front of her pony and placed her hand gently on the white spot on her forehead. "I'll love you always," she exclaimed, and she laid her head caressingly on the pony's neck.

Ralph sat on his pony, holding the reins in his hand, eager to be off. "Are you goin' to stall around all day, Candy?" he asked impatiently.

"I'm ready, I reckon. I just had to enjoy every minute of getting acquainted with my beautiful pony," she responded.

"Austin you had better help her get on the pony," Marsha suggested.

"No problem," Austin said, and he picked Candy up and set her in the saddle.

"What's her name? And what do I say to her when I want her to stop?" she asked.

"You say whoa to her when you want her to stop,

but you'll have to give her a name," Austin told her.

"Then I'll call her Happiness," she said, quick as a flash.

"That's a strange name for a pony, isn't it?" Marsha asked.

"It's a good name, 'cause that's the way I'm going to feel every minute while I'm riding her."

"What are you going to call your pony, Ralph?" Daddy White asked.

"I haven't thought of a name yet."

"Why don't you call him Joy?" Candy suggested.

"That's no name for a pony," he objected.

"Why not? Happiness and Joy go well together," Marsha said.

"Well if you say so, Mama Marsha." He looked at Austin to get his reaction.

"You might as well name him that, Ralph. There's no way you can out talk two women," Austin laughed.

"All right, but let's go, Candy. I want to ride."

"Candy, have you ever ridden before?" Marsha asked.

"No, but I can learn."

"Austin, you had better walk beside her and steady her until she gets used to riding," Marsha suggested.

"What about you, Ralph?" Austin asked as he put his arm around Candy's shoulder to steady her.

"I used to ride a horse that belonged to my friend, so I won't have no trouble," Ralph said, and started his pony toward the hill back of the house in a gallop.

Daddy White led Candy's pony in the direction Ralph had gone, and they soon came to the path that followed the fence line of the pasture. Sandy Bell was with the cows in the valley by the creek. When she saw Candy on the pony, she ran full speed to the fence and stopped. She looked hard at Candy on the pony, reared up and came down in an arch on her front feet, turned her head to the side and stabbed at the air with her horns, stamped her feet, and barked as only an angry goat can bark.

"Sandy Bell, you stop it," Candy scolded.

"It looks like you have an angry goat," Austin laughed.

"She'll have to get over it, because I'm going to keep Happiness forever," Candy declared.

"Watch Ralph," Marsha exclaimed. "He's riding like he was born to the saddle."

They all looked and saw Ralph galloping the pony along the ridge toward the river.

"You'll soon be riding like that, Candy," Austin said, stopping her pony so Marsha could catch up.

"I hope she will be more careful than Ralph," Marsha said.

"I'm sure she will," Austin returned.

"Daddy White, I'm so glad you and Mama Marsha adopted us," Candy said.

"We're glad too, blue eyes. Marsha and I have always been happy, but you and Ralph have made our home complete."

"You surely have, Candy, and we love both of you very much," Marsha said.

Chapter 13

Spring came to the Ohio River Valley early in 1938, introduced by blossoming dogwood and redbud trees on the hills and by the first green buds on willow trees along the river. At Oakcrest there were flowering crocus and narcissus and tulips along yard fences and walkways, and in the side yard, forsythia was laden with golden blossoms. In the back yard fruit trees blossomed in profusion, promising a bountiful harvest.

During the past winter the river had reached only its normal crest. Now it was going about its business as if it had never gone on the rampage of the past year. But scars from the flood remained. Muddy stains were still visible on houses, fences and trees, and there were wrecked buildings along the river's course that had neither been torn down nor rebuilt.

It had been more than a year since Candy and Ralph had come to live with the Whites. In that time they had been adopted into the family, and they had almost forgotten the trials of the past winter. The school year had been a busy one, with both of them making good grades. Ralph had become the star baseball player on the school team, and they both had become popular with their schoolmates.

The early spring made Ralph and Candy eager for the school year to end, and finally, after what seemed a very long time to them, it did end, the last week in May.

The next morning after breakfast, Candy and Ralph decided to go riding on their ponies. Roger was waiting for them when they came out of the house, and he barked, leaped in the air, and ran ahead of them to the barn.

"Look how excited he is. I believe he knows we're going riding," Candy exclaimed.

"You've spoiled that dog, lettin' him ride behind you on your pony the way he does."

"Who do you think would have ridden with me when you were fishing or helping Bill, if Roger hadn't?"

"I never thought that dog would. I don't see how he stays on, riding crossways behind the saddle the way he does."

"I taught him to do that, and he's been riding with me ever since."

They went in the barn, saddled and bridled the ponies, and led them out. Roger barked with excitement, leaped on Happiness' back and stretched out behind the saddle. Happiness only looked around at him, snorted and shook her head. She had long since grown accustomed to the dog riding on her back.

Candy and Ralph mounted the ponies and rode slowly across the pasture back of the barn. They rode up the hill and turned out the ridge toward the river. Halfway out the ridge Roger leaped off the pony and romped ahead of them. He flushed a convey of quails, and, startled by their loud fluttering, he stopped and watched with a puzzled expression at they flew away. He trotted on and soon roused a sleeping rabbit from a clump of dry grass. The rabbit raced away, and Roger ran after him, barking furiously. At the boundary fence, the rabbit went through and left Roger disappointed and frustrated.

Candy and Ralph paid only passing attention to the dog and his antics. Ralph was noticing for the first time how Candy had changed in the last year, and she was interested only in riding across the meadow in his company on this beautiful spring day.

It was strange that he had not noticed how Candy was changing before, Ralph thought. Perhaps it was because he had been so involved with the baseball team, interested in the work on the farm, and studying his lessons. Candy looked nothing like the pallid, big toothed, skinny girl she had been when he had first seen her. She certainly had changed since they had come to live with the Whites.

The bloom had returned to her cheeks; she had put on weight, and the first hint of the woman she was to become was suggested by the gentle curves that were beginning to shape her body. Her appearance pleased him, though he did not know why. He liked the fashionable riding habit she was wearing, and he thought how different it was from the used garments the Red Cross had given her after the flood.

As they were passing a locust thicket, Ralph's pony shied at some imaginary danger, and sprinted ahead. She did not try to catch up with Ralph, for she was taking pleasure in watching him. She noticed how tall he had grown, and how firm his muscles had become. His voice was beginning to change also, and she liked the masculine, huskiness when he spoke. He was wearing riding pants and a western style shirt and jacket. She had never dreamed he could be so handsome when first she had seen him.

At the end of the ridge, where they had stopped so often in the past to look down at the river, he paused and waited for her.

She rode up and stopped Happiness beside him. Joy was already cropping the fresh, spring grass as if he had not eaten all day. Happiness promptly started grazing also.

"Look!" Candy exclaimed, pointing toward the river.

He turned and saw a tugboat coming down the river, pushing three barges well-laden with coal. The captain must have seen them, for he blew two short blasts on his whistle.

Candy and Ralph waved, then turned their ponies and started down a ravine single file, with Ralph leading the way.

"I'll draw you a picture of the boat and the barges when we get back to the house," he called over his shoulder.

"That's a promise, and I won't let you forget it," she called after him.

"I'll draw it in memory of our first day out of school."

"I'll hang it in my room and keep it always," she returned.

Ralph rode in silence then, until he reached the springhouse at the foot of the hill. There he stopped, as he always did.

She rode up beside him and stopped also.

"Want a drink?" he asked.

"You know I always want a drink when we come to the spring," she replied as she dismounted.

"I bet Indians used to drink from this spring," he said as he threw his leg over the pony's neck and slid to the ground.

"What makes you think that?" she asked.

"I found an arrowhead behind the springhouse one day when I came out here by myself."

"You don't reckon there's still Indians around do you?"

"Of course not. They've all gone out west somewhere. . . . Oklahoma, maybe. I read that they're in a lot of places. Anyhow, they're not here," he assured her.

"I'm glad, Let's get our drink and ride back to the house. I want to practice on the piano."

"And I want to draw the picture I promised you, but I have to move the new calf Daddy White gave me to the back pasture first. It's too much trouble carrying water to it in the barn lot."

"You hold the ponies, and I'll get the water," she said, and she handed him the reins of her pony.

She went in the spring and came back with a bucket, filled and dripping cold water. She filled the dipper and handed it to him.

He drank deeply, emptied the dipper in the spring branch, and handed it back to her. She got herself a drink, dumped the rest of the water into the stream, and returned the bucket and dipper to the springhouse.

"Ready to go?" he asked as she mounted her pony.

"Sure, I'm ready." Joy was prancing around, eager to start back to the barn, but he held him in place and mounted to the saddle.

Happiness moved close to Joy, and Candy held her in place also.

"What do you think would have happened to us if the Whites hadn't took us in?" he asked.

"We would have stayed together anyway, and we would have made out some way. We had adopted each other, and there was no way I was going to let anybody separate us."

"I would have taken care of you, no matter what. But somethin' is botherin' me."

"What's that?"

"Now that the Whites have adopted us, does our adopting each other still count?"

Joy tugged at his bridle rein, but Ralph held him steady.

"Of course. We meant it, didn't we? Now that we have the same parents, that makes us double brother and sister," she teased.

"I don't see how you get that."

"You've heard of double cousins, haven't you?"

"Well, yes," he admitted.

"Then why can't there be double brothers and sisters?" she queried.

"Daddy White talks so much about what is legal and what is not, I've just been wondering, that's all."

"We made vows, didn't we? That makes it legal, as far as I'm concerned."

"I reckon you're right, Candy, but I almost wish we hadn't. And I almost wish Daddy White and Mama Marsha hadn't adopted us."

"Ralph White, why on earth did you say that?"

"'Cause, if you weren't my sister, I'd want you for my sweetheart."

For a moment she was silent, stunned by what he had said.

"You are the prettiest girl, and the sweetest girl I've ever seen," he said in his husky, changing voice, and he leaned across her saddle and gave her a quick kiss on the lips.

Startled, yet pleased, she drew away, hoping he had not seen the quick blush that had mounted to her cheeks.

She spurred Happiness to a sudden start and galloped up the hill, fearing that Ralph would read what was in her face if she did not get away from him.

"What's your hurry?" he called after her, but she rode on, aware of a strange, fluttering sweetness in her heart. She wanted to wait for Ralph, to talk with him, to hear him say again what he had just said, but she did not dare. The last thing in the world she wanted was for Ralph to think that she was chasing him.

Ralph had not missed her blush, but he had no idea why she had ridden away so suddenly. What he had said must have displeased her, and that was something he never wanted to do. He would have to be careful what he said to her in the future.

He soon caught up with her, but she rode with her face turned away. Neither of them spoke until they reached the barn.

"I'll take care of your pony so you can go practice," he offered in a restrained voice as he dismounted.

"Thank you," she said. She slid to the ground and held out her bridle reins to him. As he took them, their hands touched, and their eyes met. She felt a quickening beat of her heart and turned away, for she knew she was blushing again. Without a word she left him and went to the house.

He watched her go with a tinge of sadness, realizing that for the first time that some unknown restraint had come between them. After she went in the house and closed the door, he turned to the ponies, took the saddles and bridles off, and turned them out to pasture. Then he went to barn lot where his calf was lying in the shade of a tree. He got the calf up, drove it out of the lot, and started it toward the back pasture.

"Did you and Ralph have a good time riding?" Marsha asked Candy as she entered the house and came to the library where she was reading.

"Oh, yes, Mama Marsha. We always have fun," she answered, hoping Marsha would not notice how flustered she was.

"You didn't stay long." Marsha lowered her book and looked at Candy over her glasses.

"I wanted to come back and practice on the piano, and Ralph offered to take care of the ponies."

"I'm glad he is such a good brother to you."

"Me too," she answered as she turned to go change from her riding habit.

"Candy, I want to talk with you after you change. Your practice can wait."

"Do you want to talk before I change?"

"No, go ahead. We'll talk when you come back."

Candy looked at Marsha closely, but her countenance revealed nothing. Puzzled, she left the library and ran up the broad stairway and along the hall to her room. As she entered, though her heart was filled with both excitement and foreboding, she glanced around the room she had enjoyed so much since the day she had grown strong enough to climb the stairs and Mama Marsha and Dora had moved her into it. She noticed again the light blue papered walls, the white muslin curtains at the windows, the white enameled woodwork, and the highly-polished hardwood floor, half covered with expensive throw rugs.

The heavy walnut furniture was polished to a luster. On her dresser and bureau were white crocheted doilies. An attractive amber vanity set was on her dresser, and on her bureau was a jewel case that contained the jewelry and trinkets she had acquired since coming to live with the Whites.

"I never want to leave this place," she said aloud.

Her mother used to pray for the Lord to watch over her little girl and take care of her. Her mother must have had a premonition that she would not live to see her grow up. The Lord had certainly answered her mother's prayers when He gave her a home with the Whites.

Wondering what Marsha had on her mind, she changed quickly and hurried back to the library.

"I'm back, Mama Marsha," she announced as she entered.

"Candy, there's something I have to tell you," Marsha began.

"What is it, Mama Marsha?"

"I received a letter today that I think you should know about."

"You heard from my stepmother," Candy guessed as alarm spread through her.

"You precious girl, how did you know?"

"I just know, and I bet she wants to take me away from you."

"That's exactly what she wants. She has been in Florida, but now she has come back."

"I'll bet she married Jake."

"She didn't say. She only said that she wants you to come and live with her. How do you feel about that, Candy?"

"Oh, no. I never want to leave you and Daddy White," Candy wailed, going to Marsha and throwing her arms around her.

"You don't know how relieved I am to hear you say that, Candy."

"I wonder how Lillian learned my address," Candy said.

"I wondered about that too. Maybe someone showed her the article in an old newspaper about our adopting you and Ralph."

"Can my stepmother make me live with her?" Candy asked uneasily.

"Of course not. Just write and tell her you don't want to live with her. She has no legal claim on you. If she tries to make trouble, Austin will write her a letter, and, if she gives you trouble after that, he can scare her off with a threat of taking her to court for deserting you."

"Oh, I'm glad, glad," Candy cried, dancing around the room.

"There's something that troubles me though," Marsha continued, looking at her thoughtfully.

"What is it, Mama Marsh?" Candy asked uneasily.

"I find it strange that your stepmother didn't mention Ralph in her letter. Did she and Ralph not get along?"

"She—she doesn't know Ralph," Candy answered,

weighing her words carefully.

"I don't understand. Didn't your brother live at home after she married your father?"

"Ralph . . . He—he—isn't . . . He wasn't my brother then."

"Candy, I've never heard you stammer so. What do you mean, he wasn't your brother then?"

"Mama Marsha, I'd rather not tell you. Ralph and I . . ." She paused not knowing how to explain.

"Candy, I think we had better call Ralph so I can ask him about this," Marsha exclaimed. "I wonder why he's so long coming to the house."

"He was going to move his calf, but he should have finished by now."

"Then, we'll wait until he gets back."

"I wish you wouldn't ask him about it," Candy said, pale and shaken.

"I'm sorry, Candy, but I must know what this is about."

"I—I'll go find Ralph," Candy stammered, and, before Marsha could protest, she ran from the house, thinking that she must see Ralph before Marsha did. As she started to the barn, she saw him coming out.

"Ralph! Ralph! I have to see you in a hurry," she called as she ran to meet him.

"What are you so worked up about, Candy?" he asked. Knowing that Candy was always on the edge of excitement, he was only curious to know what she was excited about this time.

"Mama Marsha got a letter from Lillian, and she wants to know why Lillian didn't mention you in the letter."

"What did you tell her?" he asked, somewhat disturbed himself.

"I told her that Lillian didn't know you. Then I had to tell her that you didn't used to be my brother."

"You did blow it," he said, shaking his head. "What

did Mama Marsha say?"

"She said that she wanted to talk to you, and I ran to get you before she could ask me anything else."

"It shouldn't be a big deal. We'll just tell her how it happened."

"Do you think she'll understand."

"Of course. Anything you do is all right with her . . . almost."

"I hope you're right." She led the way to the house, trembling inside, and he followed, almost nonchalantly. When they reached the house, she paused and held the door open for him.

"Did you find Ralph?" Marsha called from the library when she heard the door open.

"Yes, I'm here, Mama Marsha," he returned,

Marsha came into the hall to meet them. "Ralph, I'm puzzled by something Candy told me," she began. "She says that you did not live with your step-mother and that you didn't used to be her brother."

"Lillian isn't my stepmother," Ralph answered calmly, as Marsha led the way back to the library.

"Then Candy must be your half sister."

"No, Mama Marsha. She's my full sister. She says we're double brothers and sisters."

"What ever are you talking about, Ralph White?" Marsha demanded, as she sank to her chair, puzzled and somewhat vexed.

"We were brothers and sisters before you and Daddy White adopted us, and Candy says that when you adopted us, that made us double brothers and sisters."

"You silly girl," Marsha laughed. "You can only be a brother or sister to the same person one time. And, Ralph, Candy is your sister, not your sisters, and you're her brother, not her brothers." She doubled over laughing.

"That's the only way I knew to say it, Mama

Marsha. I'm sorry."

Marsha laughed so hard she had to wipe tears from her eyes. "Now, back to what we were talking about," she said when she regained control of herself. "Let's see. Candy, you said that Ralph didn't used to be your brother, and he said that you told him you are double brother and sister. Please explain that to me."

Candy looked helplessly at Ralph.

"Tell her, Candy," he shrugged.

"Ralph didn't used to be my brother. The first time I ever saw him, he was floating down the river on top of his house, and I ran after him and rescued him, and . . ."

"Candy!" Marsha interrupted. "I've never known you to be untruthful, but that story is hard to believe."

"It's true, Mama Marsha," Ralph affirmed. "I don't know what would have happened to me if she hadn't come after me in a boat."

Marsha looked at Ralph, then at Candy. "Knowing you as I do, Candy, I believe you could have done that," she finally said.

"I couldn't let him drown, could I?" Candy defended.

"It seems there is much I don't know about you, Candy," Marsha said, shaking her head.

"Ralph, how did you get on top of a house that was floating down the river?" Marsha asked.

"I was alone in the house when it washed off its foundation during the flood."

"I see. Then what happened?"

"Water was rising inside the house, so I crawled out a window and climbed on top of the roof."

"That's where I first saw him," Candy interrupted.

"And you rescued him?" Marsha prompted.

"She came after me in a boat," Ralph told her again, answering for Candy.

"I see. Now, that we have that settled, tell me how

Ralph got to be your brother."

Candy bit her lower lip and rung her hands, but she did not drop her eyes from Marsha's face. "After I rescued Ralph, people kept wanting to separate us and send us off to orphan homes. I decided that maybe they wouldn't do that if we were brother and sister, so we adopted each other."

"You adopted each other! And how did you two manage that?" Marsha asked, breaking into laughter again.

"It wasn't funny to us. We were serious," Ralph said, hoping he could relieve Candy's chagrin.

"You still haven't told me how you adopted each other. Did you go before a judge?"

"Oh no, Mama Marsha. Candy mostly did it herself, but I helped her a little," he said, squirming with embarrassment.

"Candy, you amazing girl!" Marsha exclaimed, putting her arms around her. "How did you accomplish this adoption?"

"I reckon it was kind of silly," Ralph conceded.

"I don't think it was silly, but I reckon it wasn't legal," Candy admitted. "We didn't go through all that Daddy White and you did to adopt us."

"I still want to know how you adopted each other," Marsha declared, looking from one to the other.

"It was kinda like gettin' married," Ralph said.

"Getting married?" Marsha struggled to keep a straight face.

"I'd seen some couple get married," Candy said with trembling lips. "All they did was say some vows, and that made them married. So Ralph and I said some vows."

"Did you have a preacher to perform the ceremony?" Marsha asked, trying hard not to laugh.

"Candy was the preacher part of the time, and she was herself part of the time," Ralph explained.

"I see," Marsha said. "I'm not sure, but Austin may have something to straighten out, as far as the record goes. We adopted both of you as Roberts. Now which one of you was the Roberts before you adopted each other?"

"He was," Candy said, pointing to Ralph. "It's always the woman that changes her name."

"And what was your name, Candy, before you and Ralph adopted each other?"

"My name was Candy Mays, before I changed it to Roberts. Then I was a Roberts until you and Daddy White adopted us and made us both Whites."

"I'm glad you are Candy White now, and you're going to stay Candy White until the day you marry," Marsha declared, hugging her. "You too, Ralph. Only you will be a White for the rest of your life."

"Mama Marsha, I hope Daddy White won't get in any trouble for using my wrong name when you all adopted us," Candy said.

"I'm sure Daddy White can straighten that out, but I can't wait to tell him how you two got to be brother and sister."

"What will Daddy White say?" Candy asked.

"I'm sure he'll laugh, just as I did," Marsha said, still laughing and shaking her head.

Chapter 14

*O*n a late spring night, in 1941, Candy sat with Daddy White and Marsha in the chapel of Maysville High School and watched Ralph receive his diploma. She thought her heart would burst with pride, and she knew that Daddy White and Mama Marsha could not have been more pleased if Ralph had been born into their family.

It was hard for Candy to realize that the lanky boy she had rescued from the floating house, just four years before, was now a tall, handsome young man of 18. It was also hard to realize that she would be graduating from high school in only two more years.

Pride was not the only emotion Candy felt as she watched Ralph graduate. She had long known that she was in love with him, but her love was a carefully guarded secret. Ralph had always been fond of her, and she had been fond of him, but since the day at the spring, when he had kissed her on the lips, she had loved him with an undying love. That day he had said that he would like to have her for his girlfriend, but he had never mentioned the subject again. With each passing day since then, her love for him had grown. Her love for him was now strong, and sweet, and frightening, and she was sure that she would never love anyone else as she loved him.

His thought of love must have been only a passing

fancy with him, but her feeling for him had been no passing fancy. He only loved her as a sister, but she loved him with a love that filled her heart with lingering despair.

Candy looked at the girls in the graduating class, and, though she did not have a jealous disposition, jealously stabbed at her heart. Ralph had become one of the most popular boys in Maysville High School, and several of the girls had openly flirted with him, though he had given none of them more than a passing glance.

Most often her eyes rested on Jewel Pennington. She was near Ralph's age, and she was the most beautiful and popular girl in the graduating class. Jewel had been attracted to Ralph since the day he had tried out for the baseball team, but he had never shown any interest in her. Yet there was always the possibility that he might become attracted to her.

Candy was glad that, after tonight, Ralph would not be seeing much of Jewel or any of the other girls in his class. That meant she would have him all to herself, if he didn't go away to work or join the Army Air Corps. All the news of war in Europe the past year had caused him to talk often about joining the air corps, but Daddy White had tried to discourage him. He wanted him to stay at home and help run the farm.

In recent months there had been much speculation that the United States would become involved in the war. If that happened, there was no way Ralph would stay out of the air corps. The thought weighed heavily upon her and made her wish that time would turn backward to the days when she and Ralph had first met.

The morning after Ralph graduated, Candy came downstairs a bit later than usual. Now that she was out of school for the summer, she felt no need to hurry. Judge White had already gone to the courthouse when she entered the breakfast room, but Marsha was still at the table, finishing her coffee and reading the morning paper.

"Come and have some breakfast, Candy," she greeted.

"I'm not hungry, but I'll have some fruit and cereal," Candy responded as she sat down.

"Good mornin', Miss Candy," Dora greeted, as she came from the kitchen to set the table for her. "Is Master Ralph comin' down for his breakfast now?"

"I didn't hear him up, but I'm sure he'll be down soon," Candy answered.

Ralph heard them on his way down the stairs. "I'll be there in a minute," he called.

"I'll go fix your bacon and eggs," Dora told him as he entered the breakfast room.

"Good morning, Ralph. What are you going to do today?" Marsha asked.

"I was just thinking about that. It seems strange not having to hurry off to school."

"Why don't we go riding on the ponies, Ralph?" Candy suggested. "We haven't ridden them in ages."

"Say, you're right. I hardly ever think of the ponies anymore, except when I feed them."

"I'd like to ride to the spring like we used to."

"That would be fun. I'll bridle and saddle the ponies after I finish feeding and watering the calves."

"While you do that, I'll milk Baby Bell. Then I'll get ready."

"Are you going to milk goats the rest of your life, Candy?" Marsha asked.

"I suppose I will. I like goat milk. Sandy Bell kept me and Ralph from starving when we were trying to make it on our own."

"Your breakfast is ready, Master Ralph and Miss Candy," Dora said as she came from the kitchen carrying two platters of food.

Marsha soon arose and went up to her room, and Candy and Ralph were left alone at the table. She sensed that he was not in a talkative mood, so she ate her cereal in silence. After she finished eating, she remained at the table, toying with her spoon and watching Ralph.

"I'll see you in a few minutes," he said when he finished eating and arose from the table.

"I'll hurry."

Candy soon went to the barn and made fast work of milking Baby Bell. She returned to the house, gave the milk to Dora to put away, hurried to her room, and dressed in her riding habit.

"Good-bye, Mama Marsha," she called as she went out the back door.

"You and Ralph have fun," Marsha returned.

"We will. We always do."

On her way to the barn, Candy noticed that the morning was especially warm. Flags were blooming along the yard fence, and roses were blossoming in the rose bed. The morning air wafted their fragrance to her as she walked past. Pigeons rose from the barn roof, wheeled above the yard, and landed back on the roof. A woodpecker hammered on a dead tree by the drive, and a mockingbird sang from a treetop in the back yard.

"Ralph, I'm glad we decided to go riding," she called when she saw him come from the barn leading the ponies.

"I'm glad too, Candy. It seems like old times." He held Happiness while she mounted, then he swung into the saddle astride Joy, and turned him toward the ridge.

"It's been so long since we rode together," Candy said as she rode beside him.

"I reckon we've outgrown the ponies."

"Especially you have. Your legs almost drag the ground." She wished she could think of something more romantic to say.

They rode up the hill and out the ridge. At the end of the ridge, they paused, as they always did, and looked down at the river. A white tugboat was coming down the river, pushing three large barges of coal ahead of it. Puffs of smoke were coming from the smokestack. The captain blew two short blasts on his whistle.

"I wonder if he sees us?" she mused, enthralled. She waved at the captain with both hands, but Ralph only sat and watched.

"Have you ever noticed how often a tugboat has passed when we ride up here?"

"Almost every time, I think. I used to think I'd like to be a river boat captain when I grew up, but now I'd rather be a pilot."

"I wish you wouldn't talk like that, Ralph. If you become a pilot and we get in the war, you'll have to go overseas to fight. I'll worry myself to death if that happens." She blushed and covered her mouth with her hand, fearing that he would realize that she was in love with him.

"If we get in the war, I'll be drafted anyway, and I'm not going to wait till that happens."

"Ralph, that frightens me."

"Come on. Let's ride." He picked up the bridle reins and spurred Joy to a trot.

She started riding after him, but the lightness had gone out of her heart. She followed Ralph along the ridge and down the ravine, the way they had gone so often.

Ralph reached the spring ahead of her, and Joy stopped of his own accord. He stepped from the saddle as Candy rode up on Happiness.

"I'll get the water this time," he said, and he went to the springhouse door, pulled it open on its rusty hinges, and went in and dipped water into the old bucket. Candy waited without dismounting until he came out of the springhouse with the bucket filled with water.

"It seems ages since we rode to the spring," she said as he handed her the dipper.

"It really hasn't been that long."

"Two years," she reminded him. "You were only sixteen, and I was fourteen the last time we rode to the spring."

"It doesn't seem that long, but, seeing how you've grown up, I reckon it has been."

"I thought I was a grown woman when I was keeping house in the cabin."

"And I was going off like a man, looking for work so we could eat."

"I was happier back then than I had ever been, until we moved to the cave. I never liked the cave, and it has only left bad memories."

"We weren't there long."

"Long enough for me to get sick," she reminded him.

"I'll never forget how scared I was."

"Me too. I thought I was going to die."

"The best part of that was the Whites' coming and taking us home with them."

"It's been good living with the Whites, and I've come to love them like they were my own parents."

"Me too. I wish we could both live with them forever."

"We can't though. Things don't work out that way."

The ponies had been drinking from the spring branch. Now Joy started pawing the ground, anxious to be on his way back to the barn.

"Whoa, Joy. Stand still," Ralph commanded.

"You're not going to join the air corps right away, are you?"

"I don't know. Maybe I'll get a job and work awhile

first."

"There's not much work around here."

"I know. Maybe I'll go to Lexington or Cincinnati."

"If you do, I won't ever see you again."

"Of course you will. I'll come home on weekends."

"I wish you didn't ever have to go away."

He looked at her closely and shrugged. "Maybe I won't. Daddy White wants me to stay and help with the farm."

"I wish you would stay." Her eyes danced, then saddened. "If you do stay, what about Bill Hanks?"

"Bill won't mind. We work good together."

"Would there be work enough for both of you?"

"Of course. We would buy more stock, and raise more crops than Daddy White ever has."

"What if we get in the war, after you do all that?"

"Then Bill would have to manage the farm like he always has."

"I hope we don't get in the war," she said, fighting back her tears.

"I guess we all hope that."

"Ralph, I'm glad you're my brother," she said, then wished that she had not said it. For today, at least, she wished he would forget that she was his sister, even by adoption.

"I'm glad you're my sister. Saying vows like we did when we were kids was silly, I guess, but I have felt like you were my sister ever since."

She turned away, trying to hide the tears that were starting down her cheeks.

"You shouldn't be crying, Candy. We have always been close, and we have a lot to be thankful for."

"Oh, I am thankful. I am," she said, trying to keep the sarcasm out of her voice. She grabbed the bridle reins and pulled hard on them, to turn Happiness around. Then she dug her spur into her side. The pony lunged forward, startled by such treatment, and started up the ravine in a gallop.

Surprised, Ralph spurred his pony after her. When he caught up with her, she looked away. Rebuffed, he rode beside her in silence for several minutes.

"Let's slow the ponies. They'll be winded before we get to the top on the hill." He pulled on the reins to slow Joy.

Meekly she slowed Happiness to a walk and rode beside him.

"Do we have to go back to the house now?" he asked. "Let's go back and follow the spring branch to the creek and ride along it. That's the most beautiful place on the farm."

"You promised to ride down there with me years ago, but you never did."

"Today, I'll keep my promise. Come on, let's go." He stopped Joy and turned him half around.

"Thank you, but I'd rather go back to the house." She did not stop Happiness. In her heart she knew that she was being difficult, but she did not know why.

Disappointed, he rode after her, caught up, and rode beside her in silence until they reached the barn.

"Please take the saddle and bridle off Happiness," she said, as she slid from the saddle. Without a backward glance she went to the house.

Perplexed, he watched her go, then shrugged and set to work taking the saddles and bridles off the ponies.

Through the summer Candy spent most of her time indoors, reading, practicing on the piano, talking with Mama Marsha, and going out to the kitchen to visit Dora. Dora often cooked dishes her mother had never had the time or the ingredients to cook, and she loved to watch her and to smell the aroma of the cooking food. But Marsha discouraged her spending time with

Dora, especially when Candy volunteered to help with the housework.

Some mornings, after Ralph had gone to work with the cattle or in the garden, she left the house and walked down the hill and across the valley to the river. Often she walked slowly along the riverbank, listening to the sounds of the flowing water. At the first bend in the river, she always stopped and stood for a time, looking down a long, straight stretch of the river. The river helped her to forget her troubled heart and to dream of things that would never come to pass.

Other days, she stopped when she reached the river and watched the flowing water. Often she tossed a piece of driftwood in the river and watched it move with the current until it was out of sight. If her heart was especially heavy, she sometimes wished she could get on a boat and go down the river as swiftly and as easily as the driftwood had gone—not caring where she landed or if she would ever come back. She did not really want to do that, she realized. She loved Mama Marsha and Daddy White too much to ever want to leave them, and the last thing in the world she wanted to do was to cause them heartache. Her hopeless love for Ralph was what made her want to run away, she knew, but running away would not solve that. No matter where she went, she would still love him.

Something was troubling Ralph also, but she had no idea what it was. He had grown morose and silent this summer. He seldom talked to anyone beyond the usual amenities, and that made her wonder if he too were nurturing a heartache. If that were true, she had no idea what was causing it. How sad, she thought, that they could not go back to the happy, carefree days when they were younger.

Chapter 15

*O*ne morning in early October, Candy saw Daddy White's secretary, Opal, coming up the hill in her little coupe.

"Opal is coming, Mama Marsha," she called. "Daddy White must have forgotten something and sent her to get it."

"Austin almost never forgets anything," Marsha said as she and Candy went out to meet Opal.

"Hello, Opal," Candy called.

"Opal, imagine seeing you at this hour," Marsha greeted. "Did Austin forget something?"

"It's not that, Mrs. White. Judge White is sick," Opal exclaimed breathlessly.

"Most likely another one of his stomach attacks. Is he coming home?" Marsha asked.

"Not soon . . . I don't think. They took him to the hospital in an ambulance."

"Oh no," Candy cried. "What happened to him?"

"I don't really know, except that somebody found him lying on the courthouse steps and called Dr. Edwards from his office down the street. Dr. Edwards took one look at Judge White and called an ambulance for him. They were putting him in the ambulance by the time I heard what had happened and ran outside."

"Thank you for bringing us word, Opal," Marsha said, white-faced, but controlled. "Where did they take

Austin?"

"Dr. Edwards told them to take him to Good Samaritan in Lexington."

"Thank you for bringing us word, Opal. We'll go to the hospital at once," Marsha said. "Candy go find Ralph and tell him. Then you both get dressed in a hurry."

With her heart filled with fear and worry, Candy ran to the back yard gate and called to Ralph in the garden. "Ralph, Daddy White is real sick, and they've taken him to the hospital in Lexington. Hurry! We're going to Lexington."

He dropped his hoe where he was and ran to her. "I saw Opal's car. Did she bring word about Daddy White?" he asked in one breath.

"Yes. She said that somebody found him unconscious on the courthouse steps, and that they have taken to the hospital. Mama Marsha wants us to hurry."

Dora met them at the door as they were coming in. "Is Mr. White bad sick, Miss Candy?" she asked.

"We only know that they have taken him to the hospital in Lexington. We're going there to see him as soon as we can dress," Candy responded.

"Dora, tell Bill about Daddy White being sick," Ralph said. "And tell him he'll have to do the chores by himself till I get back."

"Sure, I'll tell him, Master Ralph. I know he'll be some kind of upset, but you can count on him taking care of things. I'll look after things here at the house, you know."

"I know you will, Dora," Candy responded.

While Candy was dressing, her thoughts were on Daddy White. Perhaps he was already in the emergency room at the hospital. Could he be near death? Surely not. He had always been such a tower of strength, and he had always appeared so perfectly well, except for his stomach. Lately he had complained of

infrequent chest pains, but they had all been too preoccupied to take his pains seriously. Since she had
known Daddy White, he had gone to his office at the
courthouse early every morning to take care of his
duties there, and he often had to try people for one
cause or another. Last year, he had run for reelection
as county judge. He had won by a large majority, but
the race had taken its toll. He had been unusually tired
when it was over, and he had never regained his usual
vigor. But that had not prevented him from coming
home each afternoon to help with the work on the farm.
She felt guilty that she had not shown more concern
for him on the occasions when he had complained.

In a very short time, they got in the car and started
driving swiftly, soberly, and quietly toward Lexington. When they reached the hospital and inquired at
the desk, they were told that Judge White had been
rushed to intensive care and that a team of doctors was
evaluating him. They were directed to the waiting room
on the second floor to await a report on his condition.

"I can't believe Austin has had a heart attack,"
Marsha said as she sat down.

"Mama Marsha, we have to pray for him," Candy
said, and she went to Marsha and knelt by her chair.

"Oh yes, child. Prayer has always been your strong
point. Surely, if anyone's prayer can help, yours can."

Candy took Marsha's hand, and bowed her head
and prayed silently.

Ralph had remained standing, but he now sat down
beside Marsha. His face was showing shock. He did
not know what to say, but he put his arm around Mama
Marsha's shoulder, and they waited in silence for a
report from the doctor.

Nurses whisked past the door of the waiting room
in starchy, white uniforms. Peopled walked the hall
on errands, or on the way to visit sick loved ones.
Doctors passed with stethoscopes hanging from their

necks. Traffic roared past in the street below.

At noon they heard food carts in the hall. They smelled the hot food being served, but none of them thought of going out to eat. Instead they waited and worried.

In midafternoon the specialist finally came to the waiting room to give them a report, and they all arose to meet him.

"Mrs. White, I'm Dr. Tate. Your husband is a very sick man," he began.

"Yes, doctor, what's wrong with him?"

"He has had a massive heart attack."

"Oh, oh. Is he going to live?"

"It's too early to tell. We're doing all we can. If he lives till morning, he'll have a chance."

"You mean he might die tonight?" Ralph choked.

"We hope not, young man."

Candy was clinging to Marsha and weeping silently. For once she did not speak.

"When can we see him?" Marsha asked.

"You can see him now, but he may not know you're there, because we have him sedated. Come and I'll show you the way to intensive care."

They followed the doctor to the intensive care unit and he led them to Austin's bed. Austin was wearing a hospital gown, and he was hooked up to monitoring machines. An oxygen tent was over his face, and IV needles were in his arms, feeding liquid from bottles that were hanging from supports above the bed.

They approached his bed quietly. Marsha took his hand, but there was no response.

"Daddy White," Ralph sobbed in a low, choking voice. Candy stood quietly by his bed, and her lips moved in inaudible prayer.

"Let's go," Marsha said, after a few moments, and she led Candy and Ralph back to the waiting room.

"I had better phone home. I know that Dora and

Bill must be worried sick. Besides I had better tell
Dora we won't be home tonight."

Ralph and Candy went with her to the pay phone
in the hall and waited while she called.

"Do you want anything to eat?" she asked them
after she hung up the phone.

"I'm not hungry," Ralph answered.

"Me neither," Candy said.

"I'm not either," Marsha agreed.

They went back to the waiting room and sat quietly until the last slanting rays of the sun were filtering through the curtained windows.

"I think I need some coffee," Marsha said then,
breaking her long silence. "I'm going to stay awake
all night, and I know it's going to be a long one."

"I'll be glad to get out of this place for a few minutes," Candy responded.

"Candy, I know that if you drink anything it will
be hot tea or a Coke. Ralph, do you want some coffee?"

"I don't want anything, but I'll go with you and
Candy. Maybe I ought to drink a cup of coffee so I can
stay awake with you tonight."

They went out and found a restaurant. Marsha
ordered black coffee, and Ralph ordered a cup of coffee with cream and sugar.

"I'll have a Coke," Candy told the waitress.

They waited for their drinks in silence, then drank
them.

"The coffee made me feel better," Marsha said
when she set her cup down.

"Me too," Ralph agreed.

"Nothing will make me feel better as long as Daddy
White is sick," Candy declared.

"I only meant that I feel more alert. Austin will
have to get well for my world to ever be right again,"
Marsha said as she arose from the table.

The sun was almost down when they started back to the hospital, and the lights were on inside when they entered. They returned to the waiting room and sat down. Ralph fished a pencil and some paper from his pockets and started drawing. Candy watched him and wished she had something to do that would take her mind off Daddy White. Marsha sat white-faced and silent.

After hours had passed, they became almost hopeful. But they still started up in fear, thinking that the doctor was coming with bad news, each time they heard a man's footsteps in the hall.

Near the end of the long night Candy fell asleep in her chair, but Marsha and Ralph still sat stiffly in their chairs, wide awake and staring mutely at each other.

When the first light of dawn appeared in the windows, Marsha stretched herself, got up, and walked about in the room. At last she paused beside Ralph.

"I am less worried than I was," she said softly, trying not to awaken Candy. "The doctor said that if Austin made it through the night he would have a chance, and it is almost day."

"I hope you're right, Mama Marsha. I don't know what we'd do without Daddy White," Ralph said.

Candy awoke suddenly and sat bolt upright in her chair. "Has something happened to Daddy White?" she asked fearfully.

"We haven't heard from the doctor, so he must still be alive, Candy. It's almost day, and that means that he has a chance," Ralph said.

"Oh, I'm glad. When I prayed last night I felt like he was going to be all right."

"So that's how you were able to sleep," Marsha said.

Candy stood up and stretched. "I'm hungry," she said.

"We'll go eat as soon as the restaurant opens. By

the time we get back, there may be some word about Austin," Marsha said.

Candy went to the window and looked out. "I can see the restaurant from here. I'll tell you when they open up," she said.

Ralph went to the door and looked up and down the hall. Then he went to the window and looked out with Candy.

"If both of you are going to stand there looking out, I'll look with you," Marsha said as she joined them.

"They just turned the lights on in the restaurant, so they must be open," Candy exclaimed.

"Then we'll go and eat," Marsha responded.

They left at once and went to the restaurant and ate a hurried breakfast. Then they returned to the waiting room and continued to wait for Dr. Tate to come. It was midmorning when he finally came.

"How is he, Dr. Tate? Do you have good news?" Marsha asked as they all arose.

"It's too early to make predictions, but your husband is not any worse. If there are no complications in the next seventy-two hours, there is a good chance that he'll live to go home. If he does, and, if he takes care of himself, he may have several years to live."

"Thank you, doctor. That gives me something to hope for," Marsha said.

"I know Daddy White is going to live. I just know it," Candy rejoiced.

"If Daddy White does get to go home, me and Bill will do all the work for him," Ralph said.

"You can all go up to see Judge White now," Dr. Tate told them.

When they entered Austin's room he was still under the oxygen tent, but he was awake. When he saw them, he looked up and smiled faintly, and he waved with the fingers of his right hand.

"Oh, Austin, it's so good to see you awake," Marsha greeted.

"We're praying for you, Daddy White, and I know you're going to be all right," Candy told him.

He made an OK sign with his fingers.

"Don't worry about anything at home, Daddy White. Bill and I will take care of everything," Ralph assured him.

The next three days passed without a crisis, and Austin appeared to be growing stronger. Dr. Tate assured them that he was making progress and that what remained now was a period of convalescence.

"We need to go home and see about things and get some clean clothes. Do we dare to leave him?" Marsha asked.

"I see no reason why you should not go. He's still somewhat sedated, and he will hardly miss you."

They went home late that afternoon and returned the next morning. To their relief, they found that Austin had improved. The oxygen tent was gone, and he was propped up in bed eating some broth.

"We had to go home to get some clean clothes, but we hurried right back," Marsha explained.

"I know you needed to go home," he said in a soft voice.

"Daddy White, I'm still praying for you," Candy said.

He winked at her and smiled faintly.

"Bill is taking care of things, and I helped him while we were home," Ralph told him.

"That's good, Ralph. Perhaps you should stay to help him the next time you go home."

"Daddy White, I'd like to do that, but I'll come and see you on Saturdays and Sundays."

"You do that, Ralph." He closed his eyes and appeared to sleep, and they all left his room.

Chapter 16

I have good news for you, Judge White," Dr. Tate greeted one morning after he had been in the hospital three weeks. "You can go home tomorrow."

"That is good news, but I'm not sure I'm up to it."

"We'll send you home in an ambulance. You'll have to stay in bed for awhile, but you'll be all right."

"How long will I have to stay in bed?"

"Until you're stronger. When you feel up to it, you can get up and walk about in the house, but don't climb any stairs."

"Will I be confined to the house for the rest of my life?"

"Not at all. In time you'll be able to go out. You may even be able to do some light work. We'll see."

"Thank you for all you've done, Dr. Tate."

"I wish I could have done more. I'll see you in the morning before you leave," Dr. Tate said as he was backing out the door.

Weak as he was, Austin was excited at the prospect of going home. He was watching the door with tears in his eyes when Marsha and Candy came later that morning.

"I'm going home tomorrow," he greeted.

"How wonderful," Marsha exclaimed, and she leaned over and kissed him.

"Daddy White, I'm glad you're going home,"

Candy said, smiling brightly. "Every time we go home, I miss you being there."

"I've missed being there, blue eyes. Where's Ralph? Is he working today?"

"Bill needed him for something, so he stayed to help," Marsha responded.

"I never knew Ralph would be so much help. It would be hard to do without him," Austin said.

"Austin, I've been thinking. If it's all right with you, I'm going to bring your bed down and put it in the library. That will make it easier for us to look after you, and you'll be close to all that goes on downstairs. That will keep you from feeling left out."

"And we'll be close to you when we eat," Candy added.

"That's a good idea, Marsha."

"After you're up and around, we'll move you to the back bedroom so you still won't have to climb the stairs," Marsha added.

The next day Marsha and Candy went to the hospital to check Austin out, but Ralph stayed at home to help Bill.

Dr. Tate did not come to Austin's room until almost noon. "You are doing fine, so I'm dismissing you from the hospital," he said. "The ambulance will be here to get you shortly after you have your lunch."

"Thank you for all you have done for me," Austin said brokenly.

"I want you to come back for a checkup in two weeks." He patted Austin on the shoulder.

"He should do better at home with his family," he said to Marsha. He smiled at Candy and left the room.

Shortly after Austin finished eating, two aides came and took him down on a gurney and put him in the ambulance.

"We had better go to the car and start home before they get too far ahead of us, Candy," Marsha said as the ambulance pulled away.

"I can't wait to get Daddy White home," Candy called over her shoulder, for she was already hurrying toward their car.

They got in the car, and Candy drove from the parking lot and turned toward home. "I'm going to get ahead of them and lead the way home," she said, driving as fast as she dared in city traffic.

"Good idea, Candy. I don't want to have to look at that ambulance all the way home. I don't want to be reminded of how sick Austin is."

Long before they got home, Ralph and Bill were watching for the ambulance. When they finally saw it coming, with their car in the lead, they left their work and went to the yard gate to wait. Dora had been watching from the front door for hours, and she came out on the porch.

Candy drove well past the gate, stopped the car, and bounded out. Then, waving both arms, she ran toward the yard gate, singing out, "Daddy White is home. Daddy White is home."Marsha got out of the car and went to stand beside the ambulance and watch the driver and his assistants carefully take Daddy White out on a stretcher. She walked toward the house ahead of them, and Ralph and Bill fell in line behind her. Dora hurried to hold the screen door open for them.

They carried Austin in and put him in bed, and the driver and his helper left.

Marsha, Candy, and Ralph gathered around Austin's bed, and Bill and Dora came and stood in the doorway.

"I made the trip better than I thought I would," Austin said in a weak voice.

"Daddy White, we sure are glad you're home," Candy said.

"I can't tell you how glad I am to have you home, Austin," Marsha told him.

"Don't worry about anything on the farm, Daddy White. Bill and I have all the work caught up," Ralph said,

"All of you are such a comfort," Austin said, smiling wearily. "And Bill and Dora, I appreciate all you are doing."

"Glad to do what I can, Judge," Bill said.

"Me too, Judge White," Dora joined in.

"Why don't you take a nap, Austin," Marsha suggested. "We'll all visit with you later."

Bill and Dora took that as a cue and quietly left the room.

"I'm too excited to sleep, but I think I'll rest a bit," Austin said as he closed his eyes.

They all tiptoed quietly from the room. "Ralph, you and Candy do what you need to, but I'm going to stay near Austin's room so I can look in on him from time to time," Marsha whispered.

"All right, Mama Marsha," Candy whispered in return, and she went to the kitchen to visit with Dora. Ralph went out and followed Bill to the barn.

"What are you fixing for Daddy White to eat?" Candy asked Dora when she reached the kitchen.

"I don't rightly know, Miss Candy. I thought the doctor might tell Mrs. White what he can have."

"When I was in the hospital, they gave me chicken soup, and they gave me Jell-O for desert. Maybe Daddy White can eat something like that. It sure tasted good to me."

"That's just what I'll fix for him, Miss Candy, 'less Mrs. White want's me to fix something different."

At supper time, Dora carried a steaming bowl of chicken soup, some toast, some Jell-O, and some hot tea to Austin's room. "I'm going to put supper on the table in the breakfast room for the rest of you," she told Marsha.

"Fix supper for Ralph and Candy in there, but bring

176

me something in here. I'm going to eat with Austin."

"Yes ma'am, Mrs. White. I don't blame you a bit. That's exactly what I'd do if I was you." She returned to the kitchen and soon came back with a well-filled plate and some coffee for Marsha.

"I wish we could eat in there with Mama Marsha and Daddy White," Ralph said as he and Candy sat down at the table in the breakfast room.

"Me too, but I reckon he doesn't need too much company."

"It doesn't seem right, just you and me eating at the table," Ralph said.

"We used to enjoy eating together when we were in the cabin, even if we didn't have much to eat. We could pretend we're back there."

"I reckon we could, but it wouldn't be the same. If we really could go back there, we would miss Mama Marsha and Daddy White and Bill and Dora."

"I know. I never want to leave them."

"What if Daddy White dies?"

"Don't say that, Ralph. He has to get well. He just has to."

"All right. I'll try to have faith like you do."

They talked little as they ate, and when they finished, they went to the door of Daddy White's room and looked in on him. They visited briefly; then Ralph went back to the barn to get out of the house and try to forget how ill Daddy White was.

By mid-November Austin was out of bed part of each day, able to walk about in the downstairs. Often he sat before the fire that was kept burning in the library, watching the fire burn and sometimes punching at it with the poker. Other times he read sketches from some book that struck his fancy. Always, after being up for an hour or two, he returned to bed.

One morning the last of the month, Marsha and

Candy drove to Maysville to buy groceries, and Ralph stayed home with Austin. There had been a heavy frost during the night, and the sun had come up this morning in a cold, gray sky. The blinds were drawn in the library, muting the outside light. The atmosphere of winter was in the room, augmented by the fire that burned on the hearth.

Austin sat before the fire, absorbing its warmth, and Ralph sat beside him.

"It's cold outside, but the fire feels good," Austin said, picking up the poker and punching at a smoldering log.

"It wasn't too bad when I went out to help Bill feed," Ralph replied.

"Ralph, you really like working on the farm, don't you?" Austin asked, looking at him intently.

"Yes I do, Daddy White, but I don't think I'm going to be able to stay on the farm."

"Why do you say that, Ralph?"

"I think our country is going to get in the war. If it does, I'm going to join the Army Air Corps."

"You may be right about us getting in the war. I heard on the radio that President Roosevelt has instructed our navy to sink any German submarines or warships that enter our waters. That could easily get us involved in the war."

"If we do, I'll be drafted if I don't volunteer first."

"Ralph, I don't want you in the air force or any other branch of the service if it can be helped," Daddy White said firmly.

"As long as you're sick, I won't enlist unless I see that they're going to draft me."

"I appreciate that Ralph."

"But when you get well, Daddy White, I'm going to enlist."

"I don't believe I'll ever be well, Ralph, and I need you to run the farm."

"Can't Bill run it?"

"Just between you and me, Ralph, Bill is a good worker, but he's not a good manager. If I don't get able to take charge, I'll have to depend on you."

Ralph looked at the fire for several minutes, not wanting Daddy White to know how torn he was between his loyalty to him and what he saw as his duty to his country. Young men like him would have to fight in the coming war. Somebody had to stop Hitler or he would conquer all of Europe, and the United States would be next.

"I'm not sure I'd know how to run the farm," he finally said.

"You have the intelligence to do it, Ralph, and, as long as I live, you can come to me for advice. After I'm gone, you can talk things over with Marsha. She has a good head on her shoulders, and she has a working knowledge of the farm."

"I reckon I could do it, with you and Mama Marsha helping me," Ralph agreed reluctantly.

"I know you can, but will you do it?"

Ralph did not answer at once, and Austin waited in silence. Only the ticking of the clock in the hall and the occasional cracking of the burning logs kept the silence from being oppressive.

"What do you say, Ralph? Can I count on you as long as the United States is not in the war?" Austin finally asked.

"Yes, Daddy White. I won't sign up as long as our country stays out of the war."

"That takes a load off my shoulders, Ralph," Austin said. Then he sat back in his chair and closed his eyes and appeared to sleep.

Ralph looked at him closely for a long moment, then quietly left the room and went out to the barn where Bill was finishing the chores.

Chapter 17

*A*ustin's health improved slowly, and on the first Sunday in December he was able to go to church with his family. Ralph drove the big car, and Candy sat beside him, wearing a new blue dress and a prim little felt hat perched at a jaunty angle atop her wealth of light brown hair. Daddy White and Mama Marsha sat in the backseat, dressed in their Sunday best. Ralph was wearing the new suit Daddy White and Mama Marsha had given him for a graduation present. He was thankful that they had provided him with good clothes and had taught him to dress well when the occasion demanded.

He could not help noticing how beautiful Candy was, and he was proud that she was his sister. He glanced at Daddy White and Mama Marsha in the rearview mirror. They were sitting close together, and Mama Marsha was holding one of his hands in both of hers. He could not help noticing how old and tired Daddy White looked. His hair had grayed perceptibly since his heart attack, and the lines in his face had deepened. Ralph turned his eyes on the road and tried to swallow the lump in his throat. He did not look at Daddy White and Mama Marsha again during the drive to the church.

Sunday school had apparently just ended when they reached the church, for some people were leaving and others were arriving.

"I don't feel like talking with people, so I want us to go in last and sit in the back," Austin said.

"All right, Daddy White," Ralph answered. He drove slowly around the block, then stopped before the entrance of the church.

"The parking places are all taken, so I'll let you all out, then I'll park the car," he said.

Candy bounded from the car and waited as Marsha got out. Austin got out slowly and stepped down to the pavement. Marsha took him by the arm, and Candy took his other arm. Together they walked him to the entrance of the stately old church.

Jim Howard, an old friend who was serving as usher, met them in the vestibule. "Judge White, and Mrs. White, and Candy, I'm delighted to see all of you. Judge, I'm glad you're able to come back to church."

"I'm glad to be here, Jim, though I still don't feel well."

"Jim, seat us toward the back so Austin can get out before a crowd throngs him at the close of the service. He still tires easily," Marsha said.

"Sure. I understand." He led them into the auditorium and to a seat near the back. They seated themselves just as the great pipe organ filled the auditorium with the uplifting strains of the doxology.

Candy stood with the congregation just as Ralph came into the pew beside her. Marsha remained seated with Austin.

Many thoughts passed through Candy's mind as she sang with the congregation. She had come to love this church during the years she and Ralph had lived with Judge White and Marsha, though it had taken her a long time to get used to it. It was so massive, so stately, and so beautiful, not at all like the small country church she had attended with her mother when she was a little girl.

She thought how good it was that they could all be in church together again. She and Ralph had been attending church regularly, but Daddy White and Mama Marsha had not attended since his heart attack, until today. Now that Daddy White was able to come to church again, it made her almost hope that he was going to get well.

She glanced at Ralph, and her heart swelled with pride, though it ached with unrequited love. She wished that Ralph cared for her as she cared for him, and that they could always come here together to worship. She sighed, thinking that if America got involved in the war, she and Ralph would soon be separated—perhaps forever.

After the sermon, as the congregation was singing the last hymn, Austin motioned that he was ready to go.

"I'll go get the car," Ralph whispered and hurried out.

Marsha and Candy helped Austin to his feet, and they quietly left the church.

"I didn't want to leave, but I don't feel up to shaking hands with a lot of people," Austin said while they were waiting for the car.

"I know," Marsha said.

Ralph soon came with the car, and Candy and Mama Marsha helped Austin get in. Marsha got in beside him, and Candy took her place beside Ralph.

"Stop and let Candy get a newspaper from the paper stand in front of the drugstore," Daddy White directed as Ralph pulled away from the curb.

"All right, Daddy White." He drove the car slowly and stopped in front of the drugstore.

Candy got out and got a paper. Then she returned to her seat, and handed it back to Austin.

He took it and scanned the headlines. "Not much in the paper today except war news," he commented, and wearily laid it aside.

Ralph drove them home and stopped the car by the yard gate, and they all got out and helped Daddy White to the house and to his easy chair before the fireplace.

"I wish I had felt like meeting people," he said as he sat down.

"You'll soon feel up to it," Marsha consoled.

"Dinner's 'most ready, Mrs. White," Dora called from the dining room.

"We'll be there in a minute, Dora." She turned to Austin and asked, "Do you feel up to eating at the table, or do you want your dinner carried to your bedroom?"

"I'm pretty tired. I think I'll eat in the bedroom."

"Then I'll bring my plate in there and eat with you," she responded.

"That means that Ralph and I will have the big dining room all to ourselves," Candy commented.

After Ralph and Candy finished eating, they went in to visit with Austin and Marsha, but Ralph soon excused himself and went out to look at the cattle as he did so often on Sunday afternoons.

"Turn the radio on, Candy," Austin said. "It's time for that nice chamber music they have on the Cincinnati station on Sunday afternoons."

Candy went to the table radio Marsha had put in Austin's room, turned it on, and dialed the station. But instead of the soft sound of strings coming from the speaker, an announcer was talking in an excited voice.

"I have a bulletin, just in. The Japanese have bombed Pearl Harbor," he was saying.

Austin bolted upright to listen, and the attention of Marsha and Candy was suddenly riveted to the radio.

"Early reports indicate that Pearl Harbor has been virtually destroyed," the voice continued. "It is reported that more than 300 Japanese planes attacked the harbor shortly before eight o'clock, Pearl Harbor time, dropping bombs and strafing with machine guns. The news to this hour reports that five of our best battleships and fourteen smaller ships have been sunk or badly damaged. Early reports say that 200 of our aircraft have been destroyed, and early counts indicate that the dead and wounded will number four thousand or more."

"We are at war," Austin said in a solemn voice that almost drowned out the news that was still pouring from the radio.

"Oh! Oh!" Marsha sobbed with her arms crossed over her heart. "That means Ralph will soon be drafted."

"He'll volunteer," Austin said hoarsely.

"You've been saying you didn't want him to volunteer," Marsha reminded him.

"That dastardly attack by the Japanese changes everything. If he doesn't volunteer now, I won't claim him as a son. I'd volunteer myself if I were younger and had my health."

"I'd volunteer, if I were a man," Candy exclaimed.

"Then I'm glad you're not a man," Marsha said sharply.

"That goes for me too," Austin agreed.

"I could take nurses' training and go in as a nurse," Candy suggested.

"There's no way I want a daughter of mine involved in the war," Marsha answered firmly.

"Your place is at home, Candy. There'll be things women can do without leaving home, but enough of this. Let's listen to the rest of the news," Austin said.

"Go find Ralph. He ought to know what's happened," Marsha told Candy.

"Oh yes!" Candy cried. "He has to know." She ran from the house calling, "Ralph, Ralph," at the top of her voice. Ralph did not answer, so she ran toward the barn, still calling for him.

When she was almost at the barn door, he came out, shaken by her excited cries.

"What's wrong, Candy? Has something happened to Daddy White?" he asked anxiously.

"No, Ralph. Nothing like that. It's the war. The Japanese have bombed Pearl Harbor and sunk a lot of our ships and destroyed a lot of our planes and killed a lot of our men."

"Where'd you get that, Candy? There wasn't anything like that in the paper."

"Ralph, it's coming over the radio right now. Let's hurry to the house and listen."

They started running as hard as they could. He reached the house well ahead of her and went in. When she got there he was in Daddy White's room, standing in front of the radio, listening to the announcer repeat the account of the bombing and give additional details that had become available.

When Ralph had heard most of the report, he turned the radio off and turned to Austin. "Daddy White, I'm going to enlist in the Army Air Corps tomorrow, no matter what you say," he said firmly.

"Ralph, I wouldn't claim you as a son if you didn't."

"Thank you, Daddy White." He put his arm around Austin's shoulder and hugged him. Then he turned to Marsha and took her in his arms. "I hate to leave because of you and Daddy White and Candy," he said.

"I can't tell you how I'm going to miss you, Ralph, but I know this is a price women have to pay," Marsha said brokenly.

Candy threw her arms around Ralph. "My big brother!" she sobbed. Tears were flowing down her cheeks, but she smiled bravely.

"I hate to leave all of you, but it's something I have to do," Ralph said in a half sob. He gave Candy a quick hug.

"Our prayers will go with you," Austin told him in

a husky voice.

"Indeed they will," Marsha echoed.

"I'll pray for you every day, Ralph," Candy promised.

"I'll be leaving the most wonderful family any one ever had," he said in a choking voice. "Excuse me. I want to be alone for awhile."

He turned and left the room, and no one tried to stop him. Hardly realizing where he was going, he started walking toward the high ground beyond the pasture. When he reached the end of the ridge where he and Candy had stopped so often to look at the river, he paused and looked off into space. For a long time he stood there looking, then he walked to the spring and followed the spring branch to the creek. He went to the fishing hole where he had fished so often since he had come to live with the Whites. He stood there for a long time, then he went to the pasture and looked at the cattle. He smiled grimly when he saw the ponies. He had enjoyed them so much, but they were now something from his past. He would never ride his pony again.

Sandy Bell and Baby Bell came to him to be petted, and he thought of the day Sandy Bell had come to the cabin when he and Candy had been so desperately in need of food. He could not help wondering if God had sent the goat in answer to Candy's prayers.

He wiped the tears from his eyes, then started slowly back to the house. It was almost dark when he got there. Resolutely, he put his hand on the doorknob and opened the door and went in, ready to face the sorrow that he knew his family could not hide.

His walk had not lessened his responsibility to his God and his country, but it had helped to prepare him for the heartache of leaving his family and to fortify him for whatever the future might hold.

Chapter 18

*T*he next day the United States declared war on Japan, and almost overnight recruiting stations were set up in towns and cities across the country. Young men of draft age and those who were not too old to be in the army started flocking to them to enlist. Ralph was among them. He went to the recruiting station in Maysville the day it opened and volunteered for the Army Air Corps.

He was given a physical and was promptly inducted into service. They told him to report early the following Monday, ready to leave on a troop train, but they did not bother to tell him where he was being sent for his basic training.

The morning after Ralph enlisted, Austin suddenly took a turn for the worse and stumbled to his bed. Alarmed, Marsha called the doctor and sent Candy to find Ralph and tell him that something had happened to Daddy White. With a wildly beating heart, Candy ran to the barn. Bill was feeding the stock, and Ralph was in the hayloft forking hay down into the hayrack.

"Ralph, something has happened to Daddy White," she called up to him.

"Not again," he exclaimed, dropping the pitchfork and hurrying down from the loft. "Bill, I reckon you can finish, I need to go see about Daddy White," he said.

"Of course, I'll finish. If there's anything I can do . . ."

His voice was lost as Ralph and Candy closed the barn door behind them and started running to the house.

Ralph arrived ahead of Candy and hurried to Daddy White's bedroom.

"How are you feeling, Daddy White?" he asked anxiously.

"Just one of my weak spells. I'll be all right after I rest," Austin answered, as Candy came in.

"Are you sure, Daddy White?" she asked.

"We'll withhold judgment till the doctor gets here and checks him," Marsha said.

"I wish I hadn't joined the air corps," Ralph muttered to himself. "Maybe I can get a deferment."

"You'll do nothing of the kind, Ralph. I'll be better off knowing that you're doing your duty than I will with you here fussing over me."

"But I don't want to go while you're sick, Daddy White."

"The country needs you, boy. Anyway, I'll soon be better."

The doctor arrived in half an hour and examined Austin. "This seems to be nothing more than a temporary upset," he told the family. "It may have been caused by stress."

"Ralph has joined the Army Air Corps," Marsha said evenly.

"That could have caused it. There's no way to know," the doctor said.

"Do you think he's going to be all right?" Ralph asked.

"As all right as he can be with his heart. He'll have problems off and on, but he may live a long time."

The family spent the rest of the day watching over Austin. To their relief he went to sleep early and slept soundly through the night. The next morning he was better.

"Just the same, I'm going to keep him in bed for a few days, and I'm going to have Dora to bring his meals to his room," Marsha said.

Daddy White smiled and winked at Ralph, but he did not object.

"I still think I should try to get a deferment," Ralph said.

"You'll do nothing of the kind, Ralph. I want you to go on just as if I hadn't had this little spell."

"All right, Daddy White, if you say so, but I'd rather wait until I'm sure you are going to be all right."

"Ralph, you may as well go on. Austin will worry himself sick if you don't," Marsha told him.

"I reckon you're right," Ralph agreed, but his mind was not at ease.

The rest of the week, Austin appeared to be getting better, and Ralph started looking forward to his departure on Monday.

Sunday night the family gathered in Austin's room for their last supper together. Though none of them mentioned it, they felt that it could be the last time Ralph would see Austin alive.

Ralph and Candy brought in a folding table and placed it by Austin's bed. Dora had prepared a special dinner for the occasion. She had fried steak smothered in onions, mashed potatoes, gravy, corn, and beans. She had even baked a cake and made a chocolate pudding, Ralph's favorite desert.

Even though they were eating on a folding table, Candy brought in the best china, crystal, and silver, and placed a lighted candle in the center of the little table.

"Leave the overhead light on. I like to see what I'm eating," Austin requested with a smile.

"Of course, Daddy White," Candy answered. She

turned and watched Dora place glasses of iced tea on the table. A slice of lemon, cut almost in half, rode atop each crystal glass. The amber tea turned golden under the light, and beads of moisture collected on the glasses.

Dora brought a platter of hot rolls from the kitchen. Because there was not room for them on the table, she placed them on the small table that held Austin's bed-side light.

"I've always loved the smell of hot rolls," Marsha said, attempting to make conversation.

"There's not room for all the food on the tables. I'll bring the rest of it and pass it around," Dora told them.

"Then we'll go ahead and start eating," Marsha said. "Austin, will you return thanks?"

A moment of silence passed, but Austin did not pray. "Ralph, you offer thanks on our last time to-gether," he finally said in a hoarse, broken voice.

Ralph started to pray, but he choked on his words. "I can't pray, Daddy White," he managed brokenly.

"I'll pray," Candy volunteered. "Dear Father," she began bravely, but her words ended in sobs.

"Be quiet, all of you, and I'll pray," Marsha volunteered, and she struggled through a brief prayer. When she finished, they all said, "Amen," and Dora started passing the food as if she were glad the ordeal was over.

There was little conversation while they were eating, for they were all too heavy-hearted to talk.

"Ralph, I'm proud of you, real proud," Austin finally said as they were finishing their desert. "I know you'll make a good pilot. I only wish I could go with you."

"I'll go for both of us, Daddy White, and you can stay home with Mama Marsha and Candy."

"I'd go in your place if I weren't a girl," Candy

said.

"I don't want to discuss that again," Marsha said firmly.

Candy shrugged, and said nothing more.

After the dishes and leftover food had been carried to the kitchen and the folding table had been carried out, they stayed on in Austin's room, visiting, until they saw that he was growing tired.

"I have to go pack a few things to take with me," Ralph said at last. "Daddy White, I'll see you in the morning before I leave. You too, Mama Marsha."

"Good night, Ralph. I'll see you in the morning," Austin said.

"You didn't say anything about seeing me in the morning," Candy said, pretending to pout.

"Of course I'll see you, Candy. You're going to take me to the train, aren't you? You promised."

"You know I will, Ralph. There's no way I'm going to let you leave without seeing you off. That way I'll know I'm rid of you," she bantered.

"And I won't be around to pester you," he kidded in return.

"To save time in the morning, I'll tell Dora to fix breakfast for you and Candy in the breakfast room. I'll be having breakfast in here with Austin, but I'll see you when you come to tell him good-bye," Marsha said.

"I'll say good night to everybody again," Ralph said as he was leaving. A moment later his footsteps echoed through the house as he went upstairs. The sound made Candy's heart ache, for she knew that after tomorrow she would miss his footsteps, the sound of his voice, and his presence.

"I'm going up to my room to write some letters," she said, and she hurried out so Austin and Marsha wouldn't see the tears that were threatening to flow down her cheeks.

The next morning Ralph went out and put the bag he had packed the night before in the car. He backed the car from the garage, parked it by the front gate, and went in to visit with Austin until breakfast was ready.

"This will be our last meal together," Candy said as they sat down at their usual places at the breakfast table a few minutes later.

"Only for a while," he said. "The war won't last forever."

"I know, but it's possible you won't come back." She bit her tongue, wishing she had not said that.

"Not everyone who fights in this war will come back, but I believe that I will. I do not know why. I just I believe that I will."

"I'll pray every day and every night that you will. I don't think I could live if anything happened to you." She blushed and wished that she could recall her words.

"We have to hurry. I don't dare miss the train," he said, apparently not noticing the slip of her tongue or the blush on her cheeks.

Trying to hide her embarrassment, she became very busy pouring milk over her cereal.

"Go ahead and pray so we can eat," he prompted.

"I was waiting for you to pray."

"You were the first person I ever heard pray before eating. Now that I'm leaving, I want you to be the last one I hear."

"Then I'll pray."

They bowed their heads, and she offered a short prayer in a half sob.

"I have to hurry," he said, and he started eating without looking up.

They finished breakfast and went to Austin's room.

"I came to say good-bye, Daddy White," Ralph said, taking his hand.

"Good-bye, Ralph. I'll pray for the Lord to watch over you."

"Thank you, Daddy White. I want to tell you before I go that I love you. You are the only real father I've ever had."

"I love you, Ralph. I could not be more proud of you if you had been born in our family."

"I hope to find you much improved when I come home on my first leave."

"I hope you will too. Ralph. I hate to see you go, but I'm glad you're going to serve your country," said Austin said with trembling lips.

Ralph shook his hand, then turned to Marsha and gave her a bear hug. "You're a real mother to me—the only one I can remember," he said huskily.

"Thank you, Ralph. You will write to us often?" She kissed him on his cheek.

"Of course."

"We'd better go, Candy." He took her arm and ushered her out the front door.

Bill was waiting by the car for them. "I come to say good-bye, Ralph. I sure am goin' to miss you," he said when they reached him.

"I'll miss you too, Bill. You've been a true friend."

"Mama Marsha and Dora have come to the door to watch us leave," Candy told Ralph.

He looked back at them and waved. "I'll say good-bye again," he called. They waved back as he got in the car and slid under the wheel.

"I'll drive," he said as Candy got in beside him. "There's no telling when I'll ever drive again."

"I guess I'll be chauffeur for Mama Marsha and Daddy White after you're gone," she responded.

When they came in sight of the railroad station in Maysville, they saw that the train was already on the siding waiting for the servicemen to come aboard. Several new recruits, who were going into various branches of the service, were already waiting beside the train. Some were accompanied by girlfriends, wives, or other family members.

Ralph parked the car in the nearest parking place, and they got out and walked to the back of the line.

Soon the engineer blew two short blasts of the whistle. The conductor opened the door of a passenger car and called for the men to board, and the men started moving toward the open door. A soldier and a young girl were standing near Ralph and Candy. The girl did not appear to be more than sixteen. They were holding each other in a tight embrace. Her head was on his shoulder, and tears were streaming down her face.

"When you're gone, I'm going to die. I just know I'll die," she sobbed.

"No you won't. I want you to live so I can come back to you." He kissed her passionately, then pushed her away and lost himself in the press of men in the line.

Candy took Ralph's arm and clung to it. She wished he would embrace her and kiss her as the soldier had kissed the girl, but she knew he would not.

"I have to go," he said, patting her hand.

"I know. Ralph . . . I . . ."

He turned a questioning gaze on her.

"I'll miss you," she said.

"I'll miss you too, Candy." He started toward the train with her still clinging to his arm.

"I'll pray for you."

"You do that." He started on, and reluctantly she let him go.

"You write often," she called as another soldier pressed between them.

"I will. You write."

He disappeared in the line of men, and a moment later she saw him enter the car. She lost sight of him as other men filled the doorway.

Steam hissed from the big engine, and it throbbed with power. It made her think of a great iron horse, chomping at the bit, anxious to be off for a run. Soon it would start along the iron rails that stretched out of sight in the distance. It would run along those rails and carry Ralph away from her . . . so many . . . so many miles. Perhaps she would never see him again.

She watched the windows of the car, hoping to catch another glimpse of Ralph, but she only saw strange men pressing along the aisle as they looked for seats.

The engineer blew the whistle again. Something rumbled deep inside the engine, and the train appeared to shudder.

"If only I were a man, I'd be going with you, Ralph," she murmured under her breath. "Even if that were true, I suppose we would soon be separated, so it would make little difference," she finished, trying to console herself.

The last man boarded the train and the door closed behind him. The big engine rumbled again and started puffing black smoke and cinders into the morning air. The wheels skidded on the rails, and the train started forward. The bell was ringing as the train gained speed.

She felt like the train was pulling her heart out, and she was sure that she would never get it back. She watched the cars go by, and her eyes did not leave the train until it disappeared in the distance.

After the train was out of sight and the thunder of its wheels could no longer be heard, she watched the cloud of smoke that had come from the smokestack until it vanished in the morning air. Then she turned sadly away and went back to the car and drove slowly home, thinking how lonely she would be for the rest of her life. What she had always feared had finally happened. The war had separated her and Ralph.

Chapter 19

*R*alph soon wrote that he was in Union City, Tennessee, taking his primary training. Candy and Marsha wrote back immediately. After that they wrote to him every day.

At first he answered all their letters, but at the end of the second week he wrote that they were keeping him so busy, he had little time to write letters. After that he wrote only an occasional brief letter, usually addressed to both of them and to Daddy White.

Despite his excuse for not writing, Candy felt neglected. "After all, I am his only sister," she fumed to herself. "It wouldn't hurt him to write me a decent letter once in awhile."

When one of Ralph's letters did arrive, Candy and Marsha would take it to Austin's room.

"Guess what, we have a letter from Ralph today," Marsha would announce as they entered, and Austin would brighten, even on his worst days. Then Candy would read the letter aloud. Austin would always feel better after Candy read the letter.

"I wish I could be in the war," he often said.

"You can do your duty right here," Marsha always told him. "The government wants farmers to raise all the crops they can for the war effort. It's going to take lots of food to feed the servicemen, so you need to get well and help me run the farm. There's no way we can do it without you."

"The way I feel, I'm no help to anybody," he often said.

"That's all the more reason for you to get well."

"I take all the pills the doctor has prescribed. That's all I can do," he said, turning his white, emaciated hands up in a gesture of helplessness.

In one of Ralph's infrequent letters, he wrote that he had been moved to Randolph Field, Texas, for basic training. After that, his letters conveyed much of the excitement and pride he felt in the progress he was making, and when he wrote that he had become a Flying Cadet, they were as excited as he was. They thought that surely he would be coming home on furlough soon, and they waited anxiously for a letter that would tell them when he was coming.

Finally two letters came from him on the same day. One was addressed to Marsha and Austin, and the other was addressed to Candy.

"I can't wait to read my letter," Candy cried, unconsciously holding the letter to her heart.

"I wonder if he's writing to tell us when he's coming home," Marsha said. "Let's go and tell Austin we have the letters and open them. Austin needs the lift that they will give him, and he'll really be pleased if Ralph is coming home."

Candy danced into Austin's room, holding the letters over her head, and Marsha followed.

"We have two letters from Ralph," she sang out.

"I've never known you to be that excited about letters," Austin commented.

"Daddy White, one of the letters is for you and Mama Marsha and the other one is for me."

"Are you going to read both of them to me and Marsha, or will you keep your letter to yourself?" Austin kidded.

"Of course I'll read both letters to you, Daddy

White, but I want to read mine to myself first," Candy responded.

"So you have to censor your letter before reading it to us," Marsha teased.

"I'm sure there's no big secrets in my letter," Candy bantered, "but, just the same, I want to read it first. I'll just take a peek now and see if he says anything about coming home. Then I'll read the other letter to you." She tore open her letter and took out several closely-written sheets of paper.

"I've never known Ralph to write such a long letter," Marsha commented.

"Me neither," Candy responded as she started scanning the pages. "He doesn't say anything about coming home in my letter. Mostly he's reminiscing about the past. I'll read it later." She returned the letter to the envelope and tucked it into the bosom of her blouse. She hoped they did not see how excited she was.

"If that's all he wrote about, open the other letter and read it," Marsha said.

Glad to divert attention from her letter, Candy opened their letter and started reading aloud:

Dear Mama Marsha and Daddy White:

> *This is the last letter I'll be writing from here, because I'll be shipping out tomorrow, destination unknown. I'll write again when I get to where they're sending me. Sorry they won't let me come home.*

"Oh, he's not coming home before they move him," Marsha exclaimed.

"I wonder why," Austin said. "Read the rest of the letter, Candy."

Candy had already scanned the letter. "The way he writes, I don't think he's coming home at all," she sobbed.

"How can that be?" Marsha cried.

Candy started reading aloud again:

> They're sending me somewhere to get my advanced training. It is rumored that they are sending us somewhere in Alabama.

> Daddy White, I hope you're much better by now. Each day, as I go out to train, I remind myself that I must do my best for you, and Mama Marsha, and Candy.

> I pray for all of you every night, and I want you all to pray for me.

> Love to all,

> Ralph

There were tears in Austin's eyes when Candy finished reading the letter. "I'm sorry he won't be coming home," he said brokenly.

"I worry about him. It seems to me that flying one of those fighter planes would be one of the most dangerous things he could possibly do," Marsha exclaimed.

"If I were a man, I'd do exactly what he's doing," Candy said.

"Candy, I couldn't bear it if you had to go off to war," Austin told her.

"Daddy White, I love you," Candy cried, and she bent over and kissed him on the cheek.

"When are you going to read your letter to us?" Marsha asked.

"Not until I've had time to read it alone, Mama Marsha. This is the longest letter Ralph has ever written to me, and I want to enjoy every line of it."

"I don't blame you, Candy. You can tell us what's

in it later," Austin said.

"Thank you, Daddy White," she said smiling. She was still smiling when she reached her room and closed the door and sat down to read her letter. It wasn't necessary to close the door, she knew, but she wanted to feel that she had shut the world out while she enjoyed her precious letter.

She already knew what the letter was about, but she wanted to read it slowly and savor every word. Then she would read it again and try to read between the lines. Surely Ralph must care for her a little, or he would not have written such a long letter, and he would not have recalled so many of the things they had shared.

That was exactly what he had done, she saw as she read his account of her rescuing him, of their running away from the Sanders, of their time in the cabin, and of the day they adopted each other. On and on she read, feeling that she was reliving those far-off, trying, yet happy days.

She had never realized the memory of those days meant so much to Ralph. Perhaps being separated from her had made him recall them. She hoped that this long letter was the first of many he would write to her.

She would write him a long letter tonight and mail it the minute he sent his new address. As in all her letters to him, she would not dare to tell him how much she loved him and how much she missed him, but she would try to write it between the lines. That would take some thought, but she would welcome the effort, and she would work on her letter to him as diligently as any author ever worked on a best-selling book.

She went through Ralph's letter a second time and underlined the things she wanted to read to Mama Marsha and Daddy White, though there wasn't much. The rest of the letter she would keep for herself, and, in days to come, she would read it again and again.

Ralph's next letter came from Craig Field, Alabama, where they had sent him to train on the P-47 Thunderbolt. After that he wrote more often, keeping them abreast of his progress. Sooner than they expected, he wrote that he had soloed in the Thunderbolt. He wrote:

> *I feel privileged to be flying one of these great planes, and I'm working hard to become the best fighter pilot I possibly can.*
>
> *I have more good news. I have been promoted to Lieutenant.*

Candy wrote a long letter from the family, congratulating him, and assuring him of their continued prayers. As in all their letters, she wrote that they could hardly wait for him to come home on leave.

Ralph continued to write almost every week, but he wrote little about coming home. That left them disappointed, for they could hardly wait for the day when he would come. Bill and Dora were as eager for his return as they were.

At last the day came when Ralph wrote to tell them that he had finished his training in the Thunderbolt, but he still would not be coming home. He wrote:

> *The war is so critical, we have to get men trained and sent to England in a hurry. I know I'll be going to England after I finish my training. I am not sure, but I think we will ship out from New York.*

For days Candy was distraught. But Marsha and Austin took the disappointment stoically, knowing that their disappointment was no greater than that of other fathers and mothers who had received the same kind of letters from their sons.

After many anxious days, they received a V-mail letter that Ralph had written from England. The crossing had been successful, he wrote. He was now taking the additional training that was required before he could start flying missions, guarding the big B-17 bombers on bombing runs over enemy occupied territory.

He wrote that he had met a pilot from West Virginia named David Bookman. They had a lot in common and had become good friends. David was interested in farming. He had had one year in college, studying agriculture, and he wanted to get a farm and raise cattle after the war.

"It's good to know that he has made a friend," Candy said when she finished reading the letter.

"Maybe they will look after each other," Marsha observed.

"Servicemen often form close bonds, and many of them become lifelong friends," Austin observed.

"Maybe since he has made friends with the Bookman boy, he won't be too lonely," Marsha said.

"David Bookman," Candy mused. "Ralph will probably be writing to us about him often. In time we'll feel like we know him."

"Ralph said he is from West Virginia. That's not far away. Perhaps Ralph and David can visit each other after the war is over," Marsha suggested.

"They may not both make it through the war," Candy said sadly.

"Candy! What a thing to say," Marsha scolded.

"Why did you say that, Candy?" Austin asked.

"I don't know. . . . It's a worry I sometimes have," Candy answered.

"Candy, for goodness sakes, don't ever mention that again," Marsha told her, half angrily.

"All right, Mama Marsha. In the future I'll keep my worries to myself."

Chapter 20

*O*n a late afternoon in June, Candy decided to walk to the river and see if that would lift her spirits. It was unusual for her to feel depressed, but all day she had had a feeling of impending disaster.

As she approached the river, she saw that it was high and muddy for the time of the year, and that it was racing wildly down the valley. She paused on the river bank and watched the turbulent water. Ever since the flood, she had not been able see high water without a feeling of anxiety. She reminded herself that the river would never reach Oakcrest, but that did not keep her from thinking about people who lived near the river.

She would never forget the flood that had taken her home and given her Ralph, but it seemed to her that a lifetime had passed since then. So much, so very much, had happened since the day she rescued Ralph from the river. From her earliest recollection, she had lived by the river. Often she had looked across it to the Ohio shore. She could cross the river on a bridge, but she had not crossed it many times. Always she had thought of it as a barrier that separated her from the people on the other side. She thought of the Atlantic Ocean. It was a much wider barrier, and it was now between her and Ralph, and there was no way she could cross to him.

It made her heart ache to think how many, how very many miles separated them. Besides the distance and the ocean, the war separated them. Ralph could not come to her, even if he chose to do so, and she could not go to him. Even if she should cross the ocean on a ship or a plane, it was not likely that she could find him.

He was probably lonely, even as she was, though he had made friends. What was the name of the man he had written about? She puckered her brow, trying to remember.

"Oh, oh . . . it was the fighter pilot from West Virginia . . . David Bookman," she finally said aloud.

She was glad that Ralph had made such a friend. That must help him bear the lonely hours when he was not flying.

Men were fighting over there . . . across that big ocean, and Ralph was among them, flying his big, roaring Thunderbolt, and facing death on every mission. *Where was he now?* she wondered. *He could be dead for all she knew.*

It had been a year and a half since he had enlisted. So much had happened since then; it seemed like a decade had passed. Ralph had been so busy, it probably did not seem that long to him. The passing weeks must have seemed like days to him, but to her they had been like years.

From the letters he had written, she had marked on the calendar the milestones of his career. She had marked the day he finished ground school and started flight training. She had marked the day he soloed and the day when he was promoted to Lieutenant. Another day she had marked was the day he moved to Craig Field, Alabama. She had marked the day he soloed in the Thunderbolt and the day he shipped out for England.

She was proud of him, but her fear blunted her

pride. After he had gone to England, his letters home had become even more infrequent. Now, when he did write home, wartime censoring kept him from telling where he was and what he was doing.

Not long after Ralph had gone to England, Daddy White's condition had worsened, and he had quietly died one night in his sleep. Ralph had not been able to attend the funeral.

The day of the funeral, she had sat beside Mama Marsha, weeping quietly. Mama Marsha had wept until she could weep no more, and she had thought what a comfort Ralph would have been to her if he could have been there.

After they had buried Daddy White beneath the big maple trees in the Maysville Cemetery, she and Mama Marsha had returned to Oakcrest to comfort each other, and to try, with Bill's help, to run the farm.

With a shrug she turned her mind to the future. She would graduate from high school next year. After that, she would like to take nurses' training and go into the nurses' corps, but she knew she could not. There was no way she could leave Mama Marsha. Since Daddy White had died, Marsha was broken with sorrow, and she was aging beyond reason. Perhaps, instead of the nurses' corps, she should prepare to be a teacher and get a job teaching in the county.

Crows were cawing in the distance, and she turned and saw them flying against the reddening clouds in the west. The sun's rays were filtering through an opening in the clouds. The brightness hurt her eyes, so she turned away and looked back at the big house with the aged, knurled and broken oak trees around it. The big western windows were ablaze with red and gold and amber, but the rest of the house lay in shadows.

The old house was weathered with age, and it had a lonely, almost forboding appearance. It was as lonely as it looked, she thought, especially since Dora had gone to live with her ailing mother. That had left her and Mama Marsha alone in the big house, biding their time until the war was over and Ralph could come home. If Ralph did not return, the house would remain a lonely old house, with two lonely women living in it. If she outlived Mama Marsha, as she likely would, she would live on there alone and grow old there, more lonely than ever.

"Stop it," she cried aloud, stamping her foot in frustration. "The war will end one day, and Ralph will come home. He has to! And when he does, there will be joy and laughter at Oakcrest again."

Her mind went back to that special day when she and Ralph had ridden their ponies to the spring. They had ridden to the spring many times, but she always thought of that special day. When she spoke of it to herself, as she often did, she always called it, "That day."

"That day" was the day he had said, "If you weren't my sister, I'd want you to be my sweetheart." He had never known, nor would she ever tell him—or any one else—the ecstasy and the agony that statement had caused her. And that day he had kissed her. That kiss she would never forget.

Before that day, she had only thought of Ralph as her beloved brother, but that day she had awakened to the realization that she loved him. That had made her wish she had never made those vows of sisterhood. If she had not, she would have felt free to love him in the way a budding young woman loves the young man of her choice.

Long ago it had dawned on her that, despite those vows, and despite their being adopted into the White family, she and Ralph were not related by blood. So there was no reason why they should not love each other. From that moment her love for him had grown beyond all bounds. After the war had taken him away, she had often told herself that when the war was over, he would come home, and surely he would realize how much she loved him. After that, the only sensible thing for him to do would be to declare his love for her. When she thought like that, it made her fear even more for his safety.

Usually in the daylight hours, she managed to maintain the hope that Ralph would come safely through the war and return to Oakcrest. But she spent her nights worrying, sleeping fitfully, and having bad dreams.

Often in her dreams, she saw Ralph thundering across the sky in his fighter plane, in dogfights with German fighter planes. More than once she dreamed of seeing him shot down, and the vision of his burning plane, spiraling toward the ground, always awakened her. Frightened and trembling, she always prayed for Ralph until she fell asleep again.

She traced a square in the sand with the toe of her slipper. Then she stooped and picked up a stick and started printing with it inside the square. Scarcely realizing what she was doing, she traced the letters of Ralph's name and printed beneath them, "I love you."

She arose and looked at her handiwork. Some animal would soon trample the letters she had printed and obliterate them, or high water would wash them away, but that would not change her feeling for Ralph.

"I'll always love him, and I'll wait for him until he comes home," she said aloud as she turned to go back to Oakcrest where Mama Marsha was waiting for her.

As she climbed the hill, her mind went back to the tragic day Daddy White had died. His passing and the funeral had been like a bad dream. She had come to love Daddy White almost as much as she had loved her own daddy, and his death had hurt her deeply.

She recalled the day of his heart attack. He had

been so warm and affectionate that morning, as he was leaving to go to the courthouse. He had kissed Marsha good-bye, given Ralph an affectionate slap on the back, had hugged her, called her "blue eyes," and kissed her on her cheek. Then he had gone out and climbed into his aging coupe and driven away.

Word of Daddy White's heart attack had come with the suddenness of an earthquake, and the days after that had been the most trying days she had ever lived through. She could never forget his fight for life and how they had stood by him and prayed for him until the end.

After he was gone, she and Mama Marsha had grown closer. They had both loved Daddy White, and they both loved Ralph. Now they were alone, clinging to the hope that Ralph would come back to Oakcrest when the war was over.

Halfway up the hill she paused to rest and turned back toward the river. The sun was going down, and the shadows were falling on the river. Soon the twilight would settle, and the frogs would start croaking. The birds Ralph called Bullbats would start flying high overhead and calling with their strange, throaty calls. Night-flying insects would start flying, and eerie bats would dance in the night sky. She shivered, trying to banish her thought of the bats. She loathed and feared bats, though she did not know why. In the western sky there was now a lone crow, a speck of black against a distant orange cloud. She wondered where the rest of them had gone.

She turned back toward the house as the last of the sun's light was fading from the windows. She should hurry. There were chores to be done and supper to be prepared. Now that Dora was gone, she and Mama Marsha would have to do it all.

As she continued up the hill, the setting sun cast her shadow before her. She watched the shadow moving ahead of her, and she hoped that a shadow would not move with her for the rest of her life. She wished she could walk away and leave the shadow . . . and the sadness that so often had settled upon her since Ralph had gone away and Daddy White had died.

After supper tonight, she would write to Ralph, she decided. Perhaps writing to him would make her feel better. Tomorrow she would mail the letter, and she would pray that it would reach him.

Mama Marsha came out on the front porch and stood shading her eyes with her hands against the last rays of the sun. Mama Marsha was looking to see if she was coming.

"Candy, I was worried about you," she called when she saw her.

"I'll be there in a minute, Mama Marsha," she called back.

She soon reached the porch where Marsha was waiting, and the two lonely women went in the old house and turned on the lights to drive back the darkness of the coming night.

Chapter 21

*T*he next morning Candy watched for the mail-man, as she did every morning. At last she saw him coming along the road and stopping to leave mail at almost every box. "The mailman is going to stop at our box, Mama Marsha," she called when she saw him slowing for the stop. "I'll run and see if he brought a letter from Ralph."

"Please hurry, Candy," Marsha returned, but Candy had already left the house.

Candy crossed the yard, let herself through the gate, and started running wildly down the hill. She waved to the mailman as he was pulling away, and hurried breathlessly on.

"He's written to us at last," she breathed when she opened the box and saw the V-mail letter the mailman had left. She got the letter from the box and started hurrying back up the hill.

"What did we get in the mail?" Marsha asked from the front porch as Candy approached the yard gate, puffing for breath.

"A—a—let—ter from Ralph. It's—ad—dressed to me!" She held it up and waved it over her head.

"Candy, I've never seen you so excited over a let-ter," Marsha said almost reproachfully.

"Ralph has finally written to me again," she sang out as they went in the house together.

"I'm glad he finally wrote. At least we know he was safe when he wrote the letter," Marsha said.

Still panting for breath, Candy opened the letter.

"Oh no!" she cried, as she started reading.

"Candy, you're as pale as a ghost. Is Ralph all right?" Marsha demanded.

"Oh no!" Candy cried again, and her hand went to her heart.

"Candy, what is it?" Marsha cried. "You're shaking like a leaf." When Candy did not answer, she went to her and walked her to the nearest chair and pushed her into it.

"Now let me see that letter. I have to know what's wrong." She reached for the letter, but Candy held it away.

"Ralph has fallen in love with an English girl, and they're going to get married," she wailed.

"Candy, that should not be a surprise to you. Lots of young servicemen are getting married. I do wish though that he had waited until he was older," she finished to herself in an undertone.

Candy made no reply, but sat staring at the wall.

"Candy, didn't you hear me? I declare, I think you must be in love with Ralph."

Candy turned wide eyes upon Marsha and looked at her for a long minute before she answered. "It's such a surprise that he's going to get married," she finally managed. "He has never even hinted that he had a girlfriend."

"If you are in love with him, his letter must be a shock to you."

"It's a shock, regardless of how I feel," Candy said.

"Candy, aren't you going to read the rest of Ralph's letter?"

"I'll read it later, Mama Marsha. You go ahead and read it." She held the letter out to her.

"This is the only time you have let me read one of

your letters first," Marsha said, still trying to read Candy's face. Marsha took the letter and read it through. "The girl's name is Bridgette. That's a typical English name," she mused when she finished.

"I suppose she would have an English sounding name."

"Ralph said that she's a good girl, but one can never know. A man in love can overlook a lot of faults."

"I hope she's good enough for him, and I hope he'll be happy," Candy said in a controlled voice. Then she arose and made herself busy with work that did not need doing.

Marsha watched her and shook her head knowingly.

When Candy could find no more work to do in the house, she went outside and left the door standing ajar.

"Where are you going, Candy?" Marsha called after her.

"Out to the barn," she called over her shoulder.

"Surely there's no work out there that needs doing," Marsha called back, walking to the door to watch her go.

"I think I'll go riding if I can talk Bill into bringing Happiness in from the pasture."

"I think the ride will do you good," Marsha called.

"I won't be gone long."

"Take your time. There's nothing more that needs doing in the house."

Twenty minutes later, Candy rode Happiness up the hill back of the house, along the way she and Ralph had ridden so often. At the end of the ridge she stopped the pony and looked down at the river as they had always done. The sun was bright on the muddy river. She saw that it was still flowing rapidly, as if it were in a hurry to reach its destination.

Willow and scrub bushes crowded its shores. Small birds were twittering and darting among the willows. A red-winged blackbird perched precariously on the slender shaft of some unknown shrub, but she hardly saw it.

She looked up the river and it appeared deserted. No barge was plying its waters; not even a small boat was in sight. Without thought she picked up the bridle reins she had let fall on the saddle horn and turned Happiness away from the river, then let her find her own way. From habit the pony followed the path that led to the spring.

Candy rode with bowed head, hardly aware of where she was going. There was no recognition of the familiar pathway and no notice of the wildflowers in the meadow.

A young groundhog popped from his den under a stump near the path and stood on his rear feet. He whistled shrilly as she passed, then dropped back into his den. She took no notice of him, for she was thinking about Ralph and his English girlfriend.

When the pony reached the spring, she stopped as she always had, but Candy did not dismount and go in the spring house for water. A large, green bullfrog jumped from the grass nearby and landed in the stream that flowed from the spring. Startled, she looked up as if coming from a dream.

"You lucky frog," she said aloud. "You don't have to worry about the war and English girlfriends. On second thought, though, I suppose you do have to worry about being swallowed by a big snake."

Happiness munched at the rank grass beside the stream and nodded her head up and down. Then she stepped into the stream and drank deeply of the clear, cold water.

"I hope you enjoyed your drink, Happiness," she said.

"Happiness," she said derisively. "I think I'll change her name. I have finally ridden her without being happy, and I doubt that riding her will ever make me happy again."

The pony stepped back from the stream and waited for Candy to dismount.

"I'm not going to get off today, Happiness," she said to the pony. "It's not worth the trouble to get water and drink it alone."

Her mind went back to that day when Ralph had wished she was not his sister so he could claim her for his sweetheart. She had never ceased to love him since that day, and, no matter what happened, she never would stop loving him.

Now she knew that Ralph would never come back to Oakcrest to live, and she could not imagine how she could go on living without him. Perhaps he would come home to visit after the war, and he would bring his English wife with him. If that happened, she never wanted her to even guess how she felt about Ralph. Certainly she never wanted Ralph to know.

It could be years before he came home, and by that time he and his English wife would most likely have children. Maybe there would be a little boy, and she would hold him and look at him and try to find some resemblance of Ralph in him. Perhaps she would come to love the little boy, and her love for him would ease the ache in her heart.

After a visit at Oakcrest, Ralph would undoubtedly go away and make a home for his family. Then Oakcrest would be more lonely than ever.

"Stop it," she scolded. "Ralph is not even married, and I have him coming home with a family."

The pony shifted on her feet, not understanding this sudden outburst from Candy.

"Oh, come on, Happiness, let's go," she said to the pony, and she picked up the bridle reins and turned her about and started home. When Candy reached the barn, Bill was still there, repairing a piece of farm machinery.

"Bill, Ralph used to take care of Happiness for me, but he's . . ."

"I know. He's not here any more," Bill interrupted. "Get off, and I'll take care of the pony."

"I'd appreciate that, Bill." She slid off the pony and stood for a moment petting her neck.

"I couldn't do it for a better young lady," Bill said.

"Thank you, Bill. I'm going to the house. Mama Marsha may need me."

Marsha was standing in the back door as Candy approached the house. "How was your ride?" she asked.

"So, so. It's not much fun riding alone."

"I know. Nothing seems the same to me since Austin is gone."

"I miss Daddy White and Ralph too. The house seems so lonely without them."

"We'd better write to Ralph tonight, so we can mail the letter tomorrow," Marsha suggested.

"Yes, I know. You can write him a nice motherly letter, and I'll write him a nice sisterly letter."

"Candy! I've never known you to have such an attitude!"

"Well, to tell the truth, I'm not all that happy about Ralph getting married."

Marsha looked at her and shook her head.

"I guess I shouldn't mind," Candy said, "but I didn't have anybody until I found Ralph. Since then we've been closer than most bothers and sisters."

"He's still your brother, Candy, and in time you'll come to love his wife as a sister."

"Maybe I will, but it's hard to get used to the idea of him getting married when we didn't even know he had a girlfriend."

"We should write some message for Ralph to give Bridgette. . . . tell her that we wish them happiness."

"And I suppose I'll have to tell her that I'm just bursting with happiness because my brother is marrying somebody I've never heard of."

"Candy! I can't believe you. I hope you don't let Ralph know that you have a chip on your shoulder because he is getting married."

"Of course I won't, and don't you ever hint to him or to anyone else how I feel." She pushed passed Marsha and went into the house and ran up to her room.

Chapter 22

*T*he next day Marsha and Candy mailed the letters they had written to Ralph. They thought that surely he would answer promptly, but when anxious days had passed and he had not written, they began to fear that something had happened to him.

His plane could have been shot down, and he could be dead for all they knew. On the other hand, perhaps he was so preoccupied with his new girlfriend and the upcoming wedding that he had not taken time to write. With courting his bride-to-be and flying missions to guard the big B-17 bombers on bombing raids, he had to be busy. Surely Bridgette would have notified them if anything had happened to him.

They finally concluded that he just had not taken time to write. Ralph never had been one to write letters, but that did not keep them from feeling neglected. Marsha phoned Dora and told her that Ralph was going to get married. In her straightforward way, Dora had asked if he was writing home any more than he used to, and Marsha told her that they had not heard from him for more than three weeks.

"It does look like that boy would write home more than he does," Dora said. "After all, you all are the only family he's got."

Bill showed his concern in a different way. Almost every day when he limped in from the barn with the milk or the eggs, he would remark, "I sure do miss Ralph helpin' me with the work. Heard from him lately?" When they told him they had not, he would silently leave the house and walk back to the barn with his head bowed and his shoulders stooped, dragging his bad leg.

"Bill and Dora both mean to be kind," Marsha said.

"I know, but I wish Bill would stop asking about Ralph every day. It upsets me when he does," Candy complained.

"I suppose Ralph is just too busy to write," Marsha said for the twentieth time.

"It wouldn't take him that long to write a letter," Candy said bitterly.

"I suppose you're right," Marsha agreed, looking at her askance.

After another two weeks, a V-mail letter addressed to both of them finally arrived. Candy got it from the box and looked at it quizzically. The address looked like a woman's handwriting. With her heart filled with foreboding, she hurried to the house.

"We have a letter from Bridgette, I think," she announced, putting up a bold front, when she entered. "The address looks like a woman's handwriting."

"I hope nothing has happened to Ralph," Marsha gasped. "Candy, open the letter and see."

"I was afraid to open it while I was alone," Candy exclaimed, as with trembling fingers she tore open the envelope. A picture slipped from the letter and fell to the floor. Instantly she picked it up and saw that it was a picture of Ralph and a pretty, fair-haired girl.

"It's Ralph and a girl, but surely this is not a picture of Bridgette. This girl doesen't look a day over fifteen," Candy exclaimed, handing the picture to Marsha.

"Read the letter and see if Ralph is all right," Marsha demanded, barely looking at the picture.

"Ralph is all right," Candy said when she had read halfway down the page.

"Let me see the letter, Candy, if you're not going to read it," Marsha insisted.

"Here!" Candy handed her the letter. "Sit down and read it, and I'll look over your shoulder."

Marsha sank to a chair and Candy leaned over her shoulder and they read together.

> *Dear Mama Marsha and Candy:*
>
> *I've been waiting for Ralph to write to you, but he goes to the base every morning while it is yet dark, and he doesn't come home until late at night. He finally asked me to write to you.*
>
> *We were married a fortnight ago, when he had a three day pass. We wanted to go to London for an overnight honeymoon, but because of the danger from bombing there, we went to a small village near the base.*
>
> *We love each other dearly, and we are very happy, though I worry about him when he is flying. He worries about me too, and has made me promise to go to the shelter every time there is an air raid warning.*
>
> *All the members of my family were killed by a bomb last year, so I have no one but Ralph. He has told me so much about you I feel that I know you, and I think of you as my family. Mama Marsha, I think of you as my mother, and, Candy, I think of you as my sister.*
>
> *I know I'm going to love you, and I can't*

*wait to see you. I pray that the war will soon
be over so Ralph and I can come to America.*

Love, Bridgette

There were tears in Marsha's eyes when she finished reading the letter. "She writes like a sweet, sensible girl," she remarked huskily.

"Girl is right. She's too young to be married to Ralph or to anyone else."

"Like it or not, that young girl is married to Ralph."

"Well, I don't like it. Ever since I rescued Ralph from his floating house, I've been afraid somebody would separate us, and that has done it," Candy said bitterly.

"Candy, you have no reason to feel that way. Ralph is still your brother, and he'll come home when the war is over."

"If he lives that long he may, but even if he does, it won't be the same. He'll have a wife."

"And you'll have a husband some day. . . . I hope."

"I don't want a husband, and I never expect to have one."

"Some day you may change your mind, Candy. You have plenty of time, you know. You still have another year of high school."

"After I graduate, I'm not going to marry. I'll take a job if I can find one close to home, and I'll go on living here with you."

"I'm glad you want to live with me, Candy. I hope you'll always feel that way. Even if you decide to marry someday, I hope you and your husband will live at Oakcrest. We could build you a house here on the farm, you know."

"I don't want to think about ever marrying," Candy sobbed, and she ran from the room and up the stairs to her room. There she closed the door and fell across her bed and wept until she had no more tears. Finally, she fell asleep and dreamed of Ralph and his new bride. She awoke somewhat composed and went downstairs to find Marsha.

Marsha was standing by the front window, looking out toward the road. She turned when she heard Candy's footsteps. "Are you all right, Candy?" she asked.

"I feel better. Where's that letter? I want to see the picture of Ralph's child-bride again."

"Candy, give her a chance. She may be older than you think."

"I'm sure she'll grow up in time, but I still want to see her picture. Maybe a close look at her face will help me decide if she's good enough for Ralph."

"I'm sure Ralph has already made that decision."

"I'm not sure I can trust his judgment."

"After all he's the one who has to live with her."

"I'm sorry, Mama Marsha. It's just that I feel lousy. Maybe I'd feel better about Ralph marrying her if I could meet Bridgette."

"In war times things don't work that way, Candy. After the war, if they both live through it, I'm sure Ralph will bring her home and you'll meet her."

"I want to get to know her before that. . . . maybe by correspondence. I'll write her a letter tomorrow," Candy said contritely.

The next day Candy got a letter from Ralph, but she did not take it to the house right away, for she did not trust herself to read it in Marsha's presence. Instead she walked to the river and sat down under a large sycamore tree. With her back propped against its trunk, she opened the letter.

The short letter was written on a single page. In it Ralph told her that he had decided to write her after Bridgette had mailed her letter. He had felt so alone until he met her. They were very happy together, and he could not wait until the war was over so he could bring her home to meet her and Mama Marsha.

She let the letter fall to her lap, and looked away to the hills beyond the river. She sat for a long time thinking. She thought of girls who had written "Dear John" letters to boys overseas, and she wondered how they could so easily break the promises they had made. Didn't they know that the shock and disappointment of such a letter could cause a serviceman to do something foolish that could cost him his life.

She would never have written such a letter, but she had received one. She had never dared to tell Ralph that she loved him, but she had hoped he would realize that she did, and that one day he would write and tell her that he loved her. But such a letter had never come. Instead, he had broken her heart by falling in love with another girl.

After awhile, she arose and walked to the river's edge. She stood for a long time listening to the water lapping on the shore and watching it move busily down the valley.

"I am just a silly girl," she stormed at last, with a stamp of her foot. "He never told me he loved me, and I had no reason to believe that he would wait for me."

The few letters he had written to her since he had gone into the air corps had been the kind of letters a brother would write to a sister. It was only her blind love for him that had made her expect him to love her. She had no right to be upset because he had written to share the news of his marriage with her.

It was not surprising that he and Bridgette had fallen in love. He was away from home and lonely, and he had made no promises to her or any other girl back home.

Bridgette was without a family, and no doubt she had been lonely also. It was natural that two people like them would fall in love. Ralph had said in his letter that he had felt so alone until he met her.

"You were not alone, Ralph," she said bitterly. "My love and my heart were with you all the time, but, like any stupid man with no . . . no . . . intuition, you didn't realize how I loved you. I still do," she sobbed.

"This is one letter I'll not share with Mama Marsha," she finally said to herself, and with a heavy heart she stuffed it in the bosom of her blouse and started back to the house.

Chapter 23

Candy graduated with honors from Maysville High School the next May. Bill rode in the car with her and Mama Marsha to attend the graduation ceremonies at the school, and Dora got someone to care for her mother so she could attend. She had phoned that she would meet them at the school, and that she would go home with them and spend the night. Her sister would come for her the next day.

"Daddy White would have been so proud of you, Candy," Marsha said that night on their way home in the car.

"I wish he could have been there tonight. I probably would never have graduated if it hadn't been for him—and for you."

"How do you know he wasn't there? Sometimes, when I'm alone, I feel like he's right beside me."

"Sometimes I feel the same way. Anyway, I'm glad you were there. I'm glad you were too, Bill and Dora," she ended, turning and facing them in the backseat.

"Miss Candy, I wouldn't have missed it for the world," Bill said.

"Me neither," Dora echoed.

The following Monday, a letter came from Ralph, addressed to both Candy and Marsha.

"We have a letter from Ralph," Candy announced when she returned from the mailbox.

"It's about time we heard from him and Bridgette, but she is the one who usually writes."

"I know, but Ralph wrote this time."

"I hope there's nothing wrong with her."

Candy tore open the letter and started reading.

"Oh!" she cried. "That's something."

"What's something?"

"Bridgette is pregnant!"

"Candy, I can't believe it. When are they expecting?"

"Just a minute." She scanned down the page before looking up. "The day before Ralph wrote this letter, a doctor confirmed that she is to be a mother, and Ralph wants to send her to Oakcrest."

"Why would he want to do that? You would think they'd want to be together when the baby comes."

"Ralph says she's awfully nervous. He wants to get her away from England so she won't hear planes flying over day and night, with air raid sirens going off and bombs falling."

"I imagine that seeing him go off to fly on those dreadful missions must be upsetting to her also. I wonder if he'll have trouble getting her to America?"

Candy looked at the letter again and traced the lines with her finger as she read. "He says it can be arranged for her to come. He can even get her a ride to America in one of our planes, and she can ride the train home from wherever it lands."

"Of course we want her to come. It will be exciting to have her here, and I think I'll die waiting for the baby to come," Marsha said.

Candy was so upset, she could hear her heart pounding in her ears. She did not want Bridgette to come to Oakcrest, but she knew that she did not have the right to refuse her. She had never allowed herself to hate Bridgette, but she had not been able to make herself like her either. She was not sure how she would cope with living in the house with her.

"Candy, why are you so quiet?" Marsha asked. "Don't you think it will be exciting to have a baby in the house?"

"Oh, yes. . . . sure. I was just thinking that I really won't be satisfied until Ralph comes home."

"We'll write and tell him to send Bridgette by all means," Marsha mused. "And we'll tell her how excited we are that she's coming."

"You should write the letter, Mama Marsha. Bridgette should have the word from you that she is welcome," Candy said.

"I suppose you're right. I'll write to her tonight, and we'll mail the letter in the morning."

"I have a headache, so I'm going up to my room," Candy said as she laid the letter on the table.

Marsha listened to Candy's footsteps until she reached her room. Then, with a puzzled frown, she went to the kitchen to start preparing lunch.

Candy stayed in her room for a long while, thinking. She thought of how alone she had felt after her mother had died. She had been even more lonely after the death of her father, but from the day she had found Ralph the loneliness had gone out of her heart. Perhaps that was why she had been so afraid of being separated from him.

After Ralph had gone overseas, and Daddy White had died, and Dora had gone to care for her mother, she had been lonely again, but Mama Marsha and Bill had made the loneliness bearable.

Soon Bridgette would be coming to live with them, and she could not imagine how her presence would affect her. Perhaps she would help to fill the void that the absence of Ralph had left in her heart. When the baby came, how would that affect them all? Certainly it would keep them busy, and perhaps it would bind them all together.

226

Finally, she fell across her bed and went to sleep. She had never been one to sleep in the daytime, but she did not awaken even when Marsha came to call her to lunch. Marsha had looked in on her, then had gone quietly back downstairs.

Two weeks later a letter came from Bridgette. She wrote that she was dying at the thought of leaving Ralph. She was afraid that she would never see him again, but he insisted that she come to the States anyway. It would be best for her and for the baby.

She appreciated their inviting her to come to Oakcrest, and she would come the minute arrangements could be made. Ralph was going to get her on the first Army Air Corps plane he could find coming to the States that had room for her. No matter where it landed, she would catch a train from there to Maysville. She would phone when she reached the States.

"We'll have to get ready for her," Marsha commented when they finished reading the letter. "I'll get Bill to help us rearrange Ralph's room for her."

"Bridgette can't take Ralph's place, even if she does sleep in his room," Candy said caustically.

"I think I'll like having her here. It will be like having a link to Ralph, and surely he'll write more often after she comes."

Candy did not reply, but it made her heart ache to think how seldom Ralph had written to her, even before he met Bridgette.

Bridgette arrived in America on a rainy May afternoon, tired but thankful that the plane had landed in Lexington to let her off. Lexington was less than two hours by car from Maysville, the navigator told her.

She thanked the crew, got off the plane, and found her way to a pay phone. Nervously she inserted the quarter Ralph had told her to use in the slot and dialed the number he had given her.

Marsha answered the phone and was excited to hear a young female voice, with a decided English accent, respond, "Hello. Are you there?"

"Yes, I'm here, and you have to be Bridgette."

"Yes, I'm Bridgette. The plane that brought me over just let me off in Lexington."

"In Lexington? Lexington, Kentucky?"

"Yes, in Kentucky."

"How wonderful! I'm glad they brought you that close to us. We had no idea where you would be landing."

"I didn't know either until the navigator told me on the way over. He said that Lexington is quite near Maysville."

"Yes it is. We'll come in the car and get you. Is there any place where you can wait? I'm sure they haven't finished construction on the airport. The war, you know . . . Besides it's not an air base."

"I'm near the flying service office. I'm sure I can wait there."

"Would you rather catch a taxi into town?"

"I think not. I wouldn't know my way around."

"Then we'll pick you up at the airport in about two hours."

"Thank you. I'll be waiting."

"We'll hurry. Good-bye."

"Good-bye."

"Candy, Candy, where are you?" Marsha called excitedly when she hung up the phone.

"I'm up here," Candy called back, coming from her room to the head of the stairs.

"Candy, you'll never guess what. Bridgette is in Lexington. . . . at the airport. We have to hurry and go after her."

"How on earth did she get to Lexington?" Candy

asked, starting down the stairs two at a time.

"She said the army plane that brought her from England was passing near Lexington, so they let her off there."

"I'll hurry and dress," Candy answered, and she started running back up the stairs.

It was still raining when Marsha parked the car in front of the flying service office at the airport.

Candy looked out through the rain-streaked windshield and saw a wisp of a girl standing just outside the door under an awning. She was thinly clad in a pale green dress, and she appeared to be shivering, though the temperature was not that cool.

That can't be Ralph's wife, she thought. *She looks more like a young girl than a woman who is going to have a baby.*

The girl turned toward them, and Candy recognized her from the pictures she and Ralph and sent.

"That has to be her," Marsha exclaimed, as she got out of the car and opened her umbrella.

"That's her all right, but she doesn't look big enough or old enough to have a baby," Candy remarked as she joined Marsha under the umbrella.

"Hello," the girl called when she saw them coming toward her. "Are you Mama Marsha and Candy?"

"Yes we are," Marsha returned.

"Oh, I'm glad you're here. I've been dying to see you." She started running to meet them in the rain. She had no umbrella, but she was carrying a small suitcase.

When she reached them, she looked first at Marsha, then at Candy with large, pale-blue eyes that dwarfed the other features of her small, pale face.

Candy felt Bridgette's eyes searching her face, and it pricked her conscious that she had not spoken to her.

"Here, get under the umbrella with Mama Marsha, and give me your case. I'll put it in the car for you," she said, anxious to make amends.

Still looking at her, Bridgette surrendered the case.

Wordless, Candy took it and ran to the car and put it in the floor in the back.

"We're glad you've come, Bridgette," Marsha said, and she put her arm around the girl's shoulders and led her to the car.

"You get in front with Mama Marsha, and I'll ride in the back," Candy said as she opened the door for Bridgette.

"If you don't mind, I'd rather ride in the back. I'm tired, you know, and I can rest better back there."

"Of course," Candy said, and she opened the back door for Bridgette.

"Have you had lunch?" Marsha asked as she started the car.

"Only a wee bit of a sandwich on the way over, but I don't want to make trouble."

"Nonsense. You must be starved. We'll stop so you can get another sandwich, at least. We'll have a good dinner after we get home, but in this rain it will take us longer than usual to get there."

They stopped in Lexington at a small restaurant on Broadway and ordered sandwiches. Marsha ordered coffee to drink. Candy ordered a coke, and Bridgette ordered hot tea.

"Most everyone in England drinks tea," she explained.

"So I've heard. Feel free to drink what you like," Marsha told her.

Bridgette said little while they waited for the food, but her big eyes continued to search the faces of both Marsha and Candy.

Realizing that she must be tired, Marsha and Candy said little either.

When the waitress brought their orders, Bridgette started eating at once.

"This has been the longest day I've ever experienced. It seems like a week since I kissed Ralph good-bye at the airfield this morning," Bridgette said as she finished eating.

"I had almost forgotten the difference in time between England and the United States," Candy said.

"You were following the sun. That made the day longer," Marsha said. "No wonder you were hungry. It must have been hours since you had breakfast."

"There wasn't time for breakfast. I just ate a wee bit of some pastries and had tea before we left for the airfield."

"This must have been a dreadful day for you," Candy said, realizing that her heart was going out to Bridgette.

"I have to eat for two, you know," Bridgette returned, smiling faintly. Then she finished the last of her tea.

"Do you want something more?" Marsha asked.

"I'll wait. You said we would have dinner later."

"We'll have to cook dinner after we get home," Candy told her.

"We had better be going. I'm sure Bridgette will want to rest before dinner," Marsha said as she arose from the table.

"Does it rain a lot in America?" Bridgette asked when they were back in the car and on their way to Oakcrest.

"Not really. At this time of the year, we usually have beautiful weather," Candy replied, turning to look over the seat back at Bridgette.

"Ralph told me that you have good weather except in the winter. He really got tired of the fog in England. We have a lot of it, you know."

She is always talking about Ralph, Candy thought.

*She must really love him. One thing is certain, she will
never know that I love him.*

Huddled in the backseat of the big car, Bridgette
looked even more frail than she had at the airport. Her
face was pale and her eyelids appeared almost trans-
parent. *She would be pretty if her face was not so thin,*
Candy thought. *Her eyes were large and bright with
intelligence, and her red lips seemed always on the
verge of a half smile.*

Candy found herself feeling sorry for Bridgette,
because she was alone, far from home, without friends
or family, in what was a strange, foreign land to her.
I'll be kind to her for Ralph's sake, she decided.

Bridgette said nothing more, and soon she laid her
head on the back of the seat and closed her eyes. Candy
righted herself in her seat, pointed over her shoulder,
and told Marsha with soundless lips that Bridgette was
asleep.

In lip language Marsha said that she must be tired.
They remained silent the rest of the way home for fear
of disturbing her.

Bridgette did not awaken until Marsha turned on
the drive at Oakcrest.

"Oh, I'm sorry I fell asleep," she said, sitting up.
"Where are we?"

"We're almost home," Marsha responded.

Bridgette looked out through the rain-streaked
window and saw the big house on the hill with the
large old oak trees around it. "Now I know why you
call this place Oakcrest," she exclaimed in the most
animated utterance that had escaped her lips since she
had landed in America.

"Welcome home, daughter!" Marsha called back
to her.

"Oh, oh! Will you let me call you Mother?"

"I would prefer for you to call me Mama Marsha.
That's what Candy and Ralph call me."

"I will. I'll like calling you that. And what am I to call you?" she asked, turning her remarkable eyes on Candy.

"Call me Candy, of course, and I'll call you Bridgette. After all we are sisters-in-law."

"Oh yes, Candy. I'll like that."

The car reached the top of the hill, and Marsha stopped before the yard gate.

Candy bounded out with Marsha's umbrella. She raised the umbrella and pulled the back door open for Bridgette. "Hand out your case, and I'll carry it for you," she offered.

"Thank you, I can manage, but I will share the umbrella," Bridgette said as she retrieved her case and got out of the car.

"Walk her to the house, Candy, and I'll be right behind you," Marsha said.

"I do wish the rain would stop," Candy said as they entered the front gate and started up the walk.

"Bridgette, I hope you'll feel at home with us," Marsha said as they went in the house.

Bridgette paused inside the door, still holding her case, and her eyes roamed around the entrance hall and paused on the crystal chandelier that hung above the stairway. Then they followed the stairs step by step and paused again at the landing as if she were wondering what was beyond her line of vision.

"There are many big houses in England, but I only lived in an apartment," she mused as if talking to herself.

"I take it that you were not from a large family," Candy said, to make conversation.

"Oh no. There were just four of us—Mamma, Papa, my baby sister, and me. After the others were killed by a bomb, there was only me."

"Who lives in your apartment, now that you have come to live with us?" Marsha asked as she closed her umbrella and put in the stand.

"There is no apartment now. The bomb destroyed it. Ralph and I lived in a tiny place near the base."

"I know how you must feel. I lost my house in a flood," Candy exclaimed.

"Come, Bridgette, there's no reason for us to stand here by the door. Candy will show you to your room. After you have refreshed yourself, perhaps you would like to see the rest of the house."

"I would like that very much," the girl murmured, looking at Candy and waiting for her to lead the way.

"If you fall asleep, we'll call you when dinner is ready," Marsha called after Bridgette as Candy led her upstairs.

"Thank you," Bridgette called back.

"This used to be Ralph's room, but we worked it over for you," Candy said as she ushered Bridgette into the room.

"Ralph's room," she mused, turning slowly around, still holding her case. "It looks clean . . . and nice . . . and . . . lonely," she finished lamely.

"I hope you won't feel too lonely. Mama Marsha and I will be in the house. My room is across the hall, and her's is at the end of the hall."

"I'm sorry. It's just that I was so alone after my parents were killed. That is until I met Ralph. Now he won't be with me."

"I know you'll miss him. We miss him too, so I guess we'll all be lonely together."

"Thank you for understanding," Bridgette said with tears in her eyes.

Chapter 24

*I*t did not take long for Marsha and Candy to realize that Bridgette was in poor health. Each morning she awoke with a sick stomach and a headache. She seldom ate breakfast, and when she did she soon lost what she had eaten. By midmorning she was ravenous and ate huge quantities of strange foods in strange combinations. Little of that laid on her stomach. She complained little, but she was usually in a gloomy mood. She seemed worse on Sundays than on other days, so she seldom went to church with Candy and Marsha. Some Sunday's they stayed home with her so she would not be left alone.

"I think you should see a doctor, Bridgette," Marsha said at the beginning of the second week. "When did you have your last checkup?"

"Not since the doctor in London told me I was pregnant. I suppose I should see another doctor."

"People say that young Dr. Green is good," Candy suggested.

"Then, I'll go to him," Bridgette decided.

Dr. Green examined Bridgette and appeared concerned. "You are not going to have an easy birth," he said frankly.

"What should I do?" Bridgette asked.

"I'm going to give you some medication to help your digestion, and I want you to go on a strict diet.

I'll give you a printed list of what you can eat. I want you to come in every month for a checkup, more often if you feel that you need to. And I want you in the hospital well before your time to be delivered."

"Very well, Dr. Green," Bridgette responded as if he had told her she was going to be fine.

Marsha and Candy were more concerned about Bridgette than they wanted her to know, but she was so much a child, they did not think it wise to tell her.

Bridgette appeared better after her visit to Dr. Green. On rare occasions she was in high spirits, and one week she felt well every day. That week she talked incessantly and volunteered to help with any work that was at hand.

Marsha and Candy dared hope that she was finally getting better, but their hopes were dashed the next week when she reverted to her usual depressed, moaning self.

Candy's heart went out to the suffering girl, and she almost forgot that her marriage to Ralph had destroyed the dream of happiness with him that she had so long cherished.

On one of Bridgette's better days, Candy invited her to go riding with her on one of the ponies.

"I'm not sure I can," Bridgette objected.

"Nonsense. The ride will do you good. You can ride Happiness; that's my pony's name. She is so gentle you will hardly know you are riding. Ralph's pony is more spirited, so I'll ride him."

"Maybe one day, when I'm feeling better, I'll try it," Bridgette said.

"Then you tell me when you feel up to it."

A few days later, when Bridgette was not troubled with her usual morning sickness, she said with a slight show of enthusiasm that she would like to go for a ride.

"Wonderful! I know you'll enjoy it," Candy responded. "I'll go to the barn and ask Bill to saddle and bridle the ponies, and I'll bring them to the back yard gate so you won't have far to walk."

"Thank you. I'll get dressed for the ride," Bridgette said with brightening eyes and a slight smile.

When Candy went outside, she was surprised to find that a brisk wind had started blowing. That made her wonder if Bridgette would change her mind, but, without asking her if she would mind riding in the wind, she went to the barn to ask Bill to saddle and bridle the ponies.

When Candy returned with the ponies, Bridgette was waiting by the gate.

"I didn't know the wind was blowing," she said, pushing her hair back from her face.

"You're not going to let the wind stop you, I hope."

"Oh no. I love the feel of the wind in my hair."

"Will you need help getting on the pony?"

"Not at all. I used to ride often before the war."

Mutely, Candy turned Happiness around and handed the bridle reins to Bridgette.

She took the reins, set her foot in the stirrup, and easily got in the saddle.

"Let's ride up to the top of the ridge," Candy suggested. "Ralph and I used to ride up there often. There's a beautiful view of the river from up there."

"I'd like that. I've always loved rivers. How far must we ride?"

"Not far—just up there," Candy pointed. "If you get tired, we'll turn back."

"I'm sure I won't. I'm glad we're riding while I can. Later I will be too heavy to ride."

"I always enjoy riding this time of year. The weather is usually good, though it is windy today. The grass and the trees are always green. The wildflowers are always in bloom, and the birds are always singing."

"I'm glad you invited me. I'll enjoy the ride, and I'll enjoy seeing the sights that Ralph used to see. After he comes home, I want to see them all again—with him."

Candy thought of the many times she had ridden up this way with Ralph, and she felt that she would give the world if she could to do it just one more time. "It's strange that we haven't heard from Ralph lately," she said, holding a tight reign on Joy so he wouldn't sprint ahead.

"It is strange, and it worries me. But I keep telling myself that he's so busy he hasn't taken time to write," Bridgette answered.

"Knowing Ralph as I do, he's probably just put off writing."

"I keep telling myself that we'll hear from him soon."

"Maybe we'll get a letter today. We can watch for the mailman from the top of the ridge, and, if he stops at our box, we'll ride down and get the mail," Candy said.

Candy was holding a tight rein on Joy to keep him under control, so she did not speak again until she stopped him at the end of the ridge, and Bridgette stopped Happiness beside her. They had stopped facing into the wind, and it fanned their faces, tangled their hair, and ruffled their dresses.

"Isn't the river beautiful?" Candy exclaimed. They saw that the river was rough. Wind-driven waves were racing diagonally across it and crashing on the shore, and along the shore the trees were tossing their leafy heads in the wind.

A small sailboat was moving slowly up the river, battling the wind and the current. Far down the valley a farmer was plowing corn with a tractor, and the roar of the motor came faintly to their ears.

"It's beautiful," Bridgette exulted. "No wonder

Ralph loves this place."

"He loved the farm from the day we came here to live," Candy told her.

"Ever since I've known him, he's talked about coming back here when the war is over. After I agreed to marry him, he told me that one day he would bring me to Oakcrest. Little did we dream that I would come here while he was still in England."

"I wonder what he is doing today," Candy mused.

"Flying a mission, most likely."

"That must worry you."

"What worries me is that I have no way of knowing where his mission will take him or what he will face while he is flying it. I never did know, even while I was in England."

"Wherever he is, I hope he's safe," Candy rejoined.

Joy pawed the ground, anxious to go, and Candy placed her hand on his neck to quiet him. With the other hand she held him steady. Happiness munched the grass at her feet and showed no inclination to go.

"I see the mailman's car on the road, way up the river," Candy exclaimed, pointing.

"Oh, I see it. I've finally learned what his car looks like," Bridgette said, holding her hand to her brow to shade her eyes.

They watched the car come along the road and stop at most of the mailboxes.

"He's slowing for our box," Candy said when he had almost reached it. "Let's go, Bridgette, and see if there's a letter from Ralph."

"I'm ready."

"There's a short cut around the hill. I'll lead the way," Candy offered.

"Go ahead, and I'll follow."

With difficulty Candy held Joy to a walk around the side of the hill. Happiness followed docilely, and Bridgette gave her the reign and let her have her way.

When they reached the mailbox, Candy got the mail and sorted through it.

"Oh, here's a letter from Ralph," she said, holding it up.

"Let me have it," Bridgette cried, reaching for the letter.

Candy handed her the V-mail letter, and she tore it open with nervous fingers.

"Oh, oh," Bridgette cried, as she started reading. She stopped reading, turned pale, swayed in the saddle, and caught the saddle horn to steady herself.

"What is it, Bridgette?" Candy cried, sliding off of Joy and running to her.

"Just a minute. Let me finish reading the letter." She put up her hand to stop Candy.

"What is it, Bridgette?" Candy demanded. "Is Ralph all right?"

"Here, you read it." She thrust the letter into Candy's hand.

Candy could scarcely control her emotions, for she thought that surely Ralph must be dead or dying. Uncertainly she smoothed the letter and started reading aloud.

Dear Bridgette:

I'm sorry I've been so long writing. I've been laid up in the hospital for a couple of weeks with my hands bandaged, so I couldn't write. Don't worry, I'm all right now.

Tell Mama Marsha and Candy that I love them. Tell Bill I sure would like to be there to help him on the farm. I'll be glad when the war is over and I can come home and be with all of you.

I hope you're feeling better, and I pray

*that the baby will be all right. I love you
and wish I could be with you. I'll write
again soon.*

Love, Ralph

"He must not have had a bad injury. He says he
was only in the hospital a short time, and that he's all
right now," Candy said when she finished reading the
letter.

"That letter is most unsatisfactory. I would like to
know why his hands were bandaged."

"It's strange that he didn't say what had happened
to him."

"It's clear enough that his hands were injured, and
I know how it happened. His plane was damaged in a
dogfight on one of his missions, and he crashed-landed
when he got back to England. The plane probably
caught fire and burned his hands before he could get
out," she said with burning eyes.

"You're only guessing. He may have been hurt in
some other way," Candy assured her.

"No, I'm not guessing. That kind of thing happens
to pilots every day. Ralph is going to be killed. I know
it! He may have been worse this time than he has told
me. He wouldn't tell me if he was dying."

"Oh, Bridgette, if what you say is true, he could be
killed and we wouldn't even know it."

"That's what will happen. I know it. I know how
men get shot up on those missions."

"Why have you not mentioned this before,
Bridgette?"

"Ralph's plane had never been hit before. I thought
it was because he was such a good pilot, but now I'm
worried. I wish I had stayed in England with him."

"Ralph was right to send you away from the war,
Bridgette. If you had stayed in England, there would

be no way you could protect him. You couldn't do anything but pray for him, and you can do that here."

"Let's go to the house and show the letter to Mama Marsha," Bridgette said sadly, and she started Happiness up the hill toward the house before Candy could remount.

Marsha was standing in the front door when they stopped at the gate. When she saw Bridgette's expression, she knew that something was wrong, so she hurried out to meet them.

"What's wrong, Bridgette?" she asked, looking from her to Candy, then back again.

"I got a letter from Ralph, and he's been in the hospital," Bridgette replied.

"Bridgette thinks his plane may have been hit on one of his missions, and that he may have crash landed," Candy elucidated.

"May I read the letter?" Marsha asked, making an effort to remain calm.

"I want you to read it, Mama Marsha, though Ralph didn't say much. He wrote a short letter so I wouldn't know what happened."

Marsha read the letter and handed it back to Bridgette, thinking that perhaps she was right.

"Go in with Mama Marsha, and I'll take the ponies back to the barn and get Bill to take care of them," Candy said to Bridgette.

Without a word, Bridgette got off the pony, gave the reins to Candy, and followed Marsha into the house.

When Candy returned to the house, Marsha and Bridgette were sitting in the library, talking.

"I was just telling Bridgette that she has to stop worrying about Ralph, for the sake of her baby," Marsha said to Candy as she joined them.

"How can I stop worrying when I know he may be killed any day?" Bridgette asked, directing her question to Candy.

"I told her that every woman who is married to a soldier has to face that," Marsha continued before Candy could answer.

"But that doesn't keep me from dying for him every day and every night," Bridgette lamented.

"My mama used to tell me to turn things over to God and not to worry about them any more," Candy said.

"But God isn't going to keep every soldier who has a wife from being killed. Suppose Ralph is one of the ones who gets killed."

Marsha turned to Candy and shrugged helplessly.

"When I was a little girl, my mama taught me a lot about how to handle things that go wrong, and I never have forgotten them," Candy said.

"What good will that do me?"

"Mama was the best Christian I ever knew, and what she taught me has helped me all my life. It will help you too if you'll let it."

"What could possibly help me if Ralph gets killed?"

"I don't know exactly, but mama told me that God would never forsake me, and that He would give me strength for every trial," Candy told her.

"We all have to pray for Ralph," Marsha said.

"I'm not sure I know how to pray. Neither of my parents ever prayed, that I remember," Bridgette said sadly.

"Bridgette, have you ever trusted Jesus as your Saviour?" Candy asked.

"I'm not sure what you mean, but, since I've been with you and Mama Marsha, I've realized that something is lacking in my life."

"It would have helped if you had felt like going to church more often with Candy and me on Sundays," Marsha said.

"I know. I enjoyed the few Sundays when I went."

"You need to be saved, Bridgette."

"I don't know how."

"Just a minute and I'll tell you how. Wait until I get my Bible." Candy ran up to her room, and in minutes she was back with her Bible in her hand.

"First, the Bible says that we have all sinned," she began.

"I know I've sinned. For one thing, my heart is filled with hatred. Ever since the bomb killed my parents, I have hated Germans, and I would kill every one of them if I had the chance."

"That is a terrible sin, but we have all sinned in one way or another. So none of us are fit to be God's children or to go to Heaven."

"But you and Mama Marsha . . . how did you get saved?"

"The Bible tells us that God loves us, even though we are sinners, and that He gave His Son to die for us." Candy opened her Bible and read John 3:16 aloud.

"I understand that, but what about my sins?" Bridgette asked.

"Jesus paid for your sins by dying on a cross."

"So that's why He died. I never knew that before. But how does that get rid of my sins?"

"You must tell Jesus that you are sorry for your sins and that you receive Him as your Saviour. When you do, He will save you."

Marsha was silent, but her lips were moving in silent prayer.

"Just like that?" Bridgette asked.

"Just like that." Candy opened her Bible again and read, "But as many as received him, to them gave he power to become the sons of God, even to them that believe on his name."

"I want to do that," Bridgette said soberly.

"Then let's kneel together, and, while I pray for you, you ask Jesus to save you."

Bridgette went down on her knees at once, and

Candy and Marsha knelt beside her.

Candy put her arm around the frail, troubled girl and prayed aloud that she would trust Jesus for salvation.

Bridgette wept silently, but in a moment she looked up. Her eyes met Candy's, and she smiled the most radiant smile Candy had ever seen on her face.

"You don't have to say anything. I see it in your face," Candy rejoiced.

"But I want to talk. For the first time in my life, I feel good in here." She placed her hand over her heart. "I wish I had listened to Ralph when he tried to get me saved when we first started dating. I'm going to write to him tomorrow and tell him that at last I'm saved."

With tears raining down their cheeks, the three women arose and embraced. Bridgette's getting saved had brought them together. From that day Marsha felt as if Bridgette were her own daughter, and Candy gladly received her as a sister.

Bridgette's health improved after that, and she started going to church every Sunday with Candy and Marsha. She also went shopping with them in Maysville. They wanted to go shopping in Lexington, but, because of gasoline rationing, they did not have sufficient gasoline for the trip. They had to hoard the limited gasoline they were allowed so they could take Bridgette to the doctor for checkups, go to Maysville for groceries, and go to church on Sundays. Also they were saving gas rationing stamps against the time when Bridgette would have to go to the hospital.

Ralph started writing almost every week, and Bridgette shared her letters with Mama Marsha and Candy. They talked about each letter for hours, dwelling on each shred of information he was able to give them in spite of wartime censoring. And they tried to read all they could between the lines.

At night they listened to the late news on radio,

and after it went off, they often remained up talking until it was quite late.

Almost before they realized it, Bridgette's slender form had become greatly distorted by the growing child within her. She began to feel heavy and uncomfortable, and she became ill again. In her seventh month, she became even worse.

"Bridgette, I think we had better take you to see Dr. Green today," Marsha suggested one morning when Bridgette was suffering more than usual.

"If you say so, Mama Marsha. I do feel terrible."

"I'll help you get ready," Candy offered.

A short while later they arrived at Dr. Green's office. His nurse took one look at Bridgette and told the doctor she thought he ought to see her ahead of his other waiting patients. Moments later she took Bridgette into his office.

"I want you to go to the hospital today," he told her when he finished his examination.

"But my time is not that near," Bridgette objected.

"You still belong in a hospital. Tell Mrs. White and Candy to come in here," he said to his nurse.

"Bridgette needs the care that she can only get in a hospital," he said when they came in.

"Can they handle her case in the Maysville hospital?" Marsha asked.

"I'd rather for you to take her to Good Samaritan in Lexington. They are better equipped to care for her if there should be complications."

"Can she ride in the car if we put pillows in the back seat for her to recline on?"

"That should be all right. Just make sure she is comfortable."

"Do I have to stay in Lexington alone?" Bridgette asked, near panic.

"Of course not. We'll stay with you," Candy promised.

Bridgette gave Marsha a questioning look.

"Of course we'll stay with you, just as we did with my dear husband when he was there," Marsha assured her.

"Then I don't mind going," she said, smiling faintly.

They left the doctor's office and hurried home to get ready to take Bridgette to the hospital.

Chapter 25

While Marsha and Candy were dressing and helping Bridgette pack to go to the hospital, the front door bell rang.

"I'll get it," Candy sang out as she ran to the door. To her surprise a man from Western Union was standing at the door when she opened it.

"Oh, what is it?" she asked uneasily.

"I have a telegram for Mrs. Ralph White," the man replied.

Panic flooded Candy's heart, and she swayed as if to fall.

"Are you all right, Miss?" the man asked.

"I'm fine," she managed, as she struggled to regain control. "Mrs. White is not feeling well, so I'll sign for her and see that she gets the message."

The man offered her his pad. She signed and he handed her a yellow envelope containing the telegram. She took it as if she were afraid to touch it.

"Good day, Miss," the man said. He turned and walked briskly back to his car, leaving her standing in the doorway with a wildly beating heart.

"Who was it?" Marsha called from the head of the stairs.

"A man. I'll tell you in a minute." She held up the envelope, pointed toward Bridgette's room, and in sign language said that it was for her.

"Oh!" Marsha mouthed with silent lips and ran down the stairs to Candy. "Something must have happened to Ralph," she whispered sharply when she reached Candy.

"That's what I think. We'll have to prepare Bridgette before we give her the telegram."

"There's not much we can do to ease the shock if something has happened to Ralph. . . . and who's going to ease our shock?"

"No one can do that. Let's go and do the best we can for Bridgette," Marsha sighed.

They went up to Bridgette's room and found her seated at her dresser, arranging her hair.

"Bridgette, we have a message for you," Candy said.

"We hope it is not bad news," Marsha added.

"Is it about Ralph?" Bridgette cried, turning to them a face pale with anxiety.

"You have a telegram, but I don't know who it's from," Marsha told her.

"A telegram . . ." Bridgette repeated as if not fully comprehending what she had said.

"Yes, a telegram," Candy echoed, holding the envelope out to her. Bridgette slowly reached for the envelope, tore it open, removed the single yellow sheet, and glanced at it.

"It's from the War Department," she said in a stricken voice. "Candy, I can't bear to read it. Please read it to me." As if in a trance, she handed the telegram back to Candy.

Candy wanted to tear the telegram to bits and throw it in the trash, but she managed to hold it steady and to steel her nerves to read it.

Marsha came to look at the telegram with her, and together they silently read:

I REGRET TO INFORM YOU THAT

YOUR HUSBAND, FIRST LIEUTEN-
ANT RALPH WHITE IS REPORTED
MISSING   IN   ACTION   OVER
ABBEVILLE, FRANCE SINCE SIXTEEN
AUGUST IF FURTHER DETAILS OR
OTHER INFORMATION REGARDING
HIS STATUS BECOME AVAILABLE,
YOU WILL BE NOTIFIED.

THE ADJUTANT GENERAL

"Aren't you going to tell me what it says?" Bridgette asked, looking at them with her large eyes open wide.

"Ralph is missing," Marsha said simply.

"Missing? . . . They will never find him," Bridgette wailed as she fell into Marsha's arms.

"The telegram only says that he's missing. Maybe they'll find him," Candy suggested.

"They say that about all the men who do not return from a mission," Bridgette sobbed.

"We have to hope for the best," Marsha said firmly. "And now we have to get you to the hospital."

"I'm not going to the hospital," Bridgette said in a determined voice. "What's the use?"

"Of course you're going, Bridgette. You have to think of yourself—and of the baby."

"Since Ralph is gone, what does it matter what happens to me . . . or the baby?"

"Bridgette! I'm amazed at you," Marsha scolded.

"Ralph would want you to go to the hospital," Candy encouraged.

"You could lose your baby, Bridgette, and, after Ralph is found, he would be very upset if he learned that you refused to go to the hospital."

"I don't care what . . ." She stopped with a gasp and struggled for breath. "I'll . . . be all . . . right in . . . a . . . minute," she panted, grimacing with pain.

Candy and Marsha watched her anxiously. In a moment she grimaced again, grasped her arms tightly around her stomach and gritted her teeth.

"Bridgette, I think you're about to lose your baby," Marsha said. "We have to rush you to the hospital at once. Candy, get her things together, and we'll help her down the stairs."

"Should I go get Bill to help get her to the car?" Candy asked.

"Don't be stupid, Candy," Bridgette snapped. "I can walk to the car."

"Are you sure, Bridgette?"

"Of course I'm sure. You can carry my things if you want to, but I can walk. My things are all in the case. It just needs closing."

Candy snapped the case closed and picked it up. Silently, white-faced and trembling, Bridgette walked to the head of the stairs and started down, holding to the stair rail.

Marsha took her other arm and helped support her, and she did not object.

"Candy, help her out to the car, and I'll get some pillows for her to ride on." Marsha said when they reached the front door.

Minutes later, they had Bridgette in the backseat, reclining on the pillows.

"Candy, you drive. I'm going to sit back here with Bridgette," Marsha said.

"Do you suppose Dr. Green can do something for her?" Candy asked as she started the car down the drive.

"He said she ought to be in the hospital, so that's where we'll take her," Mama Marsha answered.

"Take me to Dr. Green. I'm not hurting as much as I was," Bridgette said.

Candy glanced at Mama Marsha in the rearview mirror to get her reaction.

"We had better try for the hospital," she said in answer to Candy's unspoken question.

By the time they reached the end of the drive, Bridgette was moaning with pain again.

"I'll make all the time I can," Candy said as she turned the car toward Lexington. She pressed on the accelerator, and the big car leaped ahead. The secondary road they were traveling on was narrow and curvy, but she did not slow down except on the worst curves. Then she raced on.

Bridgette often bit her lips and groaned, but she did not cry out.

When they reached the highway, it was less curvy, and Candy disregarded the speed limit, thinking only that she had to get Bridgette to the hospital.

On a long straight stretch in the road, a state policeman was parked in a driveway. He saw the speeding car go by and pulled out after it.

"Oh, no! We have a policeman coming after us," Candy cried.

"Maybe he's just going our way," Marsha suggested hopefully, looking back over her shoulder.

"He has his flashing light on. That means he's pulling us over," Candy fumed as she slowed the car and guided it to the shoulder of the road.

"Surely he'll let us go when we tell him the circumstances," Marsha said hopefully.

"Tell him I'm dying," Bridgette sobbed.

"Oh hurry," Candy said under her breath. She rolled her window down, then beat on the steering wheel with her fist while she watched the officer slowly emerge from his cruiser and walk to where she had stopped.

"What's your hurry, Miss?" he asked Candy, then he glanced at Marsha and Bridgette in the backseat.

"I'm rushing her to the hospital." She pointed to Bridgette. "She's about to lose her baby."

"Miss, I've heard that story before," he said.

Marsha recognized the officer as one she had heard testify in her husband's court. "What she told you is the truth, Officer Preston," she said.

"Why, Mrs. White!" the officer exclaimed. "I didn't realize that this was your car."

"My daughter-in-law is about to lose her baby, and we're rushing her to the hospital. Can't you let us go?" Marsha asked.

At that instant Bridgette let out a wail of pain, and Officer Preston glanced quickly at her.

"Sorry I stopped you, Mrs. White. Which hospital are you taking her to? I'll escort you."

"Good Samaritan in Lexington."

"All right. I'll get in front and you follow me. I'll radio ahead so they'll be ready for her at the hospital."

He ran back to his cruiser, got in and pulled out, burning rubber. With his siren screaming and his light flashing, he passed them.

"I'm glad he didn't detain us any longer," Candy said as she pulled out after the cruiser and pressed hard on the accelerator..

"I think I'll die before we get there," Bridgette wailed.

"It won't take long, Bridgette, now that we have a police escort," Marsha told her.

"I hope I don't have a wreck trying to keep up with him. He's doing ninety miles an hour on the straight stretches," Candy said, braking hard to slow for a curve.

"Just don't run into the back of the cruiser when he slows down," Marsha cautioned.

"Candy, don't have a wreck because of me, but do hurry all you can," Bridgette sobbed.

"Just hold on, and I'll make all the time I can," Candy called back to her.

"I can't believe Ralph is missing. I know I'll never see him again," Bridgette sobbed between gasps of pain.

"Try not to worry about him, Bridgette. For all we know he may have bailed out of his plane and is safe somewhere," Marsha comforted, putting her arms around the girl's shoulders.

A city policeman was waiting for them in his cruiser at the city limits. He flashed his headlights at Officer Preston, then turned and drove ahead to clear traffic at the intersections. Officer Preston drove through the city at speeds approaching sixty miles an hour, and Candy followed close behind him, biting her lips and gripping the steering wheel.

When they reached the hospital, Officer Preston slowed, turned into the emergency entrance, and parked in a reserved space. Candy stopped before the entrance.

At once two emergency room attendants rolled a gurney out to the car. Candy bounded from the car and opened the rear door for them. Marsha got out and came to stand beside Candy as the attendants carefully lifted Bridgette to the gurney.

They pushed Bridgette toward the emergency waiting room. Candy followed close behind them, but Marsha paused to thank Officer Preston.

"You'll have to wait out here," one of the attendants told Candy as they pushed Bridgette into the emergency room.

"Come back and tell me how she is the minute you find out," she called as the door was closing behind them. Disappointed, she turned away and waited for Marsha.

"We have to wait here, and there's no telling when they'll tell us if she's going to be all right or not," she told her when she came in.

"I suppose that's their usual procedure. Anyway, I'm glad we got Bridgette to the hospital before she lost her baby."

"I believe the Lord sent Officer Preston to escort us," Candy said.

"I think you're right. I'm sure we were both praying all the way."

A great while latter a nurse came out, and they arose to meet her. "Are you helping with Bridgette?" Marsha asked.

"Yes, I am, and I came to tell you that she's all right."

"Has a doctor seen her yet?" Candy asked.

"Oh, yes. When we got word from the police that you were on the way, we called in an obstetrician. He was here when they brought her in."

"What did the doctor say about her?" Candy asked.

"He thinks she may have an early birth, so he has sent her to the delivery room."

"When can we see her?" Marsha asked.

"It may be awhile. I suggest that you go to the waiting room on the third floor and wait there. The doctor will come and give you a report if there is any change."

They went to the third floor, found the waiting room and went in.

"I wish we knew what's going on," Candy exclaimed as they sat down.

"So do I, but there's no point in sitting here, wringing our hands."

"I hope the doctor doesn't forget to keep us informed," Candy said a great while later.

"So do I. Let's go to the nurses' station and see if they know anything. Maybe they'll let us see her."

"Good idea. I know Bridgette doesn't want to be alone. She's probably worried half to death."

They went to the nurses' station, and a nurse looked up from her work. "May I help you?" she asked.

"We're Bridgette's family. . . . the girl they took into the delivery room some while ago," Marsha said.

"We'd like to know how she is."

"I really don't know, but you can knock on the delivery room door and ask. The delivery room is at the end of the hall."

"Thank you," Candy said, and she and Marsha hurried down the hall and knocked gently on the delivery room door.

In a moment a nurse opened the door slightly and looked out at them.

"We want to know how Bridgette White is," Marsha asked.

"She's all right, and she's been asking for Mama Marsha and Candy," the nurse smiled. "Would that be you?"

"Yes, I'm Marsha and this is Candy."

"Her doctor has gone out for a minute. This would be a good time for you to see her, but you can't stay long." She stepped aside for them to enter, then ushered them to Bridgette's room.

Bridgette was lying in her bed with a sheet pulled up to her neck. Her face was wet with tears, and she was moaning softly. She looked frail and frightened.

"I'm glad you've come," she sobbed when she saw them.

"I'm glad they let us in, Bridgette, but we can only stay until your doctor comes back," Candy told her.

"I know. They say the baby is going to come soon."

"Have you thought what you're going to name the baby?" Marsha asked.

"I haven't thought much about a name until today . . . when I wasn't hurting too much. I've decided to call the baby Ralph."

"What if it's a girl?" Candy asked.

"It's going to be a boy."

"You don't know that," Candy countered.

"The baby is going to be a boy, and I'm going to name him Ralph," she said stubbornly.

"What will you call him after Ralph comes home?"

"I don't believe Ralph will ever come home, but if he does, I'll call the baby little Ralph."

"You're not going to name him Little Ralph?" Candy questioned, smiling.

"Oh, oh," Bridgette cried, suddenly clasping her hand over her stomach. "Candy I think I'm going to die."

"I know you're hurting, but you're going to be all right," Marsha consoled.

"If you knew how much I'm hurting, you wouldn't say that," Bridgette moaned.

"We're praying for you, Bridgette," Candy said.

"I want you to. They say I may lose the baby." She grimaced with pain.

"They haven't told us that," Marsha said.

"They haven't told me, but I overheard the doctor and a nurse talking."

Just then the doctor came in. "Are you related to Bridgette," he asked, looking at Candy, then at Marsha.

"I'm Candy White, Bridgette's sister-in-law, and this is Marsha White, her mother-in-law."

"I'm Dr. Walker, Candy and Mrs. White. I am attending Bridgette."

"Is she going to be all right, doctor?" Marsha asked.

"I believe she will, though this is an early birth. . . . I'd say about two months early."

"Will the baby be all right?"

"The baby should be fine. A seven month baby is not that unusual."

"How soon do you think the baby will come?"

"I'm going to die if it doesn't come soon," Bridgette groaned.

"You may feel like you're going to die, but remember women have been giving birth to babies since the beginning of the human race," Dr. Walker told her.

"You ladies will have to go now. Wait in the waiting room down the hall, and one of the nurses will let you know how things are going from time to time."

"Thank you, Dr. Walker," Marsha said and turned to Bridgette.

"We'll be close by, and we'll be praying for you."

"We certainly will, Bridgette," Candy echoed.

"Please do," Bridgette said, smiling faintly.

They waved at her as they were leaving. The door closed quietly behind them, but it did not blot out the vision of the suffering girl.

They sat for a long time in the waiting room, grew tired, went for soft drinks from the coin operated machine in the lobby, walked the halls, watched the nurses go about their business, and looked out the windows at the passing traffic.

They were on the point of going back to the delivery room door to ask about Bridgette when Dr. Walker came to the waiting room.

"Your little English girl is having a difficult time," he said as they arose to meet him. "The baby should have been born hours ago."

"Is there anything more you can do to help her?" Marsha asked.

"She may have to have a cesarian section."

"Is that serious?" Candy asked.

"Not really. We do it quite often."

"When will you know if you have to do it?" Marsha asked.

"I'm going to give her some different medication. If that doesn't do it, we'll operate tonight."

"So soon?" Candy asked.

"She isn't strong enough to continue suffering the way she is much longer."

"You will let us know before you operate," Marsha insisted.

"Sure, and I'll let you see her before we take her to the operating room." Dr. Walker was moving toward the door as he talked.

"Thank you, doctor," Candy said tearfully.

"We haven't had lunch," Marsha observed when the doctor was gone.

"I know, and I haven't been hungry."

"We had better go find a restaurant and eat something before the doctor comes back."

"I'm not hungry, but I'll go with you."

A short distance from the hospital they found a place that sold sandwiches.

"It shouldn't take long to get something here," Candy said as they entered.

Twenty minutes later they returned to the waiting room in the hospital and again sat down to wait. The shades of the coming night soon darkened the room, and an orderly came and turned on the lights. Still they waited.

At last a nurse came to them. "Dr. Walker has decided that they have to operate on Bridgette. You can come and see her before they take her to the operating room," she said.

"We want to see her," Candy exclaimed, leaping to her feet.

"I was hoping she would get by without surgery," Marsha said as she arose.

"The doctor has done everything he can, but the baby just won't come."

They followed her to Bridgette's side in the labor room, and she looked up at them, wide-eyed with fright. "I thought you'd never come back," she sobbed.

"We wanted to be with you every minute, but the doctor wouldn't let us in," Candy responded.

"We love you," Marsha said, and leaned over and kissed Bridgette on the forehead.

"They're going to cut me open and take the baby out, and I'm scared," Bridgette lamented. "I could face a bombing raid easier than this, but I have to do it to get the pain to stop."

"We'll be praying for you," Candy promised.

"We surely will, Bridgette," Marsha told her.

"I'm glad I got saved," Bridgette said. "Even with all the pain, the Lord has been with me."

"I'm glad to hear you say that, Bridgette," Candy responded.

They came at that moment to take Bridgette to surgery. "Offer a prayer for the baby and one for Ralph while you're praying for me," she said as they lifted her to the gurney. They pushed her away, and she looked back and waved her fingers at them.

Marsha and Candy waved back, then returned to the waiting room. For a long time they sat mutely staring at each other and wishing that the ordeal was over.

"It seems that the time will never pass," Marsha said a great while later.

"I felt that way when Daddy White was in the hospital."

"It's hard to keep from worrying when they don't tell us anything."

"It's past ten o'clock," Candy said, consulting the tiny watch on her arm. "I wonder why it's taking them so long."

"I can't imagine, but no news is good news, they say."

"What do you think of Bridgette wanting to name the baby Ralph?" Candy asked.

"If the baby is a boy, I think that would be a good name for him. Perhaps a baby named Ralph will be a comfort to us if our Ralph doesn't comes back."

"I suppose you're right. At least a baby will keep us occupied, but I'll never forget that Ralph is across the ocean. . . . somewhere. I still believe that someday he'll come home."

"I hope you're right," Marsha replied, growing misty-eyed. "If he does come home after the war, I think he'll like the baby being named after him."

"I hear footsteps! Someone is coming," Candy exclaimed.

"So do I," Marsha said, turning her head to listen.

In a moment Dr. Walker appeared at the door, and they both rose to meet him.

"Bridgette has a baby boy," he announced.

"Wonderful!" Candy almost shouted. "When can we see him?"

"You can see him in the morning. He is so small—we had to put him in the incubator. Besides, visiting hours in there are over for the night."

"Is he going to be all right?" Marsha asked.

"I'm sure he will. He appears perfectly normal, except for being small. Babies smaller that he is survive all the time."

"What about Bridgette?" Marsha asked.

"She's not awake yet, but her vital signs are almost normal."

"What do you mean, almost?" Candy cried.

"She has lost some blood, and her pulse is slow. We are giving her a transfusion, and that should bring her around."

"Do we have to wait until morning to see her?" Marsha asked.

"She is sedated, and we're going to keep her in intensive care overnight. We should be able to move her to a room in the morning, and you can see her then."

"What are we going to do, Mama Marsha, just sit here and wait?" Candy complained.

"I suggest that you both go to a hotel and get a night's sleep. Call the hospital and leave your room number after you check in. If there's any change during the night, we'll call you." With that he left them.

Chapter 26

*C*andy and Marsha checked into the Lafayette Hotel on Main Street and went straight to bed. In spite of all that was on their minds, sleep soon claimed their weary bodies, and they did not awaken until after daylight the next morning.

"Oh, Mama Marsha, we have overslept," Candy cried when she awoke. She sat up in bed and squinted at the light that was filtering through the drawn window blinds.

"I can't believe we slept this late," Marsha exclaimed, putting her feet on the floor and stretching.

"Bridgette will think we have forsaken her," Candy said as she got out of bed and stepped into her house slippers. "I can't wait to see little Ralph," she called over her shoulder as she started to the bathroom.

"Hurry with your bath, Candy. I have to get in there too, you know," Marsha called after her.

They dressed hurriedly, collected their things, and left their room.

"Are we going to eat breakfast before we go to the hospital?" Candy asked on the way down on the elevator.

"I think we should at least take time for some toast and coffee. We hardly ate anything yesterday."

"I'm so worried about big Ralph and Bridgette and so excited about little Ralph, I'm still not hungry,"

Candy said.

"You had better eat something, or you'll starve before noon."

"You're right. I'll at least eat some toast and have something to drink."

The elevator thudded to a stop at the first floor, and they got off and hurried across the lobby and out the front door.

"You drive; I'm too excited to drive," Candy said on the way to the car.

"I never thought you'd turn down a chance to drive," Marsha teased, as she fished her keys from her purse and walked around to the driver's side. She got in and Candy got in beside her. As Marsha backed the car out and turned toward the hospital, Candy realized that she was biting her nails. Silently she put her hands on the seat and sat on them.

"We'll go in here, where it won't take long to get served," Marsha said as she parked the car by a hamburger place.

"The service can't be too fast for me," Candy said, and she got out of the car and danced on her toes while Marsha locked the door.

For breakfast Marsha ordered toast and coffee.

"I'll have toast and milk. I'm too nervous to drink tea or a coke this morning," Candy said.

After they finished eating, Marsha drove out Limestone and parked across the street from the hospital. They got out and hurried across the street and entered the hospital, and Candy ran to the information desk.

"Has Bridgette White been moved to a room?" she asked the receptionist as Marsha caught up with her.

The receptionist consulted her records and shook her head. "They do not list her in a room, but they may not have brought the record up-to-date if they moved her this morning," she said. "Just a minute and I'll call and find out."

In her excitement, Candy stood on tiptoes while the receptionist dialed the number. Someone answered the phone on the second ring.

"Has Bridgette White been moved to a room this morning?" the receptionist asked.

A voice crackled in the receiver, but Candy could not understand what was being said. "Thank you," the receptionist said and hung up.

"She's still in intensive care," she told Candy. "I suggest that you go to the desk on the third floor and ask about her."

"Thank you," Candy said breathlessly. "I can't believe it," she said to Marsha as she turned away from the desk. She started running down the corridor to the elevator with Marsha running close behind her.

"I think it would be quicker to walk up the stairs than to wait on the elevator," Candy grumbled as she pressed the button by the elevator door.

"Calm down, Candy," Marsha said. "I've never seen you so worked up."

The elevator stopped at their floor with a thump, and the operator slid the door open.

"The third floor, please," Candy said as they were getting on.

At the third floor, they hurried to the nurses' station and found a nurse they had not seen before on duty.

"We'd like to see Bridgette White," Candy told her.

"Her doctor left instructions that she is not to have company," the nurse said without looking up.

Candy turned away, angry and sobbing.

"Has Dr. Walker seen her this morning?" Marsha asked.

"He has not come in this morning," the nurse answered indifferently.

Marsha turned and went to Candy where she had stopped halfway down the hall.

"I can't believe that woman, and I'm not about to spend any more time in the waiting room," Candy stormed.

"Just a minute, I'll go back and ask when we can see little Ralph," Marsha said.

Together they returned to the desk and found the nurse still busy with her papers.

"When can we see Bridgette White's baby?" Marsha asked.

The nurse glanced at her watch. "Visiting hours start in there in half an hour," she said without looking up.

"We would have had time for a good breakfast," Marsha complained. "Candy, do you want to go and get something more?"

"I'm too worried about Bridgette to think of food," Candy said. "I guess we might as well go back to the waiting room." She turned and led the way back to the room where they had waited the day before.

"Maybe they kept Bridgette in intensive care overnight as a precaution," Marsha suggested.

"If that's the reason, why can't she have company?" Candy asked. "I wish her doctor would come."

"Surely he'll be here soon."

Candy did not answer, but started alternately biting her lips and her nails.

For the next half hour they watched the time and watched for Bridgette's doctor to pass in the hall.

"Something must have detained Dr. Walker, but we can go see Little Ralph," Marsha said when the time for visiting hours had arrived.

Instantly Candy was on her feet. "Let's ask a nurse in the hall how to get there. I'm not asking old poker-face anything," Candy declared.

"Candy!" Marsha scolded. "Maybe the nurse was just busy."

"And maybe she doesn't care!" Candy snapped.

They met a pleasant looking nurse in the corridor and asked her for directions to the nursery. She pointed the way, and moments later they were standing outside the glass window looking in at the babies. Candy wrote Ralph in large letters on a piece of paper and held it up for one of the nurses to see. She smiled and pointed to a small baby in an incubator at the end of the room.

"There he is!" Candy cried, pointing. "Mama Marsha, isn't he beautiful."

"Yes he is," Marsha agreed, looking at the red face of the tiny baby in the incubator.

"I wonder how long they'll keep him in there," Candy said.

"Not long, I hope. I know Bridgette must be dying to hold him in her arms."

"I wish we could see him close up," Candy said.

"Me too, but we'll have to wait."

They spent some time looking at the other babies, took another look at Little Ralph, and turned away.

"Let's go ask someone if Dr. Walker has come to the hospital this morning," Marsha suggested.

"I refuse to ask that nurse at the desk."

"Candy! I'm surprised at you."

"I'm sorry, Mama Marsha. I guess I'm not myself today. I'm sorry, Lord," she added in a whisper, deciding at that moment that she would go and inquire of the nurse who had been so insolent and that she would be especially pleasant to her.

In spite of her resolve, Candy was relieved when they found another nurse at the desk, but she decided she would still make an effort to be nice to the nurse who had affronted her when she saw her again.

The new nurse smiled pleasantly and offered to page Dr. Walker and see if he was in the hospital.

They thanked her and stepped aside to wait. Minutes later, Dr. Walker got off the elevator and came to them.

"I know you're concerned about Bridgette," he greeted.

"Yes we are," Candy replied.

"They told us she can't have company," Marsha added.

"She was slow coming from under the anesthesia last night. When she finally did, she was very weak and somewhat confused, so I ordered that she was not to have visitors."

"How is she now, Dr. Walker?" Candy asked.

"Surely she's awake by now," Marsha said hopefully.

"I saw her early this morning, and she was awake, but she was still very weak. You can see her, but make your visit brief. Come and I'll tell the nurse to let you in."

He led them to intensive care and rapped on the door. "Mrs. White and Candy have come to see Bridgette," he told the nurse who came to the door. "I'll be back to see her later," he added as they entered.

When they entered Bridgette's room, they saw her head elevated and her silver-gold hair spilling over her pillow. Her usually pale face was flushed, and her eyes were unusually bright.

"I'm glad you've come," she said faintly.

"We've been dying to see you," Marsha returned, "but they wouldn't let us in."

"We saw little Ralph and he's beautiful," Candy told her.

Bridgette smiled weakly, and caught a gasping breath. "I'm glad . . . you saw him," she said faintly.

"You have to hurry and regain your strength so we can take him home," Marsha encouraged.

"I . . . don't think . . . I'll ever get well."

"Of course you will, Bridgette. Women have their

babies delivered the way you did all the time. You just need time to regain your strength."

"Something . . . must have . . . gone wrong. I know I'm not going . . . to get well," she said with her eyes on Candy.

"Sure you will, Bridgette," Candy encouraged.

"Candy, if something . . . does happen to me, I want . . . you to take my baby . . . and raise him as your own. Will . . . you do that, Candy?"

"Bridgette, you know I will, but I'm not even going to think about it. You're going to get well."

"I'm . . . glad I got saved. Now I'm . . . not afraid . . . to die."

"We're glad you got saved too, Bridgette, but we want you to stop talking about dying. little Ralph needs a mother," Marsha said firmly.

"I'd love to . . . see him. Candy, you . . . take care of . . . him." Bridgette closed her eyes and did not speak again. Apparently she had gone to sleep or drifted into unconsciousness.

Marsha and Candy looked at each other, then walked quietly from her room.

"I can't believe she's that sick," Marsha said when they reached the hall.

"Me neither. Surely she'll get better. I can't imagine going home without her. And, Mama Marsha, can you imagine the two of us taking care of a tiny baby?"

"I'm sure we could manage, but he needs a mother. Bridgette has to get well."

"Since we can't stay with Bridgette, let's leave the hospital. I can't bear that waiting room another minute."

"I feel the same way, Candy. Let's go downtown and window-shop until noon, then go eat a good meal. We've hardly eaten anything since we left home."

"I'm not sure I can eat, but we need to get our minds off of our worries. I've been worrying about Bridgette every single minute, and, besides that, I've had Ralph on my mind."

"So have I. Maybe by the time we get home we'll hear something more about him."

They left the hospital and drove downtown and parked on Main Street. They got out of the car and walked along the street, window-shopping. They visited some of the stores, though neither of them was in a mood to buy anything. They were simply killing time. At noon they went to a restaurant and ate. Then they returned to the hospital and went to Bridgette's room and tapped on the door.

To their dismay, the nurse who opened the door told them that Bridgette had gone into a coma. Dr. Walker had called in a specialist, but he had not suggested any new treatment.

Just then Dr. Walker came.

"There's little we can do but wait and see if she comes out of the coma," he told them.

Numb with disbelief, Marsha and Candy turned away and went to look through the glass again at little Ralph. After that they returned to the waiting room and waited through the long afternoon. Near nightfall they went across the street to the restaurant and ate sandwiches. Marsha drank coffee, and Candy drank tea. After they finished eating, they returned to the waiting room and sat down to wait. Instead of going back to the hotel for the night, they would simply sit in the semi-darkened waiting room and wait.

At two o'clock in the morning a nurse came to tell them that Bridgette had quietly died without regaining consciousness.

"I can't believe it," Candy moaned.

"How sad, and she doesn't have a living relative besides us to attend her funeral," Marsha said.

"That is tragic," the nurse said, and she turned away and went about her business, leaving Candy and

Marsha standing in the waiting room, filled with grief and questioning what they should do.

"If we could only get word to Ralph," Candy sighed.

"Well, that's not possible. For all we know, he may be dead."

"I know. Just thinking of him breaks my heart."

"We'll bury her in our family plot in Maysville," Marsha said after a long silence. "After all, she is a member of the family."

"And if Ralph ever comes home, we can show him where we have buried her," Candy sighed.

"I'll call the Smith Funeral Home in Maysville and have them to pick up her body. Then we'll go home and make arrangements for the funeral."

Two days later they had Bridgette's funeral service in the church they attended. During the service, Marsha wept silently. Candy wept also, and repented of every unkind feeling she had ever had because Bridgette had married Ralph. With all her heart she wished Ralph could be there to share their sorrow.

Bridgette was buried near where Austin was buried. There was an unused lot besides her, in case Ralph was ever found and sent home for burial.

A week after they buried Bridgette, they brought little Ralph home from the hospital. True to her promise, Candy assumed the role of motherhood, but Marsha insisted that she was going to help her raise him.

"I really don't mind taking care of him, and I believe he will keep us from missing big Ralph so much," she told Marsha.

"Speaking of Ralph, we ought to contact his commanding officer and see if they have learned anything more about what happened to him."

"Oh yes, Mama Marsha, we should do that. During all the ordeal with Bridgette, I hadn't thought of doing anything to find out more about him."

"I'm sure there are others we could write."

"What about Ralph's friend, David Bookman? Maybe he knows what has happened to Ralph," Candy exclaimed.

"Of course, we'll write to him, and I'll call Congressman Duncan and see what he suggests. Surely he must know what avenues we should pursue."

The next day they wrote to David Bookman in care of Ralph's commanding officer, but they never received an answer to their letter. In the following six months, they made phone calls, wrote more letters, waited, and made more phone calls.

Finally, a letter came from Ralph's commanding officer telling them that no trace had been found of Ralph, and that he was now presumed dead.

The letter made Candy feel that she should go into a period of mourning, but the demands of caring for little Ralph kept her occupied, and her growing love for the child helped to heal the pain in her heart.

By the time little Ralph was two, he was walking all over the house. Often he crawled up the stairs to the landing and played there for hours at games of his own invention. When the weather was good, Candy took him out in the yard to play. He loved the big yard, and he loved to pluck blossoms from the flower bed and bring them to her.

One afternoon as Candy sat on the porch reading a book and keeping an eye on little Ralph, she heard a car turn into the drive. She looked up from her book and saw a battered old jalopy coming slowly up the hill. She watched it and wondered who could be coming in such an old, dilapidated car. Soon she saw an aged woman at the wheel. She stopped the car at the gate and got out. Candy thought she looked vaguely familiar, but she did not recognize her.

"Is this where the Whites live?" the woman asked in a raspy voice, and in that instant Candy knew that she was Lillian. But how could she possibly look so old and haggard? she wondered.

"Yes, Lillian, the Whites live here." She got up and walked out to the gate to meet Lillian.

"How'd you know me?" Lillian rasped.

"Lillian, don't you know me? I'm Candy."

"You're Candy? Why, you're too growd-up and fine looking to be Candy."

"But I am Candy. I have grown up since you last saw me."

"Your eyes are the same, but I never would have believed you'd grow up to be so pretty and so fine lookin'," Lillian quivered, searching her face.

"You have changed, Lillian."

"Law child, I reckon I have. I've had a hard life."

"Come in and we'll talk," Candy said, opening the gate for her.

"I just thought that, good as I was to you when you was a youngun, maybe I could get you to come and live with me." She stood with one foot inside the gate, as if she dared not enter.

"I can't do that, Lillian. My life is here now, and I have responsibilities that I can't leave."

"Have these people made a slave out of you, Candy?" Her eyes roamed over the big house, then back to Candy's face.

"Indeed they have not. They have given me a home and made me a member of the family. And I now have a little boy to take care of." She pointed to little Ralph.

"A child? . . . a little boy?" She looked at little Ralph, unbelieving. "I didn't expect to find you married."

"I'm not married, Lillian," she laughed. "I'm raising my foster brother's little boy. His daddy was killed in the war."

"Oh I see. Well, I'm glad you're not married. Men ain't no good."

"Where's Jake? I thought you were married to him."

"I was, but he left me. Don't know where he went. That's why I wanted you to come and live with me. I ain't able to work like I used to."

At that moment Marsha came to the door. "I thought I heard a car," she said.

"Marsha, this is my stepmother, Lillian, and, Lillian, this is my foster mother, Marsha. She has been a mother to me ever since I came here to live."

"Pleased to meet you, ma'am." Lillian stepped back and closed the gate. "Reckon I'll be goin'," she said as she turned toward her car.

"Don't hurry, Lillian. I want to talk with you." Candy said.

"What about?" Lillian asked, but she did not pause in her retreat.

"Lillian, if you would get right with the Lord, you would have a much better life."

"Now, that's one thing I don't want to talk about," she snapped, hurrying her pace to the car. She reached the car, got in, started the motor, and turned the car down the drive.

"Why was she in such a hurry?" Marsha asked.

"I don't think she felt at ease in your presence, Mama Marsha, and she didn't want me to talk to her about getting right with the Lord. When I lived with her, she resented my being a Christian, and I see that she hasn't changed. I guess all I can do is pray for her."

"How sad. Judging from her face, she must have had an unhappy life."

"I'm sure she has, and she doesn't realize that the way she has lived has contributed to her unhappiness."

Chapter 27

*O*ne afternoon in late June, Candy sat in the library, thinking. It hardly seemed possible that little Ralph was now a healthy, active little boy of three.

He should be healthy, she mused. He has certainly had the best of care and plenty of love. "I love him as if he were my own son, and so does Mama Marsha," she said aloud, smiling happily. "And he's had plenty of exercise to make him grow strong."

The child had had the run of the big house from the time he learned to walk, and soon he had started playing in the big yard in good weather, under her watchful eyes. Bill had spoiled him from the first, and now, holding onto Bill's hand and pestering him with all kinds of questions, he often went to the barn with him and watched while he did the chores. Bill had taught him to ride Happiness while he held him on the pony's back, and he often helped him ride the pony in the barn lot and in the big yard.

From the beginning Marsha had indulged him to the point of spoiling, and Candy had had to exercise care, lest she do the same. Little Ralph had done a lot for her and Mama Marsha, she realized. As a baby, he had seldom cried, but he had cooed and laughed a lot. He had driven away the loneliness that had settled in the big house after the death of Daddy White, the departure of Ralph and of Dora, and the death of

Bridgette. Her love for little Ralph had helped heal the hurt of losing his father. As he grew older, he filled the house with chatter and laughter and the noise of play.

She became suddenly aware that little Ralph was quiet and was on the point of getting up to go see what he was doing when she felt him tugging at her finger.

"You promised to take me walkin'," he said, looking earnestly up into her face.

She smiled down at him, thinking that every day he was looking more like his daddy. "So I did. I have just been thinking," she responded.

"Can't we go now, 'fore it gets late?" He was looking at her with eyes that reminded her so much of Ralph's eyes.

"Of course we can. You sit on the front steps while I go change to my walking shoes. Then we'll go. How's that?"

"That's fine." His eager smile warmed her heart, and with loving eyes she watched him go and sit on the top step to wait for her while she went to her room and changed her shoes.

He was watching for her when she came back, and he ran to her and took her hand. She led him down the steps, and they crossed the big yard and started across the meadow toward the river. Roger, now an old dog, romped ahead for a few yards, then stopped and waited for them to catch up. When they reached him, he whined and wagged his tail, then turned and trotted back to the house.

Soon a field lark darted up and sailed away, singing his plaintive song. Candy's mother used to call her attention to their singing in the early days of spring. "Listen," she used to say. "That is a Three Weeks, Six Day Bird, and he's telling us that is how long it will be till spring." That was only something someone had imagined, she realized. It was now the last of June, and the bird was still singing the same song.

She looked about her, seeing what she had seen so many, oh so many times, when she and Ralph had ridden their ponies across the meadow. The meadow had not been pastured lately, and the grass had grown tall, gone to seed, and turned brown in the hot dry air.

Grasshoppers were jumping from the grass, and butterflies were dancing in the wind. Overhead a lone buzzard circled against the blue sky on motionless wings, and white, billowy clouds moved across the sky like sheep in a pasture.

Little Ralph tugged at her hand. "Carry me, Mama Candy," he pleaded.

"I thought you wanted to walk," she teased as she picked him up.

"I'll walk at the river," he replied in his small-boy voice.

"You won't have long to play this time. The sun will soon go down," she said.

"Can I play till dark?"

"I suppose you can, but we'll have to walk home in the dark if you do."

"Oh, goody. I can chase lightning bugs."

"We'll see. Let's go play by the river first."

When they came in sight of the river she saw that it was calm. A barge loaded with coal was going downstream.

"Where will the boat go, Mama Candy," little Ralph asked, as he always did when they saw a boat.

"To Cincinnati, maybe, or to Louisville."

"It won't go to Orleans?"

"Maybe it will, and maybe it won't. If it does, they may put the coal on a big ship and send it way across the ocean."

"Where is the ocean?"

"It's a long way from here."

"Why will it cross the ocean?"

"To take coal to people."

"What for?"

"To burn . . . I don't know."

"How come you don't know?"

"I just don't, you little question box."

He wriggled from her arms and started running toward the river.

"Wait for me," she called after him.

He stopped and motioned for her to hurry.

She caught up with him, still thinking of the barge and its unknown destination. Little Ralph was like that. She had no idea what he would become or what he would do in life. Whatever it was, she would help him, and, like her mother did, she would endeavor to instill good principles in him. And she would lead him to the Saviour when he was old enough to understand.

She picked him up again, but he fretted. "Let me down," he pleaded, but she held him in her arms.

"I want to go play," he said, squirming.

"I'll put you down when we get to the river." She walked on, holding the child close to her heart. At the river she put him down. "Now you can play for a little while," she told him.

He ran along the river and started throwing bits of driftwood into the water.

"Let me help you. I can throw farther than you can," she said. She picked up a broken limb and threw it out in the water as far as she could. The current caught it and it started drifting down the river.

"Watch it go!" he cried in a shrill little voice, jumping up and down.

She thought of the day she had come to the river alone and had thrown driftwood in the water and watched it float out of sight. She had wished she could go away from home as easily as the driftwood had gone down the river. That had been because she loved big Ralph so desperately, and so hopelessly, and he seemed not to care for her at all.

They had heard nothing from him in all these years, and she had finally concluded that she would never hear from him again.

Perhaps he was buried in some unmarked grave in a land unknown to her. Or he may have gone down at sea and been buried beneath the waves. She now believed that he was dead, but she loved him as much as she had when he was alive. *Was that a proof of life after death?* she wondered. *Surely it was not possible to love the ashes of a person that once had lived and was now turned to dust.*

She had shown little Ralph his daddy's picture, and had told him that his daddy was a good man. "He won't be coming home, because he has gone to Heaven," she had told the child many times. "You look like him, and I want you to grow up and be as strong and good as he was." She hoped the child understood. He would in time, she knew. "Why don't you talk, Mama Candy?" little Ralph asked, looking up at her.

"Look, the sun is going down, and soon the stars will come out," she said to distract him.

"Show me the stars, Mama Candy," he cried, reaching up his arms for her to take him.

"Up there. See?" she asked as she picked him up. "That one is the evening star—I think."

"I want to go home," he said.

"All right, baby. We'll go."

"I'm not a baby," he corrected. "I'm four years old, and I'm bigger than a three year old boy." He struggled from her arms.

"So you are, and one day you'll be five years old, and you'll be bigger than a four year old boy."

She wondered if he would look more like Ralph as he grew older. She hoped he would, and she hoped he would be handsome like his daddy.

"Let's hurry, Mama Candy," he pleaded, tugging

at her finger.

"No, let's walk slowly and enjoy the coming of twilight."

"What's twilight?" he asked.

"Twilight is when the sun goes down and the shadows fall."

"Does it hurt the shadows when they fall, Mama Candy?"

"Oh you funny little boy!" she cried. and she picked him up and held him close. "No, I'm sure it doesn't hurt the shadows when they fall."

She started slowly up the hill carrying him until he made her put him down again.

What a responsibility she had to train this precious little boy, she thought. She was glad that from his very babyhood she had taught him to love the Bible, and the Sunday school, and the church. Yet there was so much to teach him.

As they walked toward the house, the sun disappeared behind a bank of clouds, and the last light faded from the sky.

"I wish it would come back," he cried.

"This day will never come back, little Ralph," she told him, "but there'll be another day tomorrow, and we'll make it the very best day we can. And we'll do that with all the other days that are to come."

"I want to be with you when the next day comes," he said with unusual seriousness for such a little boy.

"Of course you'll be with me, little Ralph."

"Mama Candy!" He tugged at her dress to be sure she was listening. "When I get big, I want to be like you."

"What a nice thing to say, little Ralph."

She picked him up and held him close, and she felt some of the sorrow and loneliness going out of her heart.

"We'll go to the house now. Mama Marsha will be

waiting for us," she told him.

"I'm hungry," he said.

"All right, baby. We'll get something to eat when we get to the house."

Her thoughts turned to the future. She was learning to live without big Ralph. She had never been interested in another man, so she had no thought of marrying, even in the distant future. Instead, she would live for this precious child, and after he grew up and married and had a family, she would live for them. Perhaps, if there were children they would call her "Grandma Candy," and that would make her life complete.

"I see a light in the window," little Ralph cried, interrupting her train of thought.

"So do I, little Ralph, and that means that we will soon be home."

Chapter 28

After lunch the next day, Bill took little Ralph riding on Happiness. "We'll be gone for awhile, Candy, 'cause I'm going to take him down to the creek and show him where his daddy used to fish," Bill said as he started to the barn, holding little Ralph by the hand.

"He'll enjoy that," Candy called after Bill. Then she went in to do some housecleaning.

A short time later an old car that had been well-worn during the war years came slowly up the drive to Oakcrest and stopped in front of the house. A stocky young man with a military bearing and a decided limp got out and started toward the house.

"Someone is coming, Candy," Marsha said in a low voice, as she drew away from the window where she had paused to look out when she heard the car.

"Who can it be?" Candy wondered, and she went to the window and peeped out from behind the drapes. "Oh, it's a strange man. I'm a sight in this housecoat, and my hair is a mess. Mama Marsha, will you . . .?" She was already running toward the safety of her room where she expected to stay until the visitor left.

"I will," Marsha called after her with a rare twinkle in her eyes. She went to the door and opened it as the young man raised his hand to ring the doorbell.

"Ma'am, is this Oakcrest Farm?" he asked through the unopened screen door.

Candy had reached her room and stopped behind her partially closed door to listen.

"Yes, this is Oakcrest Farm. I'm Marsha White; what can I do for you?"

"I'm pleased to meet you, ma'am. I'm David Bookman. I was . . ."

"Oh, you were Ralph's friend!" Marsha cried in what was a highly excited voice for her. "He wrote home about you. Do come in, Mr. Bookman." She unlatched the screen door and held it open wide.

In her room, Candy thought she was going to die of excitement. David Bookman might know what had happened to Ralph. She closed her bedroom door with a bang, threw off her work clothes and started dressing faster than she had ever dressed before. While she was dressing, she could hear Marsha and David talking as they moved toward the library. It distressed her that she could not understand what they were saying.

When Candy finished dressing, she gave her hair a hurried brushing, then started downstairs, almost forgetting to walk with the ladylike poise she had so carefully cultivated. When she entered the library, David Bookman arose to meet her. Marsha arose also.

"This is my daughter, Candy," Marsha said, "and, Candy, this is David Bookman. You remember Ralph writing home about him."

Candy's eyes met David's. They were brown, and warm, and friendly. His face was handsome, and his brown wavy hair was just beginning to thin on each side above his forehead. His smile was infectious, and, instantly, she felt drawn to him. *That must be because he was Ralph's friend,* she rationalized.

"I'm pleased to meet you, Mr. Bookman. Of course I remember Ralph writing about you, and I'm dying to ask if you know what happened to him," she said.

"I'll be glad to tell you, Miss Candy, but please call me David."

"Then call me Candy."

"I'll call you David also," Marsha volunteered. "Please sit down."

As Marsha sat down, David motioned Candy to the Queen Anne settee and took a chair facing her.

"David told me that he was one of the last people to see Ralph alive," Marsha said.

"Then Ralph is dead?" Candy questioned sadly.

"That's why I'm here, Candy. Ralph made me promise that if I made it through the war and he didn't, I'd come and tell you and Mama Marsha and Bridgette what I knew of his final flight. So I drove here from West Virginia today to keep my promise. By the way, where is Bridgette?"

"I'm sorry to tell you that she died soon after her little boy was born."

"I'm sorry. . . . A little boy," he mused with thoughtful eyes. "Where is he?"

"Our tenant, Bill Hanks, took him riding on one of the ponies. They'll be back soon, and you have to see him. He's a darling," Candy said.

"What a shame that Ralph didn't live to see his child."

"Ralph must have had a premonition that he was going to die," Marsha said.

"I think he did. He seemed especially worried about himself after he sent Bridgette to America."

"Tell us what you know about how Ralph died," Marsha suggested.

"I saw him go down in his plane. We were flying on the same mission," David elucidated. "The day he died we were flying escort for B-17 bombers over occupied France."

"I can hardly bear to think about Ralph dying, yet I want to know how it happened," Marsha said.

"Me too, but maybe it will help me to stop grieving so much if I know," Candy said.

"We had crossed the English Channel and had just made landfall over France when German fighter planes came after us. The air was full of them."

"That must have been frightening," Candy murmured as if to herself.

"It was," David replied, "and if it hadn't been for Ralph, I wouldn't be here to tell you about it."

"Why do you say that?" Marsha asked.

"Ralph saved my life that day. Three German fighters came after me at once. The closest one fired on my plane and damaged it so it was almost impossible to fly. Another German plane came up behind me to finish shooting down my crippled plane. There was no way I could get away from him, but Ralph came up behind him and shot him down. Another plane was diving at me, but the pilot turned and strafed Ralph's plane instead. He was shooting at pointblank range, and Ralph's plane started down, spinning out of control and trailing smoke. Ralph didn't bail out."

"Then Ralph's plane crashed?" Candy asked.

"Not exactly. While we were fighting the German planes, we had flown back over the channel, so Ralph's plane went down in the water. It sank within minutes."

"Then he's buried in the English Channel," Candy said as if talking to herself.

"I wonder why he didn't bail out," Marsha mused.

"I think he was killed before his plane went out of control."

"Well, now we know," Candy said tearfully. "Thank you for telling us."

"I'm glad to know that Ralph saved your life," Marsha said.

"David, how were you able to get away from the planes that were after you?" Candy asked.

"I think the good Lord was watching over me. The air was full of German fighter planes, and one of them flew by shooting into my plane again. My plane was so badly damaged I could not fight back, so I went into a spiraling dive to make the German pilot think I was going to crash."

"And did he think that?" Candy asked.

"He must have. He didn't follow me down."

"And did you crash?" Marsha asked.

"Not right away. I pulled out of the spiral just above the water and started limping toward home. It was a long, frightening flight across the channel, with my engine missing and losing oil. I finally made it across the channel, but I was almost out of gas. The engine soon sputtered to a stop, and I crashed in a field."

"Were you badly hurt?" Candy asked.

"All I remember was seeing the ground coming up at me and thinking that I was going to hit too hard. I woke up in a hospital a week later, and it was almost a year before I was able to fly again."

"Thank God, you made it," Candy breathed.

"We appreciate you telling us what happened to Ralph," Marsha said.

"I'm sorry I've been so long getting here. Near the end of the war, I was injured a second time and was in the hospital over a year."

"Are you all right now?" Candy questioned.

"I'm fine, except that I have a short leg."

Just then they heard Bill coming in with little Ralph.

"Bill, there's a man here who wants to see little Ralph," Marsha called.

Bill set little Ralph down, and he started running toward the library, but when he saw David he stopped and hid behind the doorjamb.

"I'm goin' back to the barn," Bill called. He went out and closed the door behind him.

"My, Ralph's boy is a cute little guy, but I don't like this little Ralph business. Since his daddy won't be coming home, you ought to call him Ralph Jr."

"I've been thinking about that. He'll not want to

be called little Ralph when he starts to school," Candy said.

"I think we should call him Ralph Jr.," Marsha agreed.

"So do I," Candy said, and she went and picked up the child and returned to the settee.

"Say, you look like your daddy," David said to him.

"My daddy is big Ralph, an' I'm little Ralph."

"You're not going to be little Ralph any more, baby," Candy said holding him close. "You're getting to be a big boy, so from now on we're going to call you Ralph."

He squirmed from her arms and stood beside her, looking at David. "What's your name, man?" he asked.

"I'm David, and your daddy and I were good friends."

"Will you be my friend?" Ralph asked.

"Sure I will. Want to come to me?" He held out his arms. With hesitating steps, Ralph went to David, and he picked him up and set him on his knee.

"Are you goin' to stay with us?" Ralph asked.

"I can't stay, but I'll come to see you real often, if your folks will put up with me."

Candy started to say she hoped he would, but she bit her tongue and said nothing.

"We'd love to have you come as often as you can," Marsha said. "If you want to stay overnight, I'm sure Bill will make you welcome at his house."

"If he will, I just may come and stay a day or two and look around for some land in this part of the country. Now that the war's over, I want to get into farming and maybe raise some cattle." He spoke with enthusiasm, and Candy felt his excitement.

"Ralph loved the farm," she said.

"I know. We used to talk a lot about farming. He wanted me to settle somewhere near him in Kentucky. . . . maybe go partners with him."

"Then I hope you will settle near here," she told him, blushing prettily.

"I still have a lot to do in West Virginia. My father was my last remaining relative, and he died recently. I have to settle his estate, and I'm getting ready for an auction."

"You came all this way to tell us about Ralph, when you were so busy," Candy remarked.

"Ralph had told me so much about you folks. I got to thinking about you, and I took a sudden notion to come. Next time I'll phone before I come, if you will give me your phone number."

"Of course," Candy said, and she went to the desk and wrote the number on a piece of paper and gave it to him.

He got up with Ralph still in his arms. "Ralph, I've got to go, but I'm coming back, and you and I are going to be good friends. That's a promise," he said as he folded the paper Candy had given him and put it in his pocket.

Ralph hugged David's neck. Then he wiggled from his arms.

"I like you, Ralph. Mrs. White, it's good to know you. And you too, Candy." He took her hand and held it a bit too long she thought, but she made no attempt to take it away.

"It was good of you to come," she murmured.

They followed David out on the porch and watched him go and get in his old car and drive away.

"Now that's a nice young man," Marsha remarked.

"Is David ever a-comin' back?" Ralph Jr. asked.

"He promised that he would, Ralph," she said, smiling wistfully.

"When he comes back, let's have a dinner for him and invite Bill and Dora to eat with us. I'm sure they would like to talk with Ralph's friend," Marsha said.

"I'd love to do that," Candy said enthusiastically.

Chapter 29

After David's visit, Candy could scarcely get him off her mind. Perhaps it was because he had been Ralph's friend, she told herself, but, if that were true, why did she have that strange flutter in her heart each time she thought of him?

He was an interesting man, she had to admit. He had no family, and that made her heart go out to him. He was pleasant to be around, easy to talk to, and he had integrity. After all those months in the hospital, he had kept his promise to Ralph. She must take care not to fall in love with him, she decided.

She was not as lonely as she had been before she found Ralph. She now had Ralph's child, and she had Mama Marsha and Bill and Dora, though she seldom heard from Dora. But that did not keep her from having an empty feeling locked away in her heart.

When two weeks had passed with no word from David, Candy began to believe that they would never hear from him again. Then one evening, just as she and Mama Marsha and Ralph Jr. sat down to dinner, David phoned.

Candy answered the phone, and when she heard David's voice, her spirits soared. "Where are you, David?" she cried.

"In Charleston. Came here to finish some business and decided to eat before I go home."

"Where is your home? You didn't tell us when you were here."

"My homeplace was in Boone County. I sold it today, along with some land my family owned that has coal on it."

"What are you going to do now?"

"I'm moving out of the homeplace tomorrow, and I'll store a few things I kept."

"Where are you going to live?"

"Nowhere right away. I'll come down and visit with you folks for awhile if you'll let me. Are you sure Bill will let me stay with him?"

"Bill will be glad to have you. When are you coming?"

"Let's see. This is Tuesday. I'll clear up everything here in the next couple of days, so I can come Friday afternoon, if that's all right."

"We'll be expecting you, and we want you to eat dinner with us."

"I'll be delighted to eat with you folks, Candy, and I'll be looking forward to seeing you. Give my regards to Marsha and tell Bill I'm coming."

"I'll be looking forward to seeing you," Candy replied. She blushed, wishing she had not said that.

"Good-bye, Candy."

"Good-bye, David."

She hung up the phone and danced back to the table with a bounce she had not had for a long time.

"What was that all about?" Marsha asked.

"David is coming Friday, and he agreed to have dinner with us. You did say that you wanted to have him?"

"I'm glad Mr. David is a-comin'. Is he a-goin' to stay with us?" Ralph cried in a shrill little voice.

"Mr. David is going to stay with Bill, but he'll eat dinner with us Friday night. How's that?"

"That's fine . . . I reckon."

"And we're going to have Bill and Dora to eat with us," Marsha told him.

"I know Dora will enjoy meeting Ralph's best friend," Candy mused.

When Bill came in with the milk that night, Marsha told him that David was coming, and that he wanted to stay with him.

"I'll be glad to have him bunk with me, but I'll have to clean up my place ... been needin' it for years," he said.

"David is coming Friday, and he's going to eat with us that night. We want you to eat with us too, and we're going to invite Dora. We haven't seen her for ages," Candy elaborated.

"Yeah, I'll eat with you, and I'll be glad to see Dora. You all let me know if I can do anything to help you get ready, but I'll be gettin' on now. I'm goin' to start cleanin' my place tonight," Bill said as he limped toward the door on his way out.

"Let's hurry and get supper over. I want to call Dora tonight and invite her, and she'll talk forever," Marsha said.

The next day Marsha started getting ready for company with a zest she had not had since Bridgette had died. Candy joined her and did the work of two people, excited that at last there was going to be happiness and laughter in the old house, in addition to the childish play and laughter of Ralph Jr.

Just after lunch on Friday, Candy heard a car climbing the hill and ran to the front door. "David's here!" she sang out to Mama Marsha when she saw his car.

Marsha joined her at the door, and they watched his car top the hill and stop by the front gate.

Candy went out on the porch with Marsha close behind her. "We heard your car on the hill," Candy called as David was getting out.

"I hope I didn't come too early."

"Not at all. We were expecting you," Marsha exclaimed as he came into the yard.

"We're glad you've come," Candy added.

Just then Ralph came galloping around the house on a stick horse. "Hi, Mr. David," he called, dropping his stick horse and running to him. David picked him up and hugged him. He hugged David's neck, then he wiggled from his arms and ran and stood by Candy and Marsha.

"Candy you're as pretty as a peach," he said with a mischievous smile. "Marsha, you're looking great, and, Ralph, I sure am glad to see you."

"Well, thank you. You're a handsome man," Candy kidded.

"Listen to that man flatter us," Marsha laughed.

"Where does Bill live? I want to check in at his house and get settled," David said.

"You follow the drive to where it ends behind the barn. You'll have to walk from there to Bill's house. It's down by the creek. Bill has never wanted anything but a path to his house. He'll help you carry your things from the car," Marsha told him.

"Where will I find Bill?"

"He's at his house. I'll phone and have him to meet you at the end of the drive," Candy told him.

David bowed to them and started back to his car.

"Bill knows what time we're planning dinner," Marsha called after him.

"I'll see you then," he called as he got in the car and closed the door.

They watched him drive out of sight behind the barn. Then Candy went in to phone Bill, and Marsha went in to continue preparations for dinner.

Dora was in the kitchen fussing over the food, when Bill and David arrived that evening. Marsha was seeing that everything was in place in the dining room, and Candy was pretending to be busy, while watching the door for them to arrive.

"Dinner is almost ready," she greeted. "Bill, take David to the library. You men can visit in there while we finish getting dinner on the table."

"I'm going with Bill and Mr. David," Ralph called from the head of the stairs, where they had sent him to play. His little feet resounded on the stair treads as he ran and ended with a thump when he reached the downstairs floor. He ran to David, took him by the hand, and, with Bill following, led him into the library.

Soon dinner was on the table and they all sat down to eat.

"I want to sit by Mr. David," Ralph insisted.

"All right, baby, you can sit by him," Candy told him. "I'll sit beside Ralph so I can help him cut his meat," she explained as she moved to the chair beside him.

"David, will you offer thanks?" Marsha asked when Ralph and Candy were seated.

David bowed his head and prayed, and Candy was pleased that he responded so easily and so naturally. Apparently he was accustomed to praying.

Rosy from the heat of the kitchen and beaming with pleasure, Dora started serving the food.

"David, this is Dora. She used to be our housekeeper. She's a guest now, but she still insists on serving us," Marsha said.

"I'm pleased to meet you, Dora," David greeted, smiling.

"Pleased to meet you, Mr. David. Miss Marsha, I'll get me a plate and eat, soon as I get through serving you all," she ended.

After they finished eating, David excused himself. "Bill and I will go back to the library and talk farming," he explained.

"Didn't you run out of talk about farming this afternoon?" Marsha asked, smiling.

"We talked a lot," Bill agreed.

"And we walked over your farm and looked at your cattle. Now I want to talk with Bill about some land nearby that he says is for sale."

"I'm a-goin' with them," Ralph shouted.

"All right, baby, but you be quiet and listen to the men talk," Candy said as she cleaned his face with a napkin.

He pulled away as she finished and ran to the library and climbed up in David's lap.

"Why don't you forget buying land and help manage this farm?" Bill began. "I don't mind working, but managing this farm is too much for me."

"I have some money to invest from the sale of my parents' property, and want some land of my own. If I can settle close by, maybe I can still give you a hand from time to time," David returned.

"The women need help too. They do all they can, especially with making decisions and book work, but it's too much for them."

"I could help them with the decisions if they want me to," David offered.

"I wish you would go partners with them. You could increase the herd. There's more land here than we've ever used, even in Judge White's lifetime."

"I'd still like to look at the land you mentioned."

"All right, if you say so. The land joins this place. If you buy it, you could run both places," Bill elucidated.

"Do you think the women would go along on that?" David asked.

"I think they would. They're tired of carrying the load. You could talk to them about it."

"Tomorrow I'll take a look at the land, and then we'll see."

"What land?" Candy asked as she came into the

library at that moment.

"Bill says there's some land close by that's for sale."

"It's the Ben Boltwright place, Candy. You know where it is," Bill said.

"I've heard that it's a good farm, but it doesn't have a house on it," Candy commented.

"I can build a house," David said.

Ralph wiggled from David's lap and ran to Candy. She took him in her arms and sat down near David.

"Can I see Mr. David ever' day when he builds his house?" Ralph asked.

"Maybe not every day, but real often, baby," she said.

"I'll see you all after awhile," Bill said, arising and stretching. "I've got some chores to do at the barn."

"Want me to help?" David asked.

"I'm used to doing it. Besides, this is a good time for you to talk to Marsha and Candy." He went out and closed the door behind him.

"What made you decide to look for land in Kentucky?" Candy asked David.

"I reckon hearing Ralph talk about this farm when we were overseas. Besides, I liked the looks of the country around here when I was here before."

"This is great country," she said, for lack of anything better to say.

"How do you and Marsha manage the farm with only Bill to help?" he asked.

"It's not easy, and I know Bill is overworked."

"I wonder if you and Marsha would consider taking a partner."

"You mean you'd go partners with us?"

"If you'll let me. I could share the work, and we could put more cattle on the farm."

"I don't know. You'd have to talk with Mama Marsha. I'll go get her."

"David wants to talk with you about something," she told Marsha when she found her in the dining room.

"What about?" she asked.

"He wants to go partners with us on the farm."

Marsha paused for a long minute, thinking. "Well, to say the least, I'm intrigued, but of course there is much to talk about."

She went to the library with Candy and sat down facing David. "Candy says you are thinking of a partnership," she prompted.

"Bill has told me that there's some land for sale that joins your farm," he began. "I've been thinking that if I can buy that land, a partnership might be a good thing for all of us. We could increase the herd, and I could help with the work."

"Wouldn't more land and more cattle make more work than we can all handle?" Marsha questioned.

"I'm sure it would, but with the size of the operation I have in mind, we could hire more help."

"What would Bill think of that?"

"He'd be for it. He suggested that I talk to you about a partnership on this farm. It was my idea to buy more land."

"What do you think, Candy?" Marsha asked.

"I think it's a great idea, if it will take some of the work off of you, Mama Marsha. You really are overworked." In her heart she was thrilled at the prospect of David's settling nearby.

"We'll discuss it further after you see if you can buy the land," Marsha said. "Now I must go and help Dora."

"Want me to help, Mama Marsha?" Candy asked.

"No, you stay and visit with David."

After Marsha was gone, David and Candy talked like old friends. He told her of his boyhood, growing up in West Virginia, and she told him how she had found Ralph when they were both children.

"I thought I was grown-up then," she said, smiling ruefully.

"I'll bet you were more grown-up than many girls are at twenty," he said.

"Anyway, Ralph and I got by, that is until I got sick and landed in the hospital."

"Ralph told me about that. He said he was really worried."

"I was sick, but I wasn't worried. I knew I was going to get well. But tell me about your time in England and how you met Ralph."

"The first time I saw Ralph was one morning at a briefing, when we were getting ready to fly a mission. I knew right then that he was my kind of guy, and, when we got back from the mission, I looked him up. We were friends from then on."

David talked then of the war, missions he and Ralph had flown, and dangers they had faced. She sat listening, spellbound, and hardly aware of the passing of time.

All too soon, Bill came in from the barn. "You about ready to go, David?" he asked. "I've still got a bit to do at my place before we go to bed."

"I'm sorry you have to go, David," Candy said as they arose.

She walked with him into the hall. There he paused and called toward the dining room, "Thank you, Marsha and Dora, for the good dinner."

"We enjoyed having you," Marsha told him as she and Dora came into the hall.

"I'm glad I met you, Mr. David," Dora said.

"I'll see all of you tomorrow," he said as he followed Bill outside.

The next day David went with Bill to look at the land that was for sale. They returned late in the afternoon, full of excitement. David had bought the adjoining farm.

"Now I'm ready to talk business with you and Marsha," David said when Candy let them in the front door.

"Marsha is upstairs. I'll get her," Candy responded, and she ran up the stairs and to Marsha's room. "The men are back, and David has bought the farm," she announced. Then in a whisper, "He says he's ready to talk business."

Marsha went down with her to the library where David and Bill were waiting. They all sat down, and David quickly outlined his thoughts about a partnership.

"That sounds good to me," Marsha said when he finished, "but I'd like to talk with my husband's former law partner, Mr. Nate Clark, before I make such an important decision."

"I think you should, and I'll be glad to answer any questions Mr. Clark has."

"If Mr. Clark thinks the partnership is a good idea, is it all right to have him to write the contract?"

"Of course."

"Will you want another attorney to look over the contract?"

"That won't be necessary. We'll just agree on the terms of the contract before Mr. Clark writes it. Then we'll both read it to see if it says what we have agreed on."

The following Monday they signed the contract. Two days later David got the title to his land, and the next day he and Bill cut the boundary fence of the back pasture and put in a new gate to make his land accessible from Oakcrest. In the days following, David became busy buying calves and having extra hay and grain delivered and stored in the barn at Oakcrest.

Chapter 30

When a year had passed, more than twice as many cattle as had previously been at Oakcrest were grazing at the two farms. The ponies had grown fat and lazy. Sandy Bell and Baby Bell each had a pair of beautiful, frisky kids. David had bought two pleasure horses, a mare and a gelding, and they were frolicking in the front pasture.

The old dog, Roger, had died of old age, and they had buried him by the snowball bush in the side yard. David and Candy had bought a beautiful Collie puppy and brought him to Oakcrest, and he was romping all over the place. He was a great playmate for Ralph, now five years old and more active than ever.

Dora's mother had died, and she had come back to her job at Oakcrest. A new intimacy now existed between her and Bill, and Candy and Marsha were beginning to think that it was the start of a budding romance.

David was still living with Bill, and every night he came to the house, ostensibly to talk business with Marsha, but he always stayed to visit with Candy. That pleased Ralph Jr., for he was wild about David.

In the spring, David had bought a cabin cruiser and put it on the river, and had built a dock for it across the valley from the mailbox. On Saturdays he often took Candy and Ralph Jr. riding on the river. Sometimes they anchored in a shady nook and had a picnic lunch. Occasionally they fished until Ralph Jr. grew restless and begged David to start the motor and take them riding again.

On a beautiful Saturday in June, David asked Marsha if she would keep Ralph Jr. while he and Candy went out in the boat. "It will be good for her to have a break, and there's something I want to show her that can best be seen from the river," he explained.

"I'll be glad to keep him," Marsha agreed, smiling knowingly. "I'll take him to town to get some ice cream. That will keep him happy for awhile, and he won't know you and Candy are going out in the boat."

Shorty after Marsha left with Ralph Jr., David and Candy walked happily down to the dock.

"Let's take a ride down the river first," he suggested when they reached the dock.

"I'd like that. I love to ride in the boat with the wind in my face on a hot day like this." She watched him make the boat ready, then got in and sat beside him.

He started the inboard motor, backed away from the dock, and turned the cruiser down the river. He opened the throttle, the engine roared, and the boat raced away.

Candy got up and stood in the bow of the boat, with the wind in her face and blowing her hair.

David looked at her and was sure he had never seen a prettier, more appealing girl. He was deeply in love with her. He was sure she was fond of him, but he feared that she had not recovered from the loss of Ralph. Little things she had said and done during the past year had convinced him that she had loved Ralph.

At the first bend in the river, David guided the boat toward the Ohio shore and made a wide turn toward the Kentucky side, churning up froth and sending waves scurrying away from the boat.

"There is something up the river that I want to show you," he called above the roar of the motor as he righted the boat and added power to maintain speed against the current.

Candy took the seat beside him and watched him guide the boat. He continued up the river, past Oakcrest farm, then slowed the boat, pulled it to the shore, and tied up to some willow bushes.

"The land in front of us is part of my farm," he said pointing. "It starts at the boundary line of Oakcrest and goes up the river for almost a mile."

"I thought your farm was behind ours."

"Part of it is, but it curves around to the river."

"I should have known that. I have heard you and Bill talk about part of your farm being bottomland."

"See that level spot up there on the hill? It's just a little lower than the hill where the house at Oakcrst is located."

"Yes, I see it."

"Wouldn't that make a beautiful place for a house?"

"Yes it would, but why do you ask?"

"If you'll marry me, I'll build us a house up there."

Candy looked at him, surprised, startled, and affronted. Cold anger welled up inside her. *Did he think he could buy her with a house? Well, he could forget it. She was not to be bought.*

"You did not answer, Candy," he said gently.

"Did you expect me to fall in your arms?" she asked angrily. "I'm not going to marry you for a house. I already have a place to live."

Shock and disappointment registered in his face. "That's the last thing in the world I had in my mind, Candy," he almost shouted. "I'm asking you to marry me because I love you."

She looked at him, wide-eyed with surprise. Then numerous incidents of the past year flashed through her mind. There had been tender moments during the

300

past year, times when he had shown her special kind-
ness, little things he had done to please her, and hints
she had been too blind to heed.

Since he had come to Oakcrest, she had been drawing closer to him, she realized. *Could she have been
falling in love with him without knowing it?* She must
have, for it suddenly occurred to her that she could
not imagine life without him.

He waited patiently, sensing something of the
struggle that was going on in her mind and heart.

If David should leave and not return, she would be
devastated, she realized. And Ralph Jr. would miss
him dreadfully. The child had come to almost worship him. David would make a wonderful father for
him. . . . and he would make a wonderful husband for
her. Suddenly she knew that she was in love with
David, and happiness washed over her.

"What did you just say?" she asked as if she had
not heard him.

"I said that I love you, and I want you to marry
me."

"Why didn't you tell me, you big lug?" she asked
as she melted into his arms.

Don't Miss These Great L. Walker Arnold Novels

In the past few years L. Walker Arnold, a native of Kentucky, has become a widely-read, greatly-loved inspirational author.

He has written eight novels and his life story, *The Way Things Used to Be* in the past ten years. All of them have been well received by the reading public.

Hundreds of his readers order each of his new books long before it is off the press. Many have placed standing orders for every book he writes. Thousands have written to praise his books.

Mr. Arnold's readers write that they appreciate his ability to create strong characters, his unique powers of description, and the gripping, emotion-filled stories he writes.

Titles Listed in the Order Written

The Legend of Old Faithful, Hardcover	$16.99 14.95
Out of the Night, Hardcover	$16.99 15.95
Fathoms Deep, Hardcover	$16.99
Riverman, Softcover	$ 9.99
Riverman (Audio) read by author on cassette	$ 9.99
White Angel, Paperbound	$ 1.00
Sunshine Valley, Softcover	$ 9.99
Euroclydon, Softcover	$ 9.99
Lucinda of Perryville, Softcover	$ 9.99
A Girl Named Candy, Softcover	$ 9.99

Abebooks

If L. Walker Arnold novels are not available at bookstores in your area, order from Arnold Publications.

Please include $2.25 postage and handling for one book, $3.25 for two books, $3.75 for three books, $4.25 for four books, and $4.75 for five books. We pay postage on orders over $50.00. Prices are subject to change without notice.

Arnold Publications
2440 Bethel Road
Nicholasville, KY 40356
Phone toll free 1-800-854-8571